# A HOLIDAY HOMICIDE

## ELLIE ALEXANDER

To request permissions, contact the publisher at rights@stormpublishing.co

Ebook ISBN: 978-1-80508-773-1
Paperback ISBN: 978-1-80508-774-8

Cover design: Dawn Adams
Cover images: Dawn Adams

Published by Storm Publishing.
For further information, visit:
www.stormpublishing.co

## ALSO BY ELLIE ALEXANDER

*The Body in the Bookstore*

*A Murder at the Movies*

*Death at the Dinner Party*

*A Victim at Valentine's*

*This book is dedicated to you. I'm wishing you a cozy and wonderful holiday season and hope Annie's latest mystery can provide you with a little escape from the hustle and bustle.*

## ONE

Everything inside the Secret Bookcase smelled of pine, cinnamon, cloves, and nutmeg. As I wound my way down the long hallway adorned with evergreen boughs dotted with cranberries and sprigs of holly, I couldn't contain a smile. The bookstore was my favorite place on the planet on an average ordinary day, but during the holidays, it was pure magic. Festive jazz music drifted along the corridors of the restored English country estate that now housed the largest mystery bookshop on the West Coast. I made my way to the Foyer, where dazzling golden twinkle lights greeted me, along with two small Christmas trees flanking the front doors.

It was impossible not to have a little spring in my step. I loved the holiday season—the aroma of hot mulled cider floating from Oceanside Park, binge-watching cheesy Hallmark movies, the annual holiday parade, and, of course, the buzz at the bookstore.

The entire bookshop was themed after Agatha Christie's works. The Foyer at the front of the mansion served as our welcome and checkout station. Customers could pour themselves a cup of spiced ginger tea, peppermint hot chocolate, or strong coffee with a splash of eggnog and help themselves to a cookie while they browsed the store's vast collection of mystery novels. A large desk with a cash register and space for gift wrapping divided the Foyer from the Conservatory. For December, we had strung paper bunting along the cash register and featured a display of Christmas crackers (imported from England) and pretty packages of colorful holiday candies. A small tabletop tree with handmade book-themed ornaments sat proudly in the window. I drank in notes of cranberry, peppermint, and hot cocoa from our seasonal candle display.

I stole a quick glance at the Conservatory. Every time I went into the elegant ballroom, I felt like I was stepping into the pages of a historical mystery for a Regency ball. When Hal Christie, my boss and the owner of the Secret Bookcase, renovated the property decades ago, he had started with the ballroom. It was where we held all our events with its massive ceilings, arched windows, parquet floors, chandeliers, and mintgreen walls with hand-painted murals and gold filigree. For the season, a twenty-foot spruce tree sat in the center of the room. It dripped with bejeweled ornaments and beads. Hal loved the holidays and didn't skimp when it came to decorations. Electric votive candles flickered on the bookshelves, and wreaths made with bay leaves, berries, and silky ribbons hung from each window.

Sometimes, I had to pinch myself to remember this was real. Me, Annie Murray, a former criminology student, worked among the stacks and stacks of gilded spines every day. Lately, I'd been giving a lot of thought to my future. Hal wasn't getting any younger and had generously offered to hand the reins of the bookstore over to me and my old friend and coworker Fletcher.

Fletcher and I had spent the better part of the last month reviewing potential plans. I was excited about the idea of continuing to expand on the events and activities we'd been hosting at the bookstore, but I was also pulled toward another path. Dr. Caldwell, my college professor and Redwood Grove's current lead detective, had offered me a job working for her. I thought I'd given up that life for good after my best friend Scarlet died the day before our college graduation. But now I wasn't so sure.

I sighed and flipped on the overhead lights in the Foyer.

*You can think about that later, Annie. You have work to do.*

In less than an hour, we were opening the doors for our first-ever gingerbread bake-off. Well, technically, it wasn't a bake-off. It was more of a showcase, like *The Great British Baking Show*, but with gingerbread, delicious, spicy, delectable gingerbread.

I couldn't wait.

The event was a first for me and for the store.

A few weeks ago, I'd received a call from Sugar Lester, who owned Sweet Room, a local bakery in town. Sugar wanted to partner with us to host a gingerbread-baking competition.

"Annie, you're never going to believe this. Lily Hawthorne wants to do a holiday collab with me," Sugar had gushed on the phone.

"Who is Lily Hawthorne?" I'd asked.

"Lily Hawthorne. *The* Lily Hawthorne." Sugar sounded incredulous that I didn't know who she was talking about. "She has over a million followers on social media. It's like winning the lottery. Lily happened to see a wedding cake I created that went kind of viral. She commented on the post and slid into my DMs, asking if I might want to collaborate. I'm still pinching myself. She's one of the biggest baking influencers in the country—no—in the world. She has huge brand deals with Nestlé and nearly every baking company you can imagine. I'll send you links to her stuff. You'll absolutely drool. The things she does with pastry are out of this world."

I was intrigued. "How would the bookstore be involved?" I asked, not tracking her train of thought. We didn't have commercial kitchens at the shop, and none of us were bakers, but I was open to hearing her ideas. The Secret Bookcase was doing well, but like most independent bookshops, we were always looking for ways to draw more customers into the store and find new revenue streams.

"Lily wants to do something outrageous for her holiday social. She'll come to Redwood Grove and bake a custom gingerbread house. Not just any house, something spectacular. We brainstormed ideas, and I sent her pictures of the bookstore. She thinks it's perfect. It's so iconic and quintessentially Christmassy. She'll build a replica of the Secret Bookcase. Then she'll invite everyone in the community to participate in a gingerbread contest. We're hoping you can display them at the store. You have the space. She'll kick off the event live on her social media and feature whoever wins on her site. This is a giant opportunity, Annie. You don't even know what this will do for my business, and it's going to be great exposure for the bookstore, too. Are you in?"

I didn't know Sugar well, but she had always seemed warm and friendly in our interactions. The idea of partnering with her on a holiday event immediately sent a happy buzz through my body. It would be a great way to get to know her better. Plus, her pastries and cakes were nothing short of heavenly.

Sugar had opened Sweet Room a couple of years ago. Whenever I stopped in for special cakes and pies for signings and book clubs at the store, she would greet me with a wide smile and free samples of mini chocolate chip pecan cookies or a slice of her pumpkin cream tarts. I knew she'd been involved in other community projects—donating to the annual library sale and school fundraisers, providing muffins for the senior center, and offering students deep discounts. She was clearly eager to make connections like the rest of our town. I appreciated that about her, and it made me all the more ready to see how we might work together.

The one drawback of her bakery was that it was in an old

Victorian farmhouse on the outskirts of town. She'd done an incredible job renovating the property—painting the exterior like a chocolate-covered cherry and revamping the interior with more touches of pink, pastry cases, and window seating for customers to curl up with a mug of tea and an apple strudel on a rainy afternoon. But not being on the main village square made it hard for her to get foot traffic. A partnership with a baking influencer would probably be a big boost for her business and certainly great for the Secret Bookcase, too.

It sounded like a win-win to me.

Aside from our weekly children's story time and book club meetings, we didn't have any major holiday plans for the month of December, so I guessed Hal and Fletcher would be on board with the idea. "Let me run this by my colleagues. I think it's a fantastic idea, and I'm sure they'll agree," I'd said to Sugar, already imagining dozens of gingerbread houses on display around the bookstore.

As expected, Hal and Fletcher were immediately excited about the idea.

"I'd never turn down an opportunity to draw more customers into the store, especially during the holiday season." Hal had tried to sound breezy, but I sensed more than a touch of worry in his tone. Operating costs were hefty. Heating and lighting the massive estate came with steep electrical bills, not to mention staffing, inventory, supplies, insurance, taxes, and so much more. Fletcher and I had been running numbers to explore the possibility of buying Hal out. It was potentially doable, but the financial aspect of owning a niche mystery book-store was daunting. There were so many things to consider, from future revenue to how to grow our customer base.

"No one opens a bookstore and expects to make millions of dollars," Hal continued. "But having a little extra cash sure would be nice."

"Aren't the numbers looking better than this time last year?"

Fletcher asked, a flash of concern passing over his long, angular face.

"Oh, sure. Sure. Nothing to worry about. We're fine. We're doing quite dandy." Hal changed the subject. "How's your baking prowess? Should we have a friendly little competition amongst the three of us?"

"I make a mean bowl of cereal. You might even call me a cereal killer," Fletcher joked.

Hal groaned. "That's bad, even for you, Fletcher."

"All I'm saying is baking isn't my forte. Give me a Sherlock manuscript to decipher and I'm all yours, but put me in front of a bowl of eggs and butter, and I'm a lost man." Fletcher was Sherlock Holmes's biggest fan. Our shared office was evidence of his passion, which bordered on obsession. He kept tomes of Sir Arthur Conan Doyle and had constructed his own murder board on one of the walls.

"That's it." Hal snapped his fingers together and pushed up the sleeves of his tattered cardigan. "Let's have a murderous gingerbread theme. We'll each bake something inspired by our favorite mysteries or anything mysterious to add to the competition."

For some reason, I found myself agreeing, even though my decorating skills left much to be desired. I had grown up in my family's diner, so I knew my way around the kitchen, and I enjoyed baking. Constructing an elaborate house out of cookies and frosting was another story.

Yet, here I was, on the day of the competition, preparing to showcase my creation along with dozens of others from the community.

"Annie, good morning." A familiar voice sounded nearby.

I turned to see Hal Christie strolling in through the side door that led to his private quarters on the second floor. Hal was in his late sixties with white hair, wise eyes, and a kind, inviting smile. He wore his typical bookstore "uniform," a pair of corduroy slacks and a cardigan. Today, he had a special Christmas cardigan. It was red with a white snowflake and reindeer pattern knitted across the chest and sleeves. "Are you feeling festive and ready for the gingerbread invasion?"

"Well, don't you look absolutely dapper, Mr. Christie?" I glanced down at my black skirt and tights, which I'd paired with a cream V-neck sweater. "I'm rethinking my outfit, though. I missed an opportunity here. I should have gone for a Christmas sweater. But I did wear my candy cane earrings in preparation for the gingerbread invasion." I dangled one of them for Hal's sake.

"I'd say you're very in the spirit. What's the plan, and where's Fletcher?" Hal glanced around the Foyer, his eyes landing on the typewriter clock on the wall next to the bay windows. "The influencer—is that really what we call them?" He scrunched his forehead like he couldn't quite bring himself to say "influencer."

"Yeah, influencer." I nodded with a half grin.

"She's coming with Sugar now to set up the main display, correct?"

"Yep," I said with another nod. "She and Sugar should be here any minute now. They wanted at least an hour to set up before we open to the general public. Contestants are bringing their gingerbread houses at nine. I slotted another hour for them to set up, just in case people are late or if any mishaps or touch-ups need to happen. Voting kicks off at ten this morning, and Lily will announce the winner on Sunday afternoon. She picked three o'clock because of the social media algorithms. Apparently, that's the time frame when most of her followers are active."

"I'll never understand the modern digital world," Hal said with a slight shake of his head. "I was born in the wrong era, but I promise I'll try my best not to come across as an old codger."

"What's an old codger?" I narrowed my eyes at him and pretended like I had no idea what he was talking about.

"Oh no, even my expressions are outdated. Never mind. I take it back. I'm hiding upstairs for the remainder of the day." He tugged his cardigan around his chest.

"No way." I chuckled and patted his sleeve. "I tease because I love you and I seem to remember *you* suggesting a friendly staff competition. I was up until two a.m. last night putting the finishing touches on my masterpiece. You're not getting out of this that easy."

"Fair enough." He checked down the hallway to the Sitting Room and the Parlor. "Where is Fletcher, by the way? I would have thought he would have been here at the crack of dawn."

"Me too." Fletcher was impeccably timely. I could count on one hand the number of times he'd missed work in the last ten years. Once, he was gone for a root canal, and another for his cousin's wedding. Both absences had him apologizing unnecessarily for days.

The sound of a door slamming made us both startle. "A little help, please!" Fletcher banged on the front door with his foot. He balanced a huge box in his spindly arms.

I hurried to unlock the door and let him in. "Speak of the devil. We were just talking about you."

"This gingerbread is going to be the death of me. Who said this was going to be fun?" He attempted to glare at Hal but couldn't hold it together. A smile broke through. "This is not my idea of a good time, Christie. Next time, let's have a holiday mystery movie marathon."

Hal helped him with the box. "I can't wait to see what you've concocted."

"I wouldn't hold your breath." Fletcher made a face. "This is my first and last time working with gingerbread as a medium." He wore a turtleneck, black slacks, and a casual sport coat and shifted the box precariously in his arms as he maneuvered past the drink cart.

I had a feeling Fletcher was being overly critical. In his spare time, he built miniature sets of Scotland Yard and 221B Baker Street. He was meticulous and quite artistic.

"Shall we?" Hal motioned to the Conservatory. "The tables await our confectionary creations."

"I need to go grab my house," I said, pointing down the shimmering hallway to the Sitting Room. "I set it down while turning on lights on my way in."

"See you shortly. May the best gingerbread baker win." Hal's eyes twinkled mischievously.

The Sitting Room was the perfect spot in the store to cozy up on a cool, drizzly Northern California winter afternoon. It was designed to resemble Miss Marple's house in St. Mary Mead with floral wallpaper, plush reading chairs, a tea cart, and our extensive collection of traditional mysteries. We added special touches for the holidays—soft plaid throw blankets and cushions in red and green. The bookshelves were lined with garlands of pine interspersed with bows and miniature silver and gold ornaments, and staff recommendations were featured near the tea cart with handwritten notes from each of us on why our picks would make the perfect gift.

I retrieved my creation. Rather than a house, I had decided to replicate the secret bookcase in the Sitting Room. I'd constructed gingerbread bookshelves and a little compartment behind the bookcases. When I was halfway through the painstaking task of painting book covers in red, green, and white frosting, I almost considered scrapping the entire thing, but it had come together in the early hours of the morning, and I was fairly pleased with the final result. Not to mention, it was about the experience—getting my hands sticky with frosting and eating way too many gumdrops in the process.

Our secret bookcase was by far what new customers to the

store raved about the most. A special lever on an Agatha Christie spine released a latch that forced the shelf to swing open and reveal a hidden room. Technically it was more of a closet, but nonetheless it was a very unique feature.

A memory surfaced of one of the first big events we'd hosted at the store, when I'd discovered the body of one of my former college classmates inside the hidden compartment.

I shuddered at the thought.

Those days were long behind me. I didn't need to worry about dead bodies or dwell on Scarlet's murder at the moment. It was the holiday season. We were about to have wonderful gingerbread houses filling the store and people filing in to see them. Hopefully, that meant shoppers would stay and check off items on their Christmas list. I had a good feeling our gingerbread contest was about to fill the coffers and spread some serious holiday cheer.

# TWO

I was right about Fletcher's gingerbread house. It was a replica of Charing Cross station, complete with a black wrought iron roof arching over the train platforms, curved windows, and hundreds of cookie bricks.

"How did you make the windows look like glass?" I asked him, setting my entry next to his. Clearly, he had already won.

"Spun sugar." He sprinkled edible glitter on the rooftop to make it shine.

"Okay, this is incredible. You could start your own cake-decorating business, Fletcher." I was stunned at the intricate details he'd included, like black licorice pieces cut in the shape of door handles, the outline of a body in the center of the train station floor, and cookie cutouts of Sherlock Holmes and Dr. Watson observing the crime scene.

"You are putting us to shame," Hal agreed, pointing to his sweet gingerbread cottage. White frosting clung to the eaves like bunches of fluffy fresh snow. A peppermint-candy wreath hung from the front door, and a small sign in the marshmallow snow near the pretzel picket fence pointed to St. Mary Mead.

"Here, I thought my attempt at recreating Miss Marple's village house was going to impress. Little did I know I'd be going up against a professional."

I threw my hands up in surrender. "You win, Fletcher. And from here on out, you're in charge of all the cookie baking for the store."

"No, no, no. Please don't put me through this torture again. This was pure agony. The angle is all wrong. The curvature of the roof is an utter mess." He continued to nitpick his masterpiece, tweaking the position of the candy rocks and kneeling to get a look at it from every angle.

Hal cut him off. "I do believe you're your own worst critic, Fletcher. Remember, life is perfectly imperfect. We're not machines. We made these culinary delights with our very own hands. What a gift. What a joy to be able to create." He held his palm face up in reverence, like an offering.

His perspective was a good philosophy on life and something I had been learning to embrace as well. Not so much when it came to modeling gingerbread, but when it came to letting go of being overly harsh with myself about mistakes (both real and perceived), especially those I made in my early years of trying to solve Scarlet's murder. I'd put too much blame on myself. I'd gotten so wrapped up in my obsession with solving her case that I'd lost myself along the way.

That had changed in the last few years, and I was proud of my growth. Interestingly enough, while I'd been releasing regret and stepping into this chapter of my life, I'd had more breakthroughs and insights into her murder. Maybe it was a sign I was finally ready.

Hal's voice dragged me back to the moment. "Like Annie, I hereby declare you the winner, Fletcher. Your prize will be coming soon." He paused and turned to me. "Although, *you* get bonus points for creativity, Annie. I adore that you paid homage to our hidden gem. That certainly deserves a prize as well."

"I don't need a prize," I protested. "Honestly, I had a great time making my house. Liam and I were elbow-deep in frosting and blasting Mariah Carey all night. Assuming everything goes well today, I think we could make this an annual tradition."

"Noooo, I'll be forever in misery," Fletcher wailed.

"Let's wait and see what the professionals have to say about your interpretation of Charing Cross," Hal said, beaming with pride. "I'm going to have to keep a close watch on you because I fear Sugar will try to snap you up and steal you away from us."

"Never fear, I'll run screaming." Fletcher clapped his hands to the sides of his face, dropped his jaw, and shook his head. "But seriously, thanks for the accolades. I have enough self-awareness to realize that this line of work is not my calling. Changing the subject, though, Annie, what's this about a gingerbread date with Liam?"

I felt a hot blush spread across my cheeks. Liam Donovan and I had started as rivals but lately had grown closer. Liam owned the Stag Head, a pub in the village square. He preferred historical nonfiction and obscure facts to mysteries, but he'd been coming around to my way of thinking. I'd given him a suggested reading list, and to his credit, he had breezed through the stack and returned for more recommendations. We'd been having Saturday night movie marathons so he could introduce me to some of his top historical classics—*Band of Brothers*, *Anna Karenina*, and *The Trial of the Chicago 7*. Sunday nights were for murder. I, in turn, got him hooked on *Midsomer Murders* and *Death in Paradise*.

A knock sounded on the front door, saving me from having to answer questions about my romantic life.

"I'll get it," I said eagerly, and took off before Fletcher could ask me anything else about Liam.

"Good morning, Annie." Sugar Lester thrust out her hand and grasped mine in a firm shake. She was in her mid to late thirties with silky blond hair and rosy cheeks. She wore brown leggings, matching knee-high boots, and a long-sleeve T-shirt. Her industrial navy apron was embroidered with the Sweet Room logo in canary yellow thread. "This is the one and only Lily Hawthorne." Sugar stepped to the side with a flourish to introduce the baking influencer as if she were welcoming the queen.

"Charmed. Absolutely charmed." Lily tilted her hand toward me. I wasn't sure if she wanted me to kiss it, but she pulled it back toward her face and fanned her cheeks. "What a stunner. This shop is going to play so well on social. It's a dream."

She wasn't what I expected. Her social media profiles made her seem larger than life, but in reality, she was short and petite like me, with jet-black hair cropped in a tight pixie cut and wide doe-like eyes. She was dressed in a candy cane-striped shirt and green skirt. On anyone else, it might have seemed over the top, but somehow she managed to pull it off.

"Becca, do you have everything?" Lily glanced behind them at a young woman with a large roller cart waiting at the bottom of the front steps.

"Yes, but I could use a hand unloading." Becca peered around Lily. She was tall with mousy brown hair pulled into a messy ponytail. She wore a logoed Lily Hawthorne sweatshirt that was splotched with white royal icing. Her hands clutched a box crammed with baking tools and supplies.

"No problem," I said with a smile. "I'm Annie Murray, by the way. I manage events for the bookstore, and we're thrilled to have you in town this weekend. The buzz about the gingerbread competition has been huge. We're expecting a great turnout and can't wait to see what you've built."

"Wonderful." Lily reached into her oversized bag and pulled out her phone. She clipped on a portable ring light. "Do you mind if I shoot some B-roll in the store while my supplies are unloaded?"

"Not at all." I motioned inside. "The store is all yours. At least for the next hour."

Lily drifted past me, smoothing her hair and checking the lighting.

"I can help you carry things in and recruit the rest of our team," I said to Becca and Sugar.

"That would be great. Thanks so much." Becca smiled with relief. "We need to be very careful when transporting some of the heavier pieces. I'll glue them together with royal icing once we get them in place."

"Tell me what to do." I offered my services.

She directed me to her car where we unloaded tubs of icing, piping tips, extra candies, colored sugars, and sprinkles, and carried it all into the store.

"Any chance I could get a cup of coffee?" Becca asked eagerly when we'd finished, eyeing the drink station. "I think I'm going on thirty minutes of sleep at this point."

"Of course." I motioned to the coffee. "Help yourself. And if you need something stronger, my best friend Pri is the head barista at Cryptic Coffee; I can run get you a double shot of espresso."

"There's no need for that." Becca poured herself a cup and stirred in a splash of cream. "This will do the trick." She held the mug up in thanks and gulped down a few sips.

It looked like they had packed enough supplies to open a bakery. Hal and Fletcher lent their muscles to maneuver giant sections of the house into the Conservatory. Lily disappeared while Sugar and Becca constructed their showpieces.

Becca lifted a section of gingerbread roofing from one of the tubs. Her fingers were stained from food dye. I watched with awe as she used what looked like a stainless-steel syringe to inject icing along the roofline.

"What is that?" I asked. "It looks like a torture tool from a dentist's office."

"In the business, we call it a cake-decorating gun. It's a filling injector we use to fill donuts and croissants with jams and custards." She twisted the tip to create a fluted line on the peak. "Depending on the tip, you can create a variety of effects. They're extremely versatile."

"I thought I was fancy using toothpicks and skewers on my house. I'm going to have to up my baking game," I said with a little laugh.

"Toothpicks are great for home baking. This is top quality. It set us back a hundred and fifty dollars and it's worth every cent." Becca tapped the syringe.

"That's spendy," I agreed.

She turned to Sugar. "It's the business, right? By the way, I've been meaning to ask, is Sugar your real name?"

"I'd love to be able to afford those, but my budget isn't that big yet. It's classic plastic piping bags and syringes for me." Sugar cleared space on her table and spread out a lustrous iridescent silver fabric. "Believe it or not, it is. My parents always said I was destined for a career in a bakery."

I couldn't believe the amount of assembly required to put their masterpieces together. Their gingerbread structures were at least two to three feet long and a foot tall and had dozens upon dozens of intricate, breakable parts. Sugar had told me she'd be recreating Redwood Grove to scale—including the midcentury modern and Spanish-style buildings that lined the village square, Oceanside Park, and landmarks like the historical museum and library.

"Is there anything we can do to help?" Hal asked, standing far away from the display tables, worried that he might be single-handedly responsible for sending them tumbling to the ground if he got too close.

I didn't blame him. Fletcher and I kept our distance, too, not wanting to get in Becca's and Sugar's way and not wanting to risk accidentally bumping the table and sending the ginger-bread mansions shattering into a million pieces.

Since Lily was the star of the show, her creation would be front and center on the stage, roped off with the velvet cord Fletcher had found stuffed in a box in the basement. Sugar's house had a table next to Lily. Local entries would be displayed on the tables we'd set up in the Conservatory and throughout the bookstore. Last night, after closing, Fletcher and I draped each six-foot table with red, white, and green tablecloths. Fletcher designed place cards for each entry and ballots for voting. We decorated a shipping box (something we were never in short supply of in the bookstore) with holiday wrapping paper and cut a slit in the top for people to cast their votes. It would stay at the cash register until Sunday afternoon when we'd tally the votes and hand over the results to Lily so she could livestream the winners.

There were six categories: Best Traditional Gingerbread House, Most Creative Design, Best Book-Themed, Most Festive, Best Children's House, and People's Choice. Lily sent strict instructions to include on the ballots about how readers were to judge each entry. They were spelled out on the back of the sheets we'd printed. Lily implored attendees to rank each house by overall appearance, originality, technical execution, complexity, consistency of theme, use of gingerbread, and creativity of edible ingredients.

It was an extensive list. I was sure the criteria would be no big deal in her professional circles, but I couldn't imagine families spending hours poring over every fine detail. A contest like this was subjective anyway. Plus, it was supposed to be a weekend of festive holiday fun. I hoped that Lily wouldn't take it too seriously.

"Are you ready for the reveal?" Becca asked, blocking part of the mansion with her body as she wiggled her hands to try and shake away a cramp. "This is going to go down in history as one of my biggest builds."

"You mean Lily's biggest builds?" Sugar clarified.

Becca cracked her knuckles and made little circles with her neck, releasing tension. "Technically, sure. We're a team, but as you can see, I've done the heavy lifting on this one as per usual."

"Should we wait for Lily before doing the official reveal?" I checked my watch and realized she'd been gone for almost forty minutes.

"She's doing her thing," Becca replied, sounding slightly annoyed. "She'll waltz in when she's ready to grace us with her presence."

I picked up a touch of bitterness in her tone. Maybe it was just from sleep deprivation.

Sugar swept her hand over her gingerbread interpretation of Redwood Grove. "You can see mine."

I gasped as she stepped to the side, revealing our sweet little town dusted with powdered sugar snow. Her detailed piping work was immaculate, and every shop and restaurant in the village was represented—Artifacts, the Stag Head, Cryptic Coffee, State of Mind Public House, and many more, all artfully crafted out of the spicy cookies and finished with wafer rooftops and coconut grass dyed kelly green.

"Oh, my pastry lovelies, look what I've made just for you," Lily's voice echoed through the ballroom. She twirled toward the stage, holding her phone above her face to get a good angle. A ballpoint pen was tucked behind her left ear like a college professor. "We're in the magical town of Redwood Falls and a cozy mystery bookshop."

"Grove," Becca corrected.

"Shoot. Cut. Cut." Lily punched her phone with her index finger to stop recording. "Quiet, please, I'm going to reshoot." She skirted to the other side of the room and proceeded to twirl again, repeating her phrase and dancing up to the stage. "Oh, my pastry lovelies, look what I've made especially for you. We're in the magical town of Redwood Grove at the most stunning bookstore you've ever seen. I can't even." She threw her thin wrist to her forehead. Then she reached for the pen and chomped on the tip like she was deep in thought.

Was it for effect?

"Don't you worry your pretty heads; I'm hooking you up this weekend. I'm going to take you on a full tour of this charming bookshop and the rest of the town, which is like something out of a Christmas card. It's too sweet, but you know what's even sweeter?" She paused and gnawed on the pen, motioning for Becca to move out of the way. Then she posed in front of her gingerbread mansion, extending one hand and grinning with an open mouth for the camera. "My latest and greatest masterpiece. A gingerbread replica of this English estate. Do you love it?"

Lily's interpretation of the Secret Bookcase was nothing short of jaw-dropping. I stepped closer to get a better look.

The exterior was made of sturdy gingerbread panels, meticulously piped to resemble the masonry of the English estate. Tall, arched, translucent sugar windows allowed everyone to see inside. Delicate lace curtains spun from sugar hung from each window, just like our actual lace curtains. The double front doors were constructed of chocolate with sculpted fondant handles and finished with a tiny candied holly wreath.

But it was the interior detail that took my breath away. I gasped as I peered in the windows to see gingerbread bookshelves lined with fondant books piped with titles and edible gold leaf spines. Lily had captured the Sitting Room's cozy reading nooks with gingerbread armchairs and marzipan cushions. Tiny chocolate side tables held mini mugs of hot cocoa and marshmallows. She'd even simulated the fireplace with gingerbread bricks and orange-tinted sugar crystals.

"Tell me you love it," Lily continued, bringing big energy to her viewership watching online. "Because I love, love, love it! What do you love? Is it the adorable turrets? Because if it is, I have a secret tip for that technique I'll be sharing with you soon. Or are you in love with these stained-glass windows? I'll hook you up with tips for making those, too. Be sure to tell me what you love in the comments below. I've got some great merch from my sponsors to share with you. Peace and pastries." She made a peace sign with her free hand, kissed it twice, and blew it to the camera. Then she turned off her phone and looked up at Becca. "How was that?"

"Perfect as always," Becca said with a tired smile, stifling a yawn. "You nailed it." Her tone was flat.

I felt bad for her. She was clearly exhausted, but the day was just starting. Hopefully, now that Lily's replica of the Secret Bookcase was set up, she could sneak away and take a nap. The tedious attention to detail, like the tapestries and rugs designed out of wafer paper and gingerbread Christmas trees decorated with buttercream and edible glitter, had to have taken countless hours.

It was no wonder Lily had amassed a huge and loyal following online. Her work was exquisite. It could easily grace a museum.

"What a quaint little village. You've captured the town beautifully. Did you use isomalt for the lampposts? And are those caramel bricks for the chimneys?" Lily asked Sugar. "It reminds me of my early work. You have a real future in this biz."

I couldn't tell if she was being genuine. She sounded slightly condescending. From my vantage point, Sugar's structure was equally, if not more impressive, than Lily's. Was I picking up on a touch of jealousy? Or was Lily so used to being on for the camera that she didn't realize her tone might be interpreted poorly?

Sugar didn't seem fazed. "Thank you. That's huge coming

from you," she gushed as the red circles on her cheeks deepened from Lily's praise.

Lily made a heart with her fingers. "We pastry girls have to stick together."

I was glad there wasn't any animosity between them. As for me, we had seventy-five gingerbread houses due to arrive any minute. It was go-time.

# THREE

A line of eager home bakers queued down the long gravel drive. Colorful stocking hats, puffy vests, and the jingle of bells greeted me as I stepped outside to welcome everyone.

"Happy holidays from all of us at the Secret Bookcase," I called, making sure my voice carried over the excited chatter. It was amazing to see such a great turnout. Our holiday bunting and Christmas lights were strung from the ivy-covered walls of the manor house across the long walkway, creating a shimmery canopy. "I see a lot of familiar faces," I continued. "I'll be checking you in at the front of the store, and then my colleagues, Hal and Fletcher, will direct you to your spots. Your table will have your name, the name of your entry, your entry number, and a stack of ballots. If you need any changes made, feel free to let one of us know. The event starts in just a little over an hour. I can't wait to see what you've created."

Cheers broke out.

I grinned as I propped open the doors and grabbed my clipboard. Today was going to be a great day for the community and, hopefully, for the store. I wanted the event to be a success for Hal. Steady sales were the key.

A young man was first in line. He was of medium height with sandy-brown hair tied in a long ponytail and a scruffy beard. He wore an oversized ugly Christmas cardigan with elves and lumps of coal over a T-shirt with Lily Hawthorne's face in the center. His shaggy beard desperately needed a trim, and his beady eyes put me on edge.

"You're checking in for the competition?" I asked, noticing that, unlike the rest of the crowd, he wasn't holding a gingerbread house.

"I'm here for the event. I'm a friend of Lily's." He tried to peer around me to see inside.

"Oh great. What's your name?"

"Shane. Shane Briggs." He tapped the edge of my clipboard to encourage me to look faster.

I checked my list but didn't see his name anywhere. "I don't see you on the list."

"Yeah, I'm not on the list. I'm here to help Lily."

No one had mentioned anything about other helpers. Something about his shifty body language made my internal radar go off. We had been trained in our criminology coursework to trust our instincts. I hesitated.

Becca appeared behind me, carrying an empty tub of baking supplies. She stopped short when she saw Shane. "Shane, what the hell are you doing here?"

"I'm here for the gingerbread competition." He shifted his body weight from one foot to the other.

"You followed us here?" Becca clutched the tub, holding it in front of her in a protective stance. "Again, really? This has to stop."

Followed them?

I didn't like the sound of that.

"Lily's in the middle of filming now," Becca said, firming her shoulders and planting her feet on the floor in a show of power. "You can't come in yet, and you're holding up the line."

Shane's eyes darted behind him. He reached into his pocket.

"Hey, easy, easy, what are you doing?" Becca took a step back like she was worried he was reaching for a weapon.

"It's a gift for Lily." Shane offered her a long black box wrapped with a shiny gold ribbon. "Can you give it to her? Tell her it's from me, and I'll see her soon."

Becca didn't move. "You can't just show up like this, Shane. It's creepy."

"What? It's not like I'm a stalker. This is a public event." Shane pointed to the line with his thumb. "You can't keep me from coming. It's a public event. Lily wants me here, anyway."

"No, she doesn't." Becca hoisted the tub closer to her body. "Trust me. She doesn't."

His pale face flushed with anger, but he tried again. "Just give this to her, please. I'll see her shortly." He set the gift box on the tub and walked toward the gardens.

"Keep an eye on him," Becca said under her breath. "He's Lily's superfan. The most annoying type of fan. He's convinced that he and Lily are friends. Yeah. Right. He's relentless. He shows up everywhere we go. Like everywhere."

"Will do," I promised. She left with the tub.

That wasn't lip service. I wanted the day to run smoothly. As event manager, it was my job to oversee everything. Once I finished getting through the line, I would loop Fletcher and Hal in on Shane and make sure we all watched out for him. There was such palpable, joyful energy in the air, and I didn't want anything to ruin that. Hopefully, Shane was just a bit overeager, but I wasn't going to take any chances.

After my strange encounter with Shane Briggs, the rest of the check-in process was relatively smooth. I was floored by everyone's creativity. There were gingerbread barns with marshmallow sheep, tiny Christmas village houses with gumdrop roofs, a train brimming with candies, a retro camper, and a beach house with palm trees and a pool. Laced designs, Victorian storefronts, the Eiffel Tower, snow globes, and a complete recreation of the Redwood Grove village square were some of the standouts.

I oohed and aahed over each one.

The kid entries were absolutely delightful—rainbows and unicorns, confetti, fairy gardens, and Star Wars entries were going to be hard to beat in the creativity category.

Dayton Coyle, the culinary instructor from Redwood Grove High, brought a group of students and needed assistance getting them set up since they were all in different rooms.

"It's Annie, right?" Dayton asked, looking flustered when I bumped into him in the Parlor.

"Yep. How can I be of service?" There was a whirl of activity in the moody Hercule Poirot-themed room.

"That's the question, isn't it?" He sighed and pulled a scrap of paper from his black chef coat. "It's like herding cats, but I think I've got all my students situated. Now I need to figure out where you want me."

Dayton was in his fifties. He looked professional in his crisp chef coat and tall chef's hat. He was tall and burly with a thin mustache, tattoos, and piercings. He reminded me more of a biker than a culinary instructor. "I was asked to make large quantities of my secret gingerbread for tasting, but I don't see a spot for it." He fiddled with a studded earring as he checked the room.

"Oh, yes. Sugar mentioned the tasting. We have a table reserved in the Conservatory for you." I pointed him in that direction. "It's near the stage and should be marked."

"Ah, I must have missed it." He folded the paper and tucked it back into his pocket.

"I was heading that way. Why don't you follow me?"

He fell into step with me. "Have you met the infamous Lily Hawthorne yet?"

"Yes. She's in the building and has already been filming. I'm not sure if she's posted anything yet."

"My students are huge fans. I have to give her credit. She's making baking cool again." He ran his finger over a skull tattoo on his hand. "You'd think my ink would do it, but they don't care. It's all about going viral now."

"Wait. Was baking not cool before?" I joked as we squeezed past a family balancing a gingerbread castle. "I'm so out of the loop."

"It's always been cool to me." He patted his coat. "I wear the uniform with pride, but getting kids interested in the culinary arts can be challenging. I was pleasantly surprised when Sugar called and asked if we'd be involved in the event. Thank you for hosting this. It's a great way to let the kids show off their pastry skills, and selfishly, for me, I'm eager to have people taste my super-secret recipe. I've had some interest—maybe *nibbles* is a better word—in potentially writing a cookbook. Lily is so connected; I'm hoping if she likes my cake, she might be able to put me in touch with an editor or at least steer me in the right direction. Do you know much about cookbook publishing?"

"Not really." I motioned to the shelves in the back of the ballroom. "Mysteries are our specialty. We carry a few mystery cookbooks, but unfortunately, that's the extent of my knowledge. Sorry, I wish I were more help, but it sounds like a great idea."

"Sure, no problem." He shifted uncomfortably. "I figured it was worth asking."

"Of course. My philosophy is always to ask." I hoped I hadn't made him uneasy. Aspiring authors often approached us about how to land an agent or book contract. We kept a stock of titles on publishing resources from "how to write a mystery" to agent directories in our non-fiction section of the Conservatory.

I showed him to his table. "This is you."

"Wow, great." He ran a callused thumb along the tablecloth.

"You weren't kidding. Front and center. Excellent. I'll head out to the van and bring in my gingerbread sheet cakes. Thanks for your help, and thank you again for this opportunity. It's really great for the kids."

I left him and surveyed the ballroom. Becca, Sugar, and Lily were huddled on the stage, snapping selfies. All the tables lining the room were filled with bright and cheery gingerbread creations.

"Not bad, Murray." A deep, familiar voice sent my heart rate skyrocketing. I turned to see Liam Donovan coming toward me. His dark, wavy hair fell over his right eye. He had threatened to trim it, but there was something undeniably sexy about the way he would brush it off his face.

My mind drifted back to the night of our first kiss. It was Halloween night—here at the bookstore. Hal and Fletcher had left early for trick-or-treaters. I agreed to lock up since I was due to meet Liam for dinner. I'll never forget wandering through the dimly lit aisles, my fingers lightly brushing the spines as I restocked misplaced inventory. I could hear the faint hum of revelers in the village and the sound of kids chanting for candy.

That's when Liam appeared at the end of the aisle, his silhouette outlined by the soft orange glow of a nearby plastic jack-o'-lantern. He swept toward me, with his black cape billowing behind him, his footsteps almost silent on the polished wooden floor.

"Good evening, Murray," he said with a playful smile, drawing out his words in a Transylvanian accent. His fake fangs peeked out just enough to add a touch of authenticity to his vampire costume. "I've been dying to sink my teeth into a good mystery, but perhaps I'll have to sink them into something else."

My heart flopped as heat spread up my neck. "I didn't take you for the vampire type."

"Funny, because I took you for the bookish type." He stared

at me with the flickering candlelight casting shadows across his rugged face.

Liam took a step closer, his hand reaching out to gently lift my chin. "You know," he said softly, removing the fangs, "we got rudely interrupted the last time we were alone like this, and I'm not letting that happen again."

My breath caught as I looked up into his eyes, my pulse flopping like a fish out of water. "Liam, I—"

Before I could finish, Liam leaned in, his lips brushing mine in a gentle, hesitant kiss. It was soft and sweet, tasting faintly of spiced cider. The world around us seemed to disappear, leaving us in our cozy, book-lined cocoon.

My hands found their way to his shoulders, gripping his costume as I kissed him back, my heart thudding out of control. The kiss was a mix of tenderness and desire—the kind that made me want to demand a million more.

When we finally pulled apart, our foreheads rested against each other, both of us breathing a little more heavily.

Liam smiled, his eyes twinkling with the same mischievous charm that first drew me to him. "Happy Halloween, Murray."

"That was, uh... breathtaking, literally," I said with a smile, trying to regain control of my body. "Do vampires always kiss like that?"

"Hmm. I'm not sure." Liam chuckled and wrapped his cape around me. "Maybe we should try again?"

*Stay in the moment, Annie.*

I rounded my shoulders and tried not to obsess with how soft and tender Liam's lips looked as he approached me now. "Is this a bookstore or a gingerbread factory?" he asked with a lopsided grin.

"A bit of both?" I shrugged. "I think gingerbread is quickly gaining the upper hand, though."

"It looks like it's already a success. Nice work," he said,

leaning in to kiss my head. "But my God, I've never seen this much sugar in one place in my life."

"Luckily, we're not consuming said sugar." I stuck out my tongue and pressed my hand to my stomach. "I can't even imagine how many pounds of butter and sugar is in this building right now."

"We went through our fair share last night. Long time no see, by the way. How's it going aside from the sugar overload?" He stared down at me with a slightly seductive grin.

"Good, I think." I bit my bottom lip as I scanned the room again. "I'm sort of waiting for something to happen—but fingers crossed—there haven't been any gingerbread disasters, and I think we're out of the woods by now. Everyone is set up." I knocked on my head so that I didn't jinx myself.

"How's the celebrity?" Liam glanced over his shoulder to catch a glimpse of Lily.

"She seems down-to-earth. I wondered if she would be a bit of a diva, but she's pretty chill. Her assistant, Becca, has been unpacking and constructing their work of art. Lily's been filming around the store, which should be good for us. There was one minor issue with this guy Shane. He's a superfan, but Becca asked me to keep an eye on him. Apparently, she thinks he's stalker-ish."

"Stalker-ish?" Liam furrowed his brow.

"Stalker adjacent?"

"That's not better." He scowled and shook his head.

"I'll work on my terminology, but could you be on the lookout for him, too? It's probably nothing, but you never know. He's in his early twenties with long, dirty blond hair that he wears in a ponytail and a scruffy beard. He's wearing a Lily Hawthorne T-shirt with her face on it, so I think he'll be hard to miss."

"That's a commitment—her T-shirt, huh?" Liam winced.

"Yeah, I'll be sure to watch for him. Do you want me to intervene if I see him? Is he banned from the event?"

"No, nothing like that. He seemed harmless, but I also want to be cognizant of the fact that Lily is a celebrity. She probably does have to be careful. I would hate for her to feel uncomfortable."

Liam wrapped his arm casually over my shoulder. My heart skipped a beat. "That's why everyone loves you, Murray."

Heat spread up my neck. I could smell Liam's pine-scented cologne and his minty toothpaste. Being this close to him always made me feel like I was slightly on the edge of being able to control my emotions. It was unfamiliar territory for me and hadn't gone away even as we spent more time together.

It didn't help that he was ridiculously handsome with his chiseled chin, strong arms, and eyes that, in the right light, looked as if they'd been sprinkled with gold. His forest green cable-knit sweater, jeans, and boots made him look like he'd stepped out of the pages of a modern romance novel.

I let myself fall into his firm shoulder as we wandered toward the Foyer to get ready to let the masses in. Knowing that Liam was by my side gave me a new kind of confidence. I was already excited about the event and couldn't wait to see the response from our sweet community. And now that Liam was here, it was the cherry—or holiday gumdrop—on the top.

# FOUR

The line was even bigger than before. At least a hundred happy shoppers waited in the cold—well, the California cold—to check out our first-ever gingerbread showcase. Winter in California hit differently. The grass was touched with a hint of frost, and there was a chill in the air, but by lunchtime, the temperature would rise to the mid-fifties with spotty sun. That didn't stop locals from layering with puffy vests, coats, and scarves. Our "California-cold" winters might be meme-worthy, but there was truth to the idea that forty degrees in Northern California felt like negative ten in Minnesota.

Spontaneous Christmas carols broke out as people filed inside.

I hummed along to "We Wish You a Merry Christmas" and propped the door open. "Be sure to vote for your favorites and turn in your ballots at the cash register." I pointed behind me. "We have treats throughout the store, entertainment, and we'll be offering complimentary gift-wrapping on all sales so you can put your purchases right under the Christmas tree when you get home."

It was wonderful to see such a turnout and enthusiasm.

Living in Redwood Grove taught me the importance of community and connection. After years of trying to hide away, in hopes that might temper the pain of losing Scarlet, I realized the opposite was true. Since I'd stepped out of myself and out of my head, throwing myself into the events program at the store and getting immersed in my hometown community, I'd finally began to heal.

Priya Kapoor, or Pri to me, rushed in with a woman I didn't recognize. "Annie, hi, hi, sorry I'm late. It's been a morning if you know what I mean." She wrapped her tan cashmere scarf around her neck tighter and thrust a box of pastries from Cryptic Coffee into my hands. "Do you know Kari Harris?" She nodded to the woman. "Kari works for Queen Mary Flour. We use their product in all our baked goods at Cryptic. It's superior—organic, finely ground, natural."

"Wow, keep going, you're making me blush." Kari fluffed up her curls. "What an introduction, I'm flattered, Pri."

"Nice to meet you," I said to Kari, making room for them to come inside. "It sounds like you've earned the highly coveted Pri seal of approval."

"Don't listen to Annie; she's my hype girl." Pri flashed her signature cheeky grin and blew me a kiss. "Speaking of hype, this is incredible. Is everyone in town here?"

"It feels like it." I couldn't contain a smile. "I was hoping people would come out, but you never know."

"It's very festive," Kari replied, taking in the store. Her eyes drifted to the front window display. "It's like something straight of Dickens."

"Hopefully, without the rampant poverty, bleak cold, and miserable Scrooge," Pri retorted.

Kari chuckled, tucking her bouncy curls behind her ears. I would guess that she was in her forties. She was dressed in skinny jeans, boots, and a Queen Mary Flour pullover sweatshirt. "Fair point. Without that."

"Is this your first time in the store?" I asked.

"It's my first time in Redwood Grove." Kari looked impressed as she surveyed the Foyer, her eyes landing on a stack of Christmas cookbooks.

"She's here because of Lily Hawthorne," Pri interjected.

"Are you a fan?" I checked to make sure the line had cleared and shut the door.

"More than a fan. I'm trying to woo her to collaborate with us." Kari tapped the logo on her sweatshirt. "She's impossible to get ahold of. I've tried everything—email, phone messages, sliding into her DMs. When I saw on her social media that she was going to be in Redwood Grove for the weekend, I booked a room at the Grand Hotel and told my boss I had to shoot my shot."

"Where are your headquarters?" I rearranged the tray of holiday cookies at the coffee and tea station to make room for Pri's pastries. She had boxed up a selection of their most popular items and tucked in discount cards for free kids' peppermint hot chocolate.

"Sacramento. Not too far." Kari peered into the Conservatory, trying to get a glimpse of Lily. "I would have driven halfway across the country to get a chance to pitch her on working with us. Getting her endorsement on our line of products would be huge for our brand. We're not a huge mega-producer. We're a small mom-and-pop shop, but I am prepared to offer her a nice chunk of change to sign on an exclusive with us."

*A chunk of change* sounded like a Hal expression.

"She's currently signed on with one of the big guys," Kari continued. "It's a long shot, but I've put together a custom pitch to show her the kinds of things we can offer her that corporate America can't." She patted the leather satchel tucked over her arm.

"Like what?" Pri asked.

I was wondering the same thing.

"The first and most important is personalization. A big brand is never going to change its packaging for a celebrity endorsement, but we will. We're envisioning products with Lily's face. She'll have complete control over the design and messaging. We're considering doing an entirely new line of blends for her. She won't get that anywhere else. Her followers will eat it up, literally. Do you want to see the mock-ups?" She reached for her phone.

"Your face on flour, it's the dream." Pri posed with hands beneath her chin and batted her eyelashes. "How do I get my face on coffee beans?"

"Any coffee company would be so lucky as to have your face grace their product," I said sincerely.

Kari scrolled through designs on her phone. The first was a spring line, Flour Power. The packaging featured gerbera daisies and tulips with whimsical swirls of flour dust. "I love the tagline for this one—Bloom with Every Bake."

"I love it." Pri snapped her fingers in approval.

"It's obviously too late for our holiday line this year, but if I can sign Lily, we're already planning for next year. Snowy Mill will be packaged in blues and white, depicting our original flour mill with snowflakes drifting down from the sky." She tapped the screen. "My placeholder is 'Warm Up with Lily's Winter Bakes,' but I'll come up with something even stronger."

"These are great," I said. Kari had clearly done her homework. If I were Lily, I would be impressed, but then again, Lily was probably used to getting similar proposals.

"Sorry to cut this short." Kari put her phone back in her satchel. "I want to hear more about the store, but Lily might be free, so I'm going to see if I can snag her for a minute. I can't miss this shot."

Far be it from me to keep her from her mission. Pri went to help herself to a coffee while I scooted behind the desk to ring up our first order of the day, gift-wrapping a set of Nancy Drew mysteries for a customer.

Pri came back bringing me a cranberry and white chocolate macaron. "So, did I miss anything good earlier?"

"Not really." I set a bowl of free stickers on the edge of the counter so our younger readers could grab them on the way out. "There's a bit of tension with Lily and Becca. I mean, Lily is the superstar, and Becca's her assistant, so I guess it makes sense. Their creation will leave you speechless. Seriously. You're not going to believe what they built out of gingerbread. It's amazing. Sugar's showpiece is equally great. I guess there was one brief incident earlier with a superfan who might be a stalker, but it's probably nothing."

"Might be a stalker? Um, that's pretty big. Care to elaborate on that?" She made a funny face and looked at me like I was losing it.

"I think he's harmless, but I'm keeping an eye on it."

"Boring. No juicy holiday gossip, that's so disappointing." She fiddled with a cozy cat sticker. "What about your vampire? How was your night of *decorating*?"

"We *did* decorate."

"Sure, you did. Sure. Or, you were up all night with Mr. Donovan's sexy fangs piercing your neck." Pri gave me an exaggerated wink and she stabbed her throat with her fingers.

"Uh, do you have something in your eye?" I offered her a box of tissues. Ever since I told her about our Halloween kiss, she had taken to referring to him as my vampire. I needed to come up with an equally clever nickname for Penny.

"Do you?" she shot back. "Like cartoon stars sparking for Redwood Grove's most eligible pub owner?"

I chuckled. "Decorating was nice. And I have proof of our hard labor in the Conservatory. Just look for the Secret Bookcase gingerbread. You can't miss it."

"You're no fun, Annie." Pri pressed her lips together and

scrunched her nose. She loosened her scarf and hung it on the coat rack near the door.

"Is Penny still traveling?" Penny, Pri's girlfriend, had recently moved to Redwood Grove and taken on the daunting task of renovating the old Wentworth farmhouse and vineyard on the outskirts of town.

"Yeah, she's back next week. It can't be soon enough. I've been practically pining for her. The holidays are so romantic, and I've been stuck alone for six days." Pri stuck out her bottom lip. "Do you feel sorry for me?"

"Not really. You're one of the most independent people I know, and I've never seen you pine."

"Oh, I pine, Annie. I pine." She fanned her face. "I pine hard."

I was about to toss a bow at her when a commotion broke out near the stage.

"A little help, please," Becca yelled, waving her hands above her head. "Hello, someone. We need a hand over here."

I left my post and ran into the Conservatory.

A crowd had gathered in front of the stage.

"Get him away from Lily." Becca stabbed her finger at the front of the crowd.

I couldn't see who she was referring to, but I had a sinking feeling I knew who it was.

Liam broke through everyone like a steam engine cutting through calm waters.

"Back off." Becca threw out her hands like she was trying to body-block someone.

"No, I just want to take a picture with my gift." A voice sounded through the mob of people around the stage.

I was right—it was Shane.

How had he gotten inside?

Liam had left an open space in his wake, and I could see Shane clinging to the edge of the stage for dear life.

"Lily, did you open it? I had it custom made for you." He pleaded, clawing the stage with one hand and taking photos with the other.

Becca snatched his phone out of his hand. "I'm deleting these."

Shane ignored her and looked at Lily with begging eyes. "Please open it. When you do, you'll see. You'll understand."

"Okay, okay," Lily said, trying to avoid being close to him by moving behind her gingerbread structure and putting more distance between them.

Sugar jumped off the stage and helped Liam tear Shane away. They dragged him toward the Foyer.

Becca tossed his phone back to him and scanned the crowd frantically. Red, ugly splotches erupted across her face.

"I'll be right back," I muttered under my breath.

I had to do something. I didn't want the atmosphere of the gingerbread contest to get tainted by Lily's stalker. I knew that Liam and Sugar could take care of Shane. I took the side steps onto the stage and grabbed the microphone. "Let me say a few words, and then let's officially kick this off, okay?" I looked at Lily and Becca.

"Thank you," Becca whispered, scooting closer to Lily. "He freaks me out so bad. I can't stand the way he looks at Lily."

"You mean like he's trying to undress her with his eyes?" I asked.

Becca wiped her sweaty hands on her sweatshirt. "No, like he's calculating how he's going to cut her up into tiny pieces and stuff her in a suitcase."

Geez.

I wasn't expecting that.

*Cut her into tiny pieces and stuff her in a suitcase?*

That was dark.

Bone-chilling dark.

I rubbed my arms and glanced at Lily.

She wasn't shaken up. She wet the tip of her finger and smoothed down her bangs, checking her appearance in her phone. "Becca exaggerates. Don't listen to her."

"Do you want to take a minute?" I offered. We weren't in a hurry.

Using her phone as a mirror, she pinched her cheeks for color and chewed on her ballpoint pen like a ravenous wild animal. "No. Go ahead, I'm ready. Let's do this."

"Hi, everyone, sorry about that mishap. It's been taken care of." I chose my words carefully, not wanting to inflame the situation. "Welcome to the inaugural gingerbread showcase at the Secret Bookcase." I paused. "That's a mouthful, isn't it? I'll work on that."

People chuckled. I could feel the tension drop.

That was a good sign.

"As you know, we're here today because of Lily Hawthorne." I motioned toward her.

The crowd cheered.

She pressed her hands against her chest like she was taking it all in.

"Lily, would you like to say a few words?"

She hurried to the mic. "I thought you'd never ask."

Everyone chuckled.

I sighed with relief. The moment had been smoothed over. Lily immediately captivated the crowd with stories about her baking escapades. Becca started the slideshow, which offered a glimpse behind the scenes into the hours and hours that went into crafting her pastry masterpieces. Lily had baked wedding cakes for celebrities and world dignitaries, all while never having so much as a drop of frosting on her beautifully tailored skirts and blouses.

Maybe that was selective editing.

I left the Conservatory to check on Shane. Becca's words

left me rattled. Was she serious? Was Shane dangerous? Did we need to involve the authorities?

But if that was the case, why was Lily so nonchalant?

I was grateful to have Liam on-site, and I was going to take control of the situation. I wouldn't hesitate to call Dr. Caldwell and the local police if necessary. Hopefully it wouldn't be necessary.

If we could get Shane to leave on his own accord, I would feel better.

Every event needed a glitch. If this was ours, I would address the issue, and the rest of the weekend could continue without incident.

# FIVE

Liam and Sugar had managed to wrangle Shane outside. The Foyer was empty except for Hal and Pri, who appeared to be on high alert.

"What was that all about?" Pri asked, keeping her eyes glued to the door.

Hal had taken over at the register. "Annie, why don't you go check with Liam and see if we need to alert the police?"

"Good idea."

Pri grabbed her scarf from the coat rack and tagged along with me. "Is the straggly guy the potential stalker?"

"Yeah." I nodded. "His name is Shane Briggs. He tried to get in early. He told me he was a friend of Lily's, but Becca set the record straight. She said he was an annoying fan following Lily from event to event, but it's escalated now. He's banned for the remainder of the weekend."

"Right. So, he's a one hundred percent stalker." Pri stated the obvious. "Not even stalker adjacent."

"It seems that way. He brought her a gift. Becca took it from him, and just now, he was trying to see if Lily had opened it." I had Dr. Caldwell's number. I wondered if I should text her regardless.

"What kind of gift?" Pri asked.

"I don't know. Maybe jewelry? A necklace? The box looked expensive."

We paused our conversation as we stepped outside.

Shane leaned against the side of the building. He tugged at a strand of the ancient ivy that snaked up the side of the building. Liam stood nearby, ready to jump in if necessary. Sugar paced in front of the evergreen topiaries.

"Hey, what's going on?" I asked casually, in an attempt to make Shane feel calm. Accusing him might make him bolt or do something worse. Suspects were rarely emotionally stable. It was the role of first responders to put them at ease and defuse the situation. I was glad I was trained for this.

"I just wanted to see if she got my gift." Shane yanked an ivy leaf off the vine and shook his head from side to side. "I wasn't going to do anything. I'm her biggest fan. We're friends, okay?"

"I understand, but Lily is a celebrity and has boundaries that she needs to maintain with fans."

"But we're friends," he repeated, rubbing the leaf between his fingers. "She knows me. We talk all the time in DMs. I told her I was coming and bringing her a Christmas present. She was excited." He dropped the piece of ivy, reached into his jeans, and pulled out his phone. "I can show you. I have proof."

"That's not necessary." I waved one hand to signal he didn't need to show us.

"No, look." He pointed his phone in my face. "See."

YOU'RE TOO SWEET. CAN'T WAIT. PEACE AND PASTRIES, LILY.

Shane yanked the phone away after I'd read the message.

"It's Becca, her personal assistant. She acts like she's Lily's bodyguard. She won't let anyone get near her."

"Maybe that's intentional," I suggested gently. "It could be that Becca plays the bad cop, so to speak, so that Lily gets to interact positively with her fans."

He lowered the screen and stared at it in doubt. "No. No. You don't understand. It's not like that. You don't know Lily like me. She wouldn't do that. She loves her fans. She talks about us all the time. She's called me out many times on her livestreams, thanking me for my support."

"I'm sure that's true. I don't doubt she appreciates you. My point is she simply can't interact with her entire fan base." I caught Liam's eye. He nodded, encouraging me to continue. "Becca might run interference between Lily and everyone who wants a piece of her."

The thought made me grateful for my small life in Redwood Grove. Negotiating real and digital relationships with fans must be challenging for Lily.

Shane wasn't giving up easily. He twirled his fingers through his long, mangy ponytail like he was trying to rationalize with himself internally. "Yeah, I guess, but it's different with me."

"What's your plan now, man?" Liam asked, stuffing his hands in his jeans like he had all the time in the world to chat.

Sugar continued to pace, her eyes drifting from the holiday bunting and lights strung across the drive to the front of the store. She seemed troubled. Was she concerned that this would reflect poorly on her? It wasn't her fault. Surely, Lily would recognize that.

"I was going to go back in and make sure Lily got my present." Shane started to move toward the entrance.

"I don't think that's a good idea. She's in the middle of an event." Liam frowned and held out a hand to stop him. "You seem like a smart guy. I think you know if you do that, it's going to end badly. You don't want that to happen, man. Then we'll have to get the authorities involved and ruin everyone's Christmas fun."

I appreciated his approach. He was showing Shane he was looking out for him.

"You don't want that for Lily either." Liam was confident and easygoing, staring at me with interest. "This is her big day. You don't want to be the guy who makes her have to call off the event."

It was a good tactic.

I could see Shane starting to come around. He nodded slowly, like he agreed, but wasn't quite ready to admit it.

"Yeah, that's true." He hung his head and kicked the ground.

"Do you want me to ask Becca about your gift?" Liam offered.

Seeing him handle Shane like a pro made me fall even harder for him. His relaxed style had brought my blood pressure down. I could tell it was doing the same for Shane.

"Not Becca." His ponytail flopped as he shook his head. "She won't tell you the truth. She'll lie, say she gave it to Lily, and keep it for herself."

"Okay, Sugar knows Lily well. They're working together on the event." He turned around. "Sugar, would you be willing to check with Lily?"

"Me? Now? I don't know her that well." She scowled and leaned back to look through the front windows.

Was she waiting for someone?

"No time like the present." Liam gave her a look to let her know it wasn't really a request.

"Fine." She glanced at her watch and took off in a full sprint. "I'll be right back."

"Where are you staying?" I asked Shane. It was important to keep him engaged.

"I got an Airbnb a couple blocks from here, near the park." He nodded toward the English gardens where bundles of twinkle lights intertwined with greenery and felt ornaments hung from the taller topiaries and bay laurels.

"I think I know the place," I said. "You should stop at Cryptic Coffee on your way back. They have great holiday drinks right now."

"Yeah. Maybe." He made an X in the dirt with his foot. "I don't know what I'm going to do now. I was planning on hanging out with Lily."

Was he more delusional than he seemed?

I glanced at Liam. His expression mirrored my curiosity. Was Shane making this up, or did he really believe he and Lily were friends?

Unless I was missing something, there was little chance Lily would have agreed to that plan.

Sugar returned, adjusting the straps on her apron while still keeping an eye on the bookstore. "I checked, and Lily got the gift. She said to please pass on her huge gratitude, and she's sorry about Becca, but we really need to get moving."

"What is it?" Shane wrapped his arms around his chest and stared at her like he was in a police interrogation room.

"What's what?" Sugar huffed and looked at me, Liam, and Pri for support.

I shrugged.

"What's the gift?" His distrust was palpable. Something about his tone shifted that I didn't like. His gaze was hard, and I picked up on a hint of fury in his voice. "The gift. What did I give Lily?"

"Oh, a pen. A nice pen. A custom-engraved pink Montblanc pen with Lily's name and logo." Sugar whistled. "A very expensive pen."

"Exactly. That's why I wanted to make sure she got it," Shane said, throwing his hands out like we had all missed the plot. "Is this like small-town mentality? None of you believe me, but I'm the only person around here telling the truth. I saved for a long time to afford that pen. She mentioned on one of her livestreams that Montblanc pens are her favorite, and you've probably already noticed that she has a habit of chewing on her pens. This one is solid. There's no way she can chew through it."

The guy had it bad for Lily. I hated hearing he was spending his hard-earned cash on extravagant gifts for the internet star.

"I should really get back inside," Sugar said, peering around Liam, trying to look into the store. "Lily and I are supposed to do a livestream together, and I don't want to miss it."

"Go," I said. "Everything's good here."

She left in a hurry, like she was worried she was missing out on whatever was happening inside.

"Are you feeling calmer?" I asked Shane, assessing his mannerisms.

He sagged against the wall. "Yeah, I'll take off. I'm glad she got the gift. I'll send her a DM. She'll probably suggest we hang out once the event is over."

"Sounds good." Liam clapped him on the back and pointed him toward the village square.

We turned to go back inside. "I'm going to let Fletcher and Hal know to be on the lookout in case he tries to sneak back in. If he does, it's an automatic call to the police."

"Good idea." Liam waited for me to go first, holding the door open. "I think he's okay. He seems fairly benign, but I wouldn't take any chances either."

After checking in with Hal and Fletcher, I took a minute to listen in on the livestream.

"You guys have to check out Sugar's Sweet Room," Lily said to her online viewers. "It's like the cutest little real-life ginger-bread house you've ever seen. I'll share pics soon, but it's so adorable I'm telling you, you should book your trip to Redwood Canyon and come get a taste of this sugary sweetness for yourself."

I had to suppress an eye roll. She was laying it on thicker than the buttercream on the gingerbread houses. I understood she had to be over-the-top for her social followers. Why was it so hard for her to get our town name right?

"Isn't her village the best? I'll give you a close-up later, but I have to tell you, I might have some real competition for once." Lily fanned her face for the camera and gave an exaggerated wink. Then she addressed the crowd. "Does anyone in our live audience have questions?"

Hands shot up.

Lily picked Dayton out of the crowd. "It looks like we have a legit chef with us. What's your question?"

Dayton balanced a plate of his gingerbread cake on his palm like a waiter at an expensive restaurant. "I'm hoping you might want to try my world-famous gingerbread. I'm the culinary instructor at Redwood Grove High, and my students baked this batch, especially for you."

"How could I turn down such an offer? Come up. Come up. Let me taste it." Lily handed her mic to Sugar so she could take a bite. She closed her eyes and savored the cake like a sommelier appraising a new vintage of wine. A curious look passed across her face. "I know this recipe."

Dayton beamed, but there was something more sinister behind his eyes like he was taking personal satisfaction in watching her reaction. "Ah, thank you. It's nostalgic, isn't it? I've perfected it over many years to resemble my grandmother's spiced gingerbread. The card next to the plate has the original recipe attached. Give it a look."

Lily picked up the recipe card. She scanned it briefly and then shook her head, tossing the card on the floor like it was contaminated. "No." She shook her head and took another bite, her eyes narrowing as her cheeks sucked in. "I know *this* recipe."

Dayton chuckled uncomfortably, twisting one of the piercings in his ear like he was setting an old watch. "It's a real winner, isn't it?"

"Let's chat offline. I don't think this is the appropriate place or time. I'd love to hear about how *you* developed this recipe." Lily studied him with new interest, her eyes shrinking as she scowled. She looked as if she wanted to say more, but instead, she set the tasting slice down and reached for the microphone. "Other questions?"

"Are you looking for new partners?" Kari shouted. "Queen Mary Flour would love to work with you."

Lily covered her microphone and apologized to the camera. "Sorry about that, my pastry lovelies. Someone was trying to get a free shoutout, and you know how I feel about that. Not cool. Not cool." She shot Kari an icy glare.

Kari waved a brochure and a handful of papers. "We have an offer that you won't want to refuse. It's very generous, and as everyone here knows, our organic brands are unmatched."

"Enough." Becca jumped forward and cut her off. "This is not the time or place for solicitations."

Lily took the phone off its stand and moved closer to the tables, completely ignoring Kari's blatant attempt to pitch her in such a public forum. "Now, what you've all been waiting for—gingerbread. Let me walk you through each step of my ultimate Christmas cookie triumph."

She proceeded to detail her work while Becca and Sugar looked on.

"I know I've taken up way too much of your precious time this morning, but before I sign off, let me show you Sugar's gingerbread village. It's simply adorable. It's a scale model of this quaint little town, and I have it from the baker's lips that she spent six weeks—that's right—six weeks cutting out the dough and piping royal icing on each of these incredible pieces."

Sugar flushed with pride.

Lily positioned the phone in front of her face. "That's what I call pastry commitment."

I watched in horror with the rest of the crowd as Lily turned toward the table, angling her phone above her head with her hand. She must have lost her footing because the next thing I knew, she tripped and stumbled, falling into Sugar's Redwood Grove replica and sending it shattering on the floor.

# SIX

"Oh no, what have I done?" Lily threw her hand over her mouth but kept her other clutched on her phone to keep recording. "We've had a pastry explosion here. I can tell you accidents happen to the best of us, but this is a gingerbread massacre, you all. Yikes."

Becca and Sugar dropped to their knees to frantically try to pick up the pieces. It was futile. There was no repairing the village.

"I'm going to sign off, my beauties, and put my piping skills to the test. Maybe I can work my pastry magic with this mess. More updates from me soon. Kisses." She blew a kiss and turned off her phone.

Sugar's face lost all its color. I thought she might cry.

Becca scooped up the bigger pieces and stacked them on the table.

Everyone whispered and mumbled, unsure whether to help or look away. It was like driving by an accident on the side of the road and not being able to pass by without sneaking a peek.

I took charge again. The carolers we hired to serenade shoppers waited in the Foyer in their Victorian-era costumes. Now was as good a time as ever to have them spread some holiday cheer.

"Can you do your first set in the Conservatory?" I asked, nudging them toward the ballroom. "Maybe three or four songs, and then you can stroll through the bookshop. We have displays in each room."

Their harmonies distracted guests. People moved away from Sugar's butchered gingerbread village and swayed to the music.

Lily tried to console Sugar as they arranged heavy gingerbread walls and parts of the shingled roofline on the table, but Sugar pushed her away with such force that I thought for a second Lily might topple off the stage.

Becca pulled Lily to the side and whispered something in her ear. They looked back and forth from the broken display to Sugar.

Lily finally nodded and reached for the mic. "That was unscripted, wasn't it? As they say, we have too many cooks in the kitchen, so I'm going to dart out and see if I can help in another way. More soon. Peace and pastries." She held up a peace sign as she stepped over the collateral damage. She left the stage with a pink pen tucked behind her ear.

Was it Shane's gift?

"I'm so, so sorry." She blew Sugar a kiss from the bottom of the stage. "I'll make it up to you."

Sugar gave her a fevered stare. Her body went completely rigid as she uttered something under her breath that I couldn't make out.

Lily took the cue she wasn't wanted and power walked toward me.

I straightened a stack of papers on the edge of the counter. The Foyer was quiet. Everyone was consumed with the mayhem in the ballroom.

"You saw that, right?" she asked me, wincing and munching

on the pen with so much force I thought she might break a tooth. "I can't believe I did that. You don't happen to have any extra gingerbread lying around in the back, do you?"

"No." I shook my head, wondering if she was picturing stacks of gingerbread slabs piled between the boxes of books we stored in the basement.

"Are these the ballots?" She reached for the stack of paper. "I'm going to start judging. I'm only going to make it worse if I hang around. Sugar is furious with me," she said to me.

"Yeah, you can take this stack, or you can grab one in any of the book rooms. We made sure to leave them everywhere."

"Good. My followers are super eager to see the local entries." She removed the pen from her mouth and tucked it behind her ear.

Upon closer inspection, it had to be the gift from Shane. It was pink and silver. Her name was engraved on the pen, along with an inscription I couldn't make out.

"That's a beautiful pen," I said, hoping to prod her.

"Isn't it? It's a gift from a fan. My fans spoil me. I'm so lucky. In fact, I need to post about it because fans like the recognition and it encourages other fans to engage, you know?"

I didn't know, but I also didn't like her reasoning. It sounded as if she was trying to coerce her fans to send her expensive gifts.

"Okay, sweets. I'm off to check out these novice bakers. Let me know when you're ready for your shining moment. I want you and this incredible store to blow up, too. Okay?" She waved with her fingers and headed toward the Sitting Room.

I watched her go, feeling torn. What was Lily up to? I supposed her level of fame naturally bred narcissism, but the more time I spent around her, the less I liked the way she treated the people who had put her on her pedestal. She didn't seem overly empathetic or distraught about ruining Sugar's display. How could she be so cavalier about breaking it?

I grabbed a broom and dustpan from the cleaning closet and went to help Sugar and Becca clean up.

"That sucked, I'm so sorry." I handed Sugar a recycled trash bag. "I'm guessing you're not able to salvage much?"

She shook her head, her chin quivering. "I'm stunned. It's so many hours wasted, and the worst part is that none of Lily's followers even got to see my work. At least if she'd filmed before she crashed into it, it would have been immortalized on her social media. I didn't even take pictures this morning because we were so busy setting up. I can't believe it."

"I can," Becca said, rolling her eyes and tossing chunks of gingerbread into the trash bag.

"What does that mean?" Sugar asked, her mouth stretching into a snarl as she stared at a gingerbread stag head in her hand with despair.

"Do you really think she tripped?" Becca sounded doubtful as she tossed a chunk into the garbage bag.

"What?" I was interested to hear more—was she implying Lily ruined Sugar's gingerbread entry on purpose?

Becca pointed to the stage floor. "There's nothing here. What did she trip on?"

"Why would she do that?" Sugar's chin trembled like it was fighting to contain her emotion. "She wouldn't do that on purpose. She's a baker and a pastry artist. She knows more than anyone here the amount of time and love I poured into this project. You were at my bakery. You saw how much time I spent on this. I don't understand how she can be so cavalier."

"You're seeing the unfiltered Lily." Becca dumped another handful of broken cookie pieces into the bag. "All I'll say is Lily doesn't like being shown up."

"How was I showing her up?" Sugar asked, bending to pick up a turret. "I wasn't trying to show her up. I've idolized her for years."

"And that's exactly how Lily likes to keep things. She's great with adoration. But not so much with anything that threatens to unseat her." She moved her box of expensive pastry tools to the far side of the table. "No one touches these, understood? Hands off."

"I won't touch them." Sugar shook her head with such force it made me dizzy. "But that wasn't my goal."

"I'm not suggesting it was." Becca closed the box like it contained rare precious gems and swept pieces of gingerbread into her arms. "Just be careful around Lily. I've learned to give her a wide berth. As long as she's got a sparkling tiara on her head, she's fine, but she won't share her crown."

"She'll just smash someone else's crown," I said, feeling awful for Sugar and trying to wrap my head around Lily's personality. She was a puzzle. Part of her seemed genuinely upset about ruining Sugar's display, but I had picked up touches of self-importance. Maybe Becca was correct.

"Yep." Becca tapped her forehead like I'd nailed it.

"That's awful." Sugar's hands began to quake. Her fingers turned clawlike as she clenched and unclenched her fists. "Can I take a minute? I'm feeling a little shaky."

"Go ahead," I encouraged her. "I'll sweep up. Don't worry about it."

"Thanks." She gave the shattered pieces a parting, wistful glance.

I wished I had a magic wand that I could wave to put it back together for her.

Becca watched her go. "I hope I didn't make things worse."

"I don't think they can get much worse than this." I gestured to the shattered gingerbread. "It is hard to imagine why Lily would intentionally sabotage her. Like Sugar said, Lily must have put in the same hours."

"Yeah. Something like that." Becca scoffed. "Listen, I need to track her down and make sure she's not going off script. You've got this?"

"Yep. No problem." I finished sweeping up while Becca left to find Lily.

Aside from the early incident with Shane and Sugar's broken castle, the event was running smoothly. People strolled from one table to the next, admiring the entries and perusing the bookshelves. Nearly everyone had an armful of books to purchase, which made my bookselling heart happy.

The holiday season would be the last push to keep us in the black for the remainder of the year and give Hal a little cushion for next year. January and February were notoriously slow in the bookselling world, particularly because our shop was way off the beaten path. Redwood Grove wasn't exactly a hotspot for tourism.

After I cleared the remnants of Sugar's castle, I washed my sticky fingers and joined Fletcher at the register. "Pri and Liam both left for work. They said they'd catch up with you later. Too bad they missed the drama."

"Or maybe it's better," I said. "I was just wishing I had missed it."

We spent the next hour ringing up sales, wrapping boxes, and sending happy customers off with holiday packages. The music from the carolers wafted through the store, and I had to refill the coffee and cookie station at least three times.

Everyone had great things to say about the gingerbread competition.

"How do we choose?" one of our regular customers lamented. "They'll all so creative. The kids' entries are outstanding. We have some real talent in Redwood Grove. Tell me this is going to be an annual tradition."

Fletcher folded his hands together. "Your wish is our command."

I was pleased customers were enjoying the experience and equally happy to be ringing up so many sales. I could be biased, but there was nothing better than waking up on

Christmas morning to find a pretty stack of books under the tree.

The ballot box was stuffed full as we approached the lunch hour. We had to empty it and make room for more votes. The small bell above the front door jingled merrily as customers left the store with bundles of cheerfully wrapped gifts and cups of hot chocolate to go.

I did a walk-through of the store, taking a few minutes to soak in the atmosphere. The entire bookstore hummed with the murmurs of quiet conversations, the rustling of pages, and the lilting sounds of instrumental Christmas carols. The scent of ginger, nutmeg, and cloves wafted from the Sitting Room and Parlor, where readers were curled up with mugs of strong tea and stacks of new reads.

I started at the back of the store. The Dig Room, our children's area themed after *Death on the Nile* with sandboxes, antique maps, and pyramids, had cleared out. Parents had taken their young readers home for lunch and naps. I returned discarded books to their shelves and lit the electric camp lanterns that hung from the ceiling. They were paired with red, green, and yellow dinosaur light strings. We had wrapped some maps and wall art in Christmas paper to resemble presents.

After tidying up, I peeked into the Mary Westmacott Nook to check on our romance readers. I stopped to admire gingerbread displays and chat with customers, offering suggestions for hard-to-shop-for readers and reminding everyone to vote for their favorite creations. I was particularly impressed with the houses on display, including Jane Austen's Pemberley with fondant columns and a blue-tinted pond made from rock sugar candy, an Italian villa from *Under the Tuscan Sun* constructed with terracotta-colored cookies and edible marzipan grapevines, and Green Gables with carrot-shaped shortbread and a pretzel stick fence.

Readers lingered in the Sitting Room, enjoying cups of tea

and listening to the carolers. I looked around for Becca, Lily, and Sugar. I hadn't seen them since the incident. The other gingerbread houses in the cozy reading room were intact. All of the entries would remain on display through the end of the weekend. Lily offered to let us keep her rendition of the bookstore. It would be impossible to break it down and transport it anyway. Having her signature piece for the rest of the holiday season would be another way to draw readers into the store.

I headed into the Parlor, which was also quiet. The art deco room had its own aesthetic for Christmas. We'd gone with more of a *Great Gatsby* theme to match the 1920s vibe. I'd always imagined that Poirot would score an invite to one of Gatsby's lavish parties had he traveled to America. The room was festooned with tinsel and pom-poms. Black and gold feathers were displayed in champagne bottles, and a foil fringe divided the front of the room from the bookshelves.

A couple lingered by the tables, pondering over their votes.

"It's an impossible task," the young man said, agonizing over his ballot. "They're all so good."

"I know." I approached them to get a closer look at a Poirot-inspired dining scene, complete with tiny fondant teacups and pastries, powdered sugar footprints, a gingerbread letter, and a marzipan dagger. "I'm declaring that Redwood Grove is the most talented town in California. Prove me wrong."

They chuckled and continued to vacillate over whether to rank Poirot's afternoon tea or a Gothic dark chocolate mansion higher.

I picked up a few discarded cups and napkins. A couple of books needed reshelving—the bane of every bookseller. Not a day went by that we didn't spend a large portion of our time placing books back in their intended spot on the shelves. The fact that our bookstore was made up of many rooms made the task even more daunting.

I brushed the shiny gold strings to the side, letting them

rustle behind me as I headed for the bookshelves. It was like walking into a secret room at a speakeasy behind a wall of glittery fringe. When Fletcher had suggested stringing the retro gold and silver streamers from the ceiling, I hadn't anticipated it would have such a cool effect.

I checked the spines to see where the books belonged alphabetically. The back half of the dark and moody room was empty except for the rows and rows of gilded spines and leather-bound collections.

As I went to place the first title on the shelf, I came to a halt.

Lily was sprawled on the floor near the shelves. A notebook and the fancy pink pen Shane had gifted her were next to her.

Had she passed out?

I stuffed the books on the shelf and dropped to the floor.

"Lily, Lily, are you okay?" I shook her gently.

She didn't respond.

My stomach felt like lead.

Something was terribly wrong.

I didn't like the lifeless look in her eyes or the way her body flopped from side to side, as I tried to revive her.

"Lily, it's Annie. Stay with me."

I checked for a pulse in her wrist and then neck.

Nothing.

There was no sign of a heartbeat or breathing.

She was dead.

# SEVEN

"I need help! Someone call 911!" I yelled as I raced back through the wall of shiny foil fringe and flagged the couple down. "We need help. Call 911."

They dropped their ballots and followed me toward the back bookshelves.

I started CPR and rescue breathing. What had happened?

What could have caused Lily to just drop dead?

There were no obvious signs of injury.

This couldn't be happening.

The couple looked ghostly white as they relayed questions from emergency services.

"Tell them she's not breathing, and there's no pulse."

"An ambulance is on the way," the young man said, sounding as shaky as I felt. "What can we do?"

I used my arm strength for chest compressions. "Can you go find Hal? He should be in the front by the cash register. Tell him what happened and that I need him to keep people out of here until the authorities arrive."

They raced off to track down Hal.

I ignored the trembling feeling in my arms and kept pumping with all my might.

It didn't make sense. Lily was young and healthy.

Why had she collapsed?

Her airway wasn't constricted.

There were no gaping wounds, bumps, or bruises.

What were the other possibilities?

A heart attack?

Drugs?

Could Lily have an addiction problem?

She hadn't appeared to be under the influence of anything, but then again it had been a couple of hours since our last interaction.

People didn't just drop dead.

Something must have happened.

But what?

My muscles ached as I continued CPR, losing track of time and focusing fully on my task until the paramedics arrived.

"We'll take it from here, miss." One of them gently tore me away from Lily's body and helped me to my feet.

"She's not breathing," I said, trying to shake off the daze. "I checked her airway and don't see any obvious signs of trauma."

The paramedic thanked me. "Why don't you take a minute?"

I let them attend to Lily and inched slowly toward the front. Part of me didn't want to leave. Not until I knew for sure that she was dead.

The shimmery foil strands hanging from the ceiling looked like they were moving wavy lines. Or maybe that was just my vision.

I stumbled out of the Parlor and found a crowd gathering in the hallway.

"What's going on, Annie?" Hal's voice cut through the fog.

He blocked the entrance with his body, keeping everyone at arm's length.

"It's Lily. She collapsed," I whispered, not wanting to freak people out more.

"Let's come this way." He motioned to one of our regular customers. "Don't let anyone in until the police arrive. I'm going to get Annie a drink." Then he wrapped an arm around my shoulder and led me toward the front of the store. "You look quite pale, my dear, which makes me think it must be bad."

I nodded, not trusting myself to speak.

"Was there an accident?" His face was etched with concern.

"I don't know. I don't understand what could have happened. I found her unconscious on the floor, but she looked fine." I shook my head, glancing behind us and trying to erase the memory. "How? I don't get it."

"Was there anyone else nearby?" Hal fiddled with a loose string on his cardigan.

"Um, not really. There was one young couple in the room. They were looking at the gingerbread houses. Otherwise, most of the store had cleared out."

We paused at the Foyer.

Fletcher managed the cash register. "What's going on?" he mouthed, tallying a sale.

Hal gave him a nod to let him know we needed a minute. "Shall we go find a seat in the Conservatory?"

"Uh, yeah." I let him guide me into the room, where he directed me to an empty chair near Dayton's table. The table was a festive masterpiece. Gingerbread bundt cakes in a variety of intricate designs were displayed on ceramic cake stands. Bright red and green holly berries were artfully arranged around the platters, along with candied cranberries that glistened like little jewels underneath the chandeliers.

"Sit. I'll be back in a moment."

I was too stunned to move. I needed a minute to collect my thoughts and calm my nerves. I knew I was trained for situations like this, but it didn't make them any easier. I closed my eyes.

Bad idea.

The image of Lily's lifeless body flashed like a movie.

Hal appeared with a cup of tea. "Drink this."

I took the tea, wrapping my hands around the mug and inhaling deeply through my nose.

"Let me get you a slice of cake. A touch of sugar might help." Hal moved toward Dayton's table.

I was close enough to overhear their exchange but not present enough in my body yet to want to join in the conversation. I used a trick from my early training to hyper-focus on the details around me to center myself back in my body. Silver candleholders topped with crisp white tapered candles cast a soft glow over the table. Bowls filled with peppermint bark, spiced nuts, and chocolate truffles were scattered between small tasting slices of cake.

My stomach rumbled at the cake's fragrant dark crumb topped with whipping cream and freshly grated nutmeg.

"Why are the paramedics here?" Dayton asked Hal, catching my eye and studying me like he expected to see a gaping wound. "Is there a medical emergency?"

"Yes." Hal picked up a slice of cake. "The authorities are in charge of taking care of the situation."

"My students all checked out with me an hour ago, but I wonder if I need to make sure it's not one of them." Dayton sounded worried. He massaged his temple, careful to avoid the black stud on the base of his eyebrow.

I winced at the thought of having a piercing that close to my eye.

"It's not." Hal didn't elaborate, scooping a handful of nuts and chunks of peppermint bark onto the plate.

"Should we do something?" Dayton asked, his eyes narrowing as they drifted from one end of the ballroom to the other.

"Not until the paramedics and police direct us." Hal was firm and direct but gentle. I appreciated his natural ability to put people at ease. "Let me give this to Annie, and I'll keep you posted as we learn more."

I sipped the tea. Hal sat on the edge of the chair and handed me the plate. "How are you feeling? You look like you have a spot of color again. That's a good sign."

I forced a smile and took the cake from him. "I'm coming back into my body slowly but surely."

"There's no need to rush it. Take your time."

I took a bite of the cake. Maybe it was the blur of finding Lily and my body's reaction to shock, but the cake was the most delicious thing I had ever tasted. It was moist and tender and infused with warming spices. A light, sugary glaze finished the cake. I gobbled it in four bites and then polished off the nuts and peppermint bark.

"Shall I get you another slice?" Hal asked, starting to get up. "I like seeing you eat. That's also a good sign."

"No. I'm good, but that hit the spot." I set my plate on the floor and took a long, slow sip of the tea. "I wonder if Dr. Caldwell is on her way?"

"I would imagine that's highly likely." Hal nodded and then shook his head slowly. "This is not going to be good for business or our dear community. I hate the thought that a young woman died here. What a tragedy."

"I still don't understand. Could she have had a stroke or a heart attack? She's so young, but I suppose she was under a lot of stress." My thoughts drifted to Shane. Could Lily have been more worried about him than she let on? What if seeing him spiked her blood pressure?

"I suppose it's possible." Hal sounded doubtful.

That seemed like a long shot.

Lily was in her twenties.

Maybe she had a health condition that she kept private? Or an issue that had gone undiagnosed?

Once my mind latched onto a puzzle, it was nearly impossible to let go. And Lily's death was certainly a puzzle.

We sat in silence for a while.

I was grateful for Hal's comforting presence and for letting me take the lead. He sat next to me, sipping his tea in an easy silence, holding space for us. I knew he would be there if and when I was ready to talk.

Before that happened, Dr. Caldwell arrived with another team of police officers. She was short and petite, with glossy silver hair and oversized black glasses. The police officers accompanying her wore standard blue uniforms, whereas she was dressed more casually in black slacks and a pullover sweater.

"Do you want me to speak with her first?" Hal asked.

"No. I feel much more normal again." I rested my teacup on the plate and stood up. "I found her. Dr. Caldwell will need my statement."

Hal squeezed my shoulder. "I'm here if you need anything."

"I appreciate that." I leaned in and gave him a hug.

Dr. Caldwell caught my eye and waved me toward her. Her ability to read a room or any situation was unmatched. I could tell from the way her gaze ping-ponged from the Conservatory to the Foyer, and down the hallway that she was taking everything in, including the nearest exits and potential escape routes.

"Annie, how are you?" She patted my arm. Dr. Caldwell wasn't effusive. Not to imply that she didn't care deeply. She did, but touch wasn't her love language.

"I'm okay. I found her." I nodded toward the hallway. "She was passed out in the Parlor. There were no obvious signs of trauma or injury. It's unsettling that she just dropped dead. She seemed to be young and healthy."

Dr. Caldwell made a quick note. "Care to walk with me?"

"Sure." I fell in step with her. Having her on the scene made me acutely aware that I owed her an answer. She had been heroically patient with me, but it was time for me to commit to my next chapter.

"Any observances prior to finding the deceased?" She scanned the entry to the Sitting Room as we passed.

"Yeah, there were a few incidents. I'm not sure if any of them are connected to her death because I can't figure out how she died." I told her about Shane and how Lily had accidentally ruined Sugar's gingerbread castle.

"Aside from Shane, were there any indications of conflict?"

I knew Dr. Caldwell was mapping a landscape of the events leading up to Lily's death. It was common practice in any investigation whether the death was from natural causes or otherwise.

"She's a celebrity. She has a large following. Becca, her personal assistant, seems to run interference between Lily and her fans. People were eager to have face time with her. We did have one incident with a superfan, Shane Briggs. Becca shared that he shows up to all of Lily's events, but we took care of it and sent him on his way." I paused.

Could Shane have come back into the store without me seeing him?

It was possible.

"Everyone wanted to pitch her," I continued. "Dayton, the high school culinary instructor, wanted her endorsement on his gingerbread cake recipe, and Kari Harris is in town to try to *woo* Lily to sign on with her flour company. She literally said 'woo.'

All of the attention made me feel sorry for Lily. How do you know who your real friends are when everyone you meet has an angle and wants a piece of you?"

"Good question." Dr. Caldwell made another note and ushered the group that had gathered outside of the Parlor away. "Please step aside. But do not leave the premises until someone on my team has had a chance to speak with you."

There was no doubt that she was in charge. Customers scattered, making room for us to step inside.

"Let me speak with the paramedics. Hang tight." She proceeded to push through the shiny Christmas decorations.

I couldn't believe there was a dead body behind the dazzling gold streamers.

Hal said it best—it was a terrible tragedy. I wondered about Lily's family and friends. Dr. Caldwell would have to contact them and break the news that she wouldn't be coming home for the holidays. My mind drifted to Scarlet. When her body was found the day before graduation, it felt like a nightmare I couldn't wake up from.

I'll never forget her parents showing up at our apartment flanked by two police officers. That day is forever etched in my brain. Scarlet's mom's sobbing screams. Her dad dropped to his knees. I wanted to run, to flee. But I sat in stunned silence on the tattered yellow couch that we'd scored for twenty dollars at the Goodwill and lugged home by hand, petting Scarlet's cat, Professor Plum, and trying to process how my best friend could be gone. My mind refused to accept that I'd seen her hours earlier on the quad. She was upbeat and happy, eager for our grad ceremony, and ready to spill a secret she'd been keeping from me. A secret that went with her to her grave.

Scarlet had been close to cracking the cold case we'd been assigned by Dr. Caldwell. Or, at least, she was convinced that she had tracked down Natalie Thompson's killer. Natalie had vanished during our first year of college. She worked as an executive assistant at Silicon Summit Partners. By all accounts, Natalie had been a valued employee. During her first few years working at the investment firm, she received glowing praise from her colleagues as well as promotions and bonuses. But something changed the year she died. According to reports from her family and friends, Natalie became withdrawn and paranoid. She went to the local authorities and reported that she'd stumbled upon a corruption scheme involving not only her bosses but other high-powered and high-profile businesspeople in the community. The police blew her off as "overly dramatic," claiming that she'd had an affair that had gone wrong and was simply seeking personal revenge.

I'd read the police report, and it was maddening. They completely dismissed Natalie. The officer had noted that she was: "Young, pretty, and bitter she hadn't landed a husband."

Scarlet and I had been outraged when we studied the reports and subsequent interviews with Natalie's coworkers after her disappearance. If the police hadn't been negligent, Natalie and Scarlet would still be here today.

I'd been trying to piece together Scarlet's final days for the last decade. She had tracked down a source, "Bob," who she met with hours before she died. The problem was I had no idea who Bob was, and clearly, she'd used an alias for his name. I'd scoured company records and reached out to every employee at Silicon Summit Partners with very little luck. Most people had kind things to say about Natalie but claimed they could provide nothing further. Many simply didn't respond to my requests. And a handful told me without hesitation that I should never contact them again. They, of course, went straight to the top of my "persons of interest" list.

A little over a month ago, I'd had my first big break. Mark Vincent, a former employee who had worked for the company when Natalie went missing, agreed to meet with me. He had since moved to the East Coast but was visiting San Francisco for a consulting job. We had a meeting lined up on Monday. I'd been preparing for our meeting like it was finals week in college.

Lily's death resurfaced so many memories. I hoped that Dr. Caldwell would be able to determine what had killed her and provide her family with some sense of peace.

# EIGHT

Dr. Caldwell's voice tore me from my thoughts. "Annie, did you hear me?"

I shook my head and rolled my shoulders. "Sorry, I guess I drifted off there for a minute."

She bobbed her head without judgment as if she understood and found it perfectly normal for me to be daydreaming as she investigated Lily's death. "I've completed my initial assessment and released the body. Like you, I find the circumstances around her death suspicious."

"Suspicious?" That could mean that Dr. Caldwell wasn't yet willing to rule out other causes, albeit accidental or homicidal. Knowing she had also picked up concerning detail about Lily's death was validating. I had no desire to be right about potential foul play, but I was glad my instincts aligned with hers.

"Yes." She set her black leather bag on one of the wingback chairs near the bust of Hercule Poirot. Then she tapped her fingers together. "When was the last time you saw Lily?"

"Probably an hour and a half or two hours ago. She left the Conservatory right after she tripped and broke Sugar's creation.

She was planning to judge each of the entries and shoot more for social media. We were busy at the register. I was wrapping orders and chatting with customers. I don't have a recollection of seeing her again, but I guess she could have slipped by us at some point."

Dr. Caldwell stared out the stained-glass windows. "The only exit is through that door to the main hallway, correct?"

"Yes." I frowned. Did she suspect Lily had been murdered? My heart thudded against my chest. Could Shane have snuck in while we were distracted by ringing up orders and gift wrapping? "Do you know the cause of death?"

Her narrow lips tugged down. "No. As you mentioned, there are no visible marks or bruising. There are no signs of a struggle. It doesn't appear that she choked or had an issue with her airway. We don't see any indications of a drug overdose. You'll likely remember from your studies that there tend to be some clear signs that point to drug usage—a bluish tint around the lips and fingertips, changes in pupil size, odors, drooling or frothing at the mouth. None of those are present here. It could be a sudden cardiac arrest. That's the most logical explanation. However, my instincts tell me something else could be at play."

"Do you think she was poisoned?"

"Perhaps. Every possibility is on the table. I'm not ruling anything out at this phase." She ran her hands along a collection of hardcover Raymond Chandler novels. "Did you happen to notice if she ate or drank anything?"

"Dayton's cake!" I clasped my hand over my mouth. "Dayton practically pushed his cake on Lily. He said he had a secret recipe he begged her to try in front of everyone. It would have been awkward for her to say no because he commandeered the Q&A session to get her to taste it."

"And did she?"

"Yes. She had a strange reaction to it, too." I felt more like myself talking through the facts with Dr. Caldwell. Piecing out everything I remembered while it was fresh made my breathing return to normal and it was good to feel like I was actually helping.

"Can you elaborate on *strange*?" Dr. Caldwell reached for her notes.

"She mentioned something about knowing the recipe—recognizing the taste. I found it odd at the time. She didn't seem pleased about it and told him they should talk offline later. Actually, she seemed pretty furious."

"Hmm." Dr. Caldwell made a note. "How long was this before you found her?"

"About the same time." I looked at the ceiling as I retraced my movements. "Two hours, probably. Lily addressed the crowd, opened it up for questions, and then she tripped and fell into Sugar's house. Although, that was also a bit unusual. Becca hinted that it wasn't an accident."

Dr. Caldwell leafed through her notebook. "To recap. Lily ingested the cake an hour and a half to two hours before falling unconscious?"

"Yes, that's correct." From our previous experiences together, I could tell she was formulating timelines and documenting the window of death. If Lily had been poisoned, knowing how much time had transpired would help direct the coroner during the autopsy.

"Did Becca elaborate on why she believed Lily intentionally destroyed Sugar's entry?"

"She hinted Lily was extremely jealous. She didn't come across that way, but then again, she was a social media influencer. It was her job to lean into that role. Her camera was always recording." I raised my eyebrows and used my hand to mimic Lily. "It was glued to her. She was constantly checking her appearance and checking in with her followers."

"Well, that could be quite helpful. Maybe we'll get lucky,

and her phone will clue us into what she was doing shortly before her death."

"She was livestreaming. You could check her social feed, too." I wondered how many people had captured clips from earlier in the day. I'd seen dozens of phones recording Lily's speech. Maybe someone had captured more.

"I've already directed my team to do that very thing." She gathered her bag and notebook. "We'll be gathering witness statements for the next few hours. Please do let me know if you notice anything else unusual and I'll be in touch soon."

I left her to conduct her interviews and returned to the front. Sugar was slumped on the counter with her head buried in her hands.

Fletcher caught my eye and shrugged like he had no idea what to do. I made a face and lifted my hands.

"No, you," he mouthed, gesturing to Sugar like she might implode.

I rolled my eyes and stifled a laugh. I adored Fletcher, but messy human emotions were not his forte. That was fine. I could do the heavy emotional lifting for both of us.

"Sugar, are you okay?" I patted her shoulder gently, not wanting to startle her.

She flinched, but when she realized it was me, she sat up and twirled her hair around her finger. "Annie, oh God, this is the worst day of my life. I thought it was going to be the best day of my life, but now it's the worst."

"Do you want to talk? I know for myself in situations like this, it helps to process my emotions with a friend. I can't take away what happened, but I can listen." I pointed to two open chairs in the Conservatory.

"I don't want to keep you from work. I know you have a ton going on." She glanced around the empty Foyer.

"Go, I insist," Fletcher said a little too eagerly. "I'll holler if we get busy."

A woman crying on his counter was not Fletcher's cup of tea, to say the very least.

"Text me if you need me." I patted my phone. I could keep an eye on the front from the Conservatory, but since Dr. Caldwell and her team were starting to interview witnesses, I had a feeling things would stay slow for a while. The Parlor was officially closed off as the crime scene, but the rest of the store was open for browsing and shopping. That didn't stop a handful of curious onlookers from trying to get a peek behind the door. Fortunately, Dr. Caldwell assigned one of her team to stand guard, so that was one thing we could cross off our list.

"I can't believe this is happening," Sugar said as we walked together. "Everything was fine a while ago, and then she fell into my replica, and it all fell apart."

Was the accident the impetus for Lily's death? I observed Sugar's body language. She ran her fingers together like she was trying to cleanse her hands. Could it be a sign of guilt?

I wanted to give her the benefit of the doubt, and I really didn't want to have to consider her as a suspect. The more time I had spent with Sugar these last few weeks preparing for the event, the more I had come to like her. We had a lot in common and had bonded over royal icing techniques and fails. But I had to treat her like any other person of interest in the case.

She was probably speaking figuratively, but nonetheless, her words got my attention.

I waited for her to sit. The Conservatory was equally quiet. The tables with the gingerbread entries looked lonely in this new light. The earlier festive and joyful atmosphere had been replaced by a palpable melancholy. Dayton was packing his tasting display, and a handful of customers wandered the shelves searching for a new read or a holiday gift. The carolers were long gone, and a soft, purplish late-afternoon light flooded through the large windows.

"Did you see what happened?" My eyes drifted to the stage where Lily's masterpiece sat alone.

"You mean when Lily died? I saw her about five minutes before, and she was fine." She stretched her hands like she was warming up for a yoga class and cracked her knuckles with a loud pop.

I flinched ever so slightly.

That wasn't my question, but this was even better information.

"Where did you see her?"

"Becca wanted us to pose for photos with some of the kids. We were in the Dig Room. Lily was fine then. Fine. Well, that's not true. She complained of a headache and some chest tightness. But Becca told her it was probably stress and she should drink more water."

"Did she?"

Sugar focused her gaze on the Christmas tree, craning her neck toward the ceiling and then looking at me with confusion. "Did she what?"

"Drink water," I nudged. If Lily was poisoned, there was a possibility someone could have slipped something into her drink.

"No. Why?" Sugar studied me like she was unsure.

"Just curious. I never saw her again after the accident. I wondered if maybe I missed her. The drink station is in the Foyer, but I was busy wrapping."

"Oh, yeah, well, anyway. She must have already not been feeling well, but I can't believe she died. It was a heart attack, right?"

"I don't think the police know yet."

Sugar smoothed her apron. "Becca told me Lily has had issues with her heart. It's the only thing that makes sense."

If that were true, she was right, and Dr. Caldwell would

likely close the case quickly. But it also seemed convenient that she was suddenly mentioning health issues now.

"I hadn't heard Lily had a heart problem." I watched her carefully. Prior to today, Sugar had always been upbeat and bubbly. Something had shifted. It might be she was rattled and distraught over Lily's death, or it could be a serious case of guilt.

Then again, could the easiest explanation be the truth? Maybe Lily had a fatal heart attack. I wasn't quite sure which was worse.

"That's what Becca told me." Sugar absently ran her finger back and forth on the trim of her apron. "She said Lily went off her medication a couple of months ago and has been having breakthrough issues."

"Has Becca spoken with the police?"

Sugar shrugged. "I have no idea. She may be speaking with them now. I haven't seen her for a while."

This was crucial information. Once we were done, I needed to fill Dr. Caldwell in if Becca hadn't already. "What happened with the gingerbread? Did Lily trip?"

"I thought so, but now I'm not so sure."

"Why?"

"A lot of things have started coming out."

"A lot of things? Like what?"

"I'm an idiot. I thought Lily was here to give me and the entire town a boost. I guess I'm more naïve than I realized because I thought she was using her social platform for good, but damn, was I ever wrong." She traced the yellow stitching on her apron as if trying to stitch her thoughts together.

Sugar didn't strike me as naïve.

"You should see some of her posts and things she said about me." Her hands clenched into tight fists. She pounded them on her knees in a rhythmic pattern like she was keeping the beat with the Christmas carols playing overhead.

"You mean on social media?"

Sugar reached into her pocket and took out her phone. She scrolled until she found what she was looking for and handed it to me.

SWEET ROOM IS CAKE-LEVEL CRINGE.

FAKE IT TILL YOU MAKE IT, BUT THIS GIRL CAN'T BAKE.

WENT TO SWEET ROOM TODAY, AND HER CUPCAKES SHOULD COME WITH A WARNING: MAY CAUSE DISAPPOINTMENT.

#DOUGHNOTRECOMMEND

My hand instinctively went to my heart. I felt terrible for Sugar. Each caption was paired with a bright photo of Lily and Sugar, grinning for the camera like old friends, but the captions and comments in the post were horrid. It was painful to read them, and they didn't have anything to do with me. I knew people could be cruel online for no reason, but this seemed intentional—almost targeted.

"I don't understand," I said to Sugar. "Why would Lily post such unkind things?"

"I don't understand either. It came out of nowhere. The morning was going so well. My DMs were blowing up with orders and requests for custom cakes, and then I got tagged in these posts, and now I'm getting spammed and hate messages."

"Lily posted these?" I tipped my head to the side to get a better look at her face. She was clearly upset by the online vitriol. I would be, too. I couldn't imagine what I would do if readers online said similar things about the Secret Bookcase.

"Yeah." Her voice rose. She jabbed her hand in the air. "I have no idea why. I didn't think there was any chance she intentionally knocked my gingerbread structure over, but after seeing this, I'm not sure. I thought things were going well."

"When did she post these?" I checked the comments to see if there was a time stamp.

"Minutes after she destroyed my Redwood Grove replica. I don't get it. I thought we were getting along well. I mean, I haven't seen her that much this week, but our interactions have been good." She stared off toward the tree again.

"You didn't see her?" That was potentially a point of interest. "Wasn't she at the bakery with you?"

"Not really. She popped in and out, but I've mainly been working with Becca." She glanced at the logo on her apron. "Lily showed up a couple of times for photo ops, but we did all the work."

This was painting a new picture of the influencer. I wanted to ask her more, but we were interrupted by a police officer who was prepared to take her statement.

"I'm sure you are already planning to, but you should tell them all this." I didn't want to sound condescending, but this could be critical information, especially the piece about Lily's potential heart condition.

"I will." She shoved her phone in her apron pocket.

I left her, feeling more confused than before. On one hand, if Lily had a heart problem, that could explain why she'd collapsed, but on the other, it sounded like Lily had a vendetta against Sugar.

Was there a chance that Sugar could have had a hand in Lily's death? Was she concealing her rage? Maybe she was seething internally about Lily ruining hours and hours of tedious baking and construction, especially knowing that Lily hadn't been a part of it. Could Sugar have exacted her revenge?

# NINE

The rest of the afternoon was relatively uneventful compared to finding Lily's body. Dr. Caldwell and her team continued taking statements, surveying the scene, and collecting evidence —not that there was much for them to go on. I spent the remainder of my shift trying to maintain as much composure as I could. I also snuck upstairs to my shared office with Fletcher a couple of times to jot down notes about the events leading up to Lily's death. Cataloging the facts and the timeline helped my brain settle and gave me a sense of purpose.

As the day began to wind down, customers dwindled. We rang up final sales and reshelved misplaced books and candles. After Fletcher locked the front door and turned the sign to CLOSED, Becca and Sugar were the last two people left in the store.

Sugar took a load outside to her van.

"I'm locking the back," Fletcher said, dangling his keys.

"What now? What am I supposed to do now?" Becca asked, slumping on the edge of the counter. She looked worse than she had at the start of the day. Her hair was frazzled, and her eyes were bloodshot.

Had she been crying?

That wouldn't be unexpected, especially given her relationship with Lily.

I wondered how close she and Lily had been. Were they more than colleagues? Had they been friends? My exchange with Sugar was top of my mind, so I used the opportunity to ask her about the nasty posts on social media.

"I wish I had more to offer you, but it's probably best to wait and see what we learn from Dr. Caldwell." I chose my words carefully, not wanting to upset her more. "Sugar showed me Lily's social. I can't believe she said such awful things about Sweet Room and Sugar's baking."

Becca's sigh made her entire body crumple. "That's what I was trying to warn her about earlier. Lily had a mean streak. She didn't like to be shown up."

"How was Sugar showing her up?" If I stepped back and observed their creations objectively, Lily's replica was superior. Did her insecurities run that deep?

"Any perceived threat sent her over the edge. That probably impacted her health. She was super high-strung."

I listened with interest, hoping she would say more. My perspective of Lily was different. Had she been a little self-absorbed? Yes. But I hadn't seen any evidence of her being high-strung.

"The detective doesn't want me to leave town yet, and I wouldn't dream of it. Not until we have some concrete answers. I want to provide her family with some level of comfort, but that's not going to happen until the police tell us how she died." Becca rubbed her jaw. "I told her she should be more careful. She was terrible about taking her medication. I organized her pills for her every morning, and yet, still, she would forget. Sometimes, I wonder if she intentionally didn't want to take them. They made her tired and sluggish. She said they impacted her ability to bring good energy to the camera. I told her that wasn't true. Her fans adore her no matter what, and if anything, if she had been honest and authentic with them about her health problems, they would have rallied around her."

"Was her heart issue serious?" I cleaned the counter with a soft rag.

Hal and Dr. Caldwell chatted nearby in the Conservatory. I figured she was probably briefing him on what they'd learned thus far.

"Not as long as she was consistent with her medication." Becca sighed, her entire body crumpling like a deflated balloon. She dug her fingers into her jaw and made slow circles like she was attempting to release bottled-up tension. "It's partially my fault. I should have forced her to take it."

"I don't think you can force a grown adult," I said truthfully. Although Becca's guilt was clear and understandable. I felt the same way about Scarlet. I had replayed the day she died with dozens of other potential scenarios where I followed her or took her place, but none of them brought her back, and what I had come to learn was the only person responsible for her death was her killer.

"No, not Lily." Becca attempted to smile. "She didn't take direction from anyone. Certainly not me."

Sugar appeared with another load. She must have over-heard us because she mumbled something under her breath. I turned to her and was about to ask her to repeat whatever she'd said.

"Forget it. It's nothing." She waved me off and untied her apron, draping it over one shoulder. "I'm taking all the supplies back to my bakery for now."

"How long have you worked with Lily?" I asked Becca as I rearranged cozy holiday stickers—cats nestled under a Christmas tree constructed from books, cups of holiday cheer, and my personal favorite, a gingerbread house with books for windows and the words MERRY BOOKMAS written in an elegant scroll across the roof.

"*For* Lily. I worked *for* Lily, not with her," Becca said, an edge creeping into her voice.

"I think that was true for everyone in her orbit," Sugar added.

Why was she being so quiet?

She had barely said anything.

Was she still fuming about Lily's last social media posts?

That would get under my skin, too. I didn't blame her. If someone had said the same kinds of awful things about the Secret Bookcase, I would have gone on the defensive.

"Yeah, you're right about that," Becca agreed. "I've been working for her for three years. I got my start as an unpaid intern. Once I'd proven my worth and loyalty to her, she brought me on full-time. Although she promised me a growth track, that never happened." She paused, searching for the right words. "I don't know what to do now. I haven't posted anything publicly. The police asked me not to. They need to notify her family. Once that happens and word gets out, do I keep her accounts running? Shut them down? Transfer them over to me? She has such a strong and loyal following I would hate to see her fans not have a space to connect. We're really a third space for a lot of them. I know it sounds strange to have a digital place as a hangout spot, but that's what we created. There is real community amongst her fan base."

I started to respond, but she cut me off.

"Oh no! I've been so distracted and frankly in shock that Lily's gone that I didn't even think about the competition. What do we do now? Do we cancel it? Do you want to take over as lead judge, Sugar?" Her words tumbled out in a breathless rush.

Sugar looked stunned. "Me? Uh, I guess. I don't know. You want me to take over Lily's social?"

"I wasn't thinking that exactly, but yeah, sure, now that you mention it, that could work. Why don't you do a takeover for the remainder of the weekend? No one needs to know the truth—not yet. Her fans are going to start to ask questions if she's not online soon. She's usually logging hours livestreaming each day. I posted a few pics an hour ago, but if you could do an update from the store now, closing out the day, I think that would satisfy everyone. Tomorrow, we can do everything from your vantage point. Yes, yeah." Her breath was quick and stilted like she was rapidly making a new plan on the fly. "That will be good—we'll go with the sweet, local angle. I can weave in some footage I shot today of Lily. No one will have any idea. That will buy us time until the police tell us what to do next. I'll work on a pitch and some talking points tonight."

"Um, I don't know," Sugar repeated, sounding uncomfortable as she tugged on her apron strings. "You want to pretend like Lily's still alive?"

"No, I don't want to, but we need to do whatever is necessary to protect Lily's family. The police were very clear about not saying a word publicly. They explained that tracking down her family may take a little while. Of course, I gave them their contact info, but Lily's fans are hyper-focused on her every move. You met Shane. He's already commented twice, and I'm going to have to respond to him soon. The algorithm will start dropping views if I don't. Fans are going to get suspicious. We hyped this weekend up. We can't just go silent. Once, I was stuck in traffic after we had done a gallery of wedding cake posts. Lily was at the event, so I was tasked with responding to comments, but I couldn't get to them for an hour. We lost so much traffic because of that. Views fell off a cliff, and her followers were furious that she wasn't communicating with them. Someone actually called her out for getting an inflated ego. Lily built her brand by connecting authentically with her fans. That never changed from when she had fifty followers to five hundred thousand. In fact, when she hired me, that was her top priority, making sure if she was busy, I could respond as her. I spent weeks reading back through her previous posts and comments to learn her style and be able to mimic her voice."

I had a new appreciation for how much pressure Lily must have been under. Becca was also correct about police procedure when no family was present. Witnesses could help with identifying victims, whether accidental or natural, but Dr. Caldwell would need to locate and inform Lily's next of kin. Sometimes, tracking down family members came easily. Hopefully, that would be true in this case since Becca was well-connected. Often, finding family members and relatives was its own investigation. Dr. Caldwell would have access to law enforcement databases. She could search vehicle registrations and even scour social media if necessary.

"What do you say? We could do a quick five-minute livestream right now in the Conservatory just to wrap up the day." Becca pulled out her phone as if she were ready to film immediately.

"Uh, I'm not sure." Sugar hesitated, removing her apron from her shoulder and twisting it on her lap. "It feels wrong."

I agreed. "Maybe we should take a beat and think this through. Perhaps even check in with Dr. Caldwell."

Sugar gave me a relieved smile. "Yeah, I second that."

"I will be doing all of the above," Becca replied in a biting tone. "I'll need to coordinate with Lily's family, her agent, you, and the police to issue a formal statement. In the interim, we need to save face. You know as well as anyone how intense her fans are. Imagine if word gets out and her family is in the dark. How terrible will we all feel then? This is a strategic PR move."

That was a fair point.

I hesitated. This was new territory for me.

"What would I even say?" Sugar asked.

"Thank everyone for following along today. Let them know that the first round of votes is in, and tomorrow, we'll chat more about your process as a baker." Becca tapped her phone. "This is a huge opportunity for you to step into the spotlight and shine while protecting Lily's family."

"Okay, I guess." Sugar gnawed on the inside of her cheek. She looked like she was prepping for a root canal.

I winced internally. It felt gross to proceed as if nothing had happened, but if Becca was right about Lily's fan base, it probably wasn't the worst idea. At least for today. By tomorrow, Dr. Caldwell should know more about the cause of death and have had a chance to get in touch with Lily's relatives.

I watched them set up the shot on the stage.

Dr. Caldwell and Hal joined me in the Foyer.

"What a day, Annie. How's our girl holding up?" Hal asked, buttoning his cardigan.

"All things considered, I'm still upright, so I'll take that as a win." I flashed him a double thumbs-up.

Dr. Caldwell's smile was strained and faint. She looked exhausted. "It's been a long day, and I have a long night ahead of me. Thank you both for your time and assistance."

"Is there anything else we can do?" I asked.

She pressed her glasses on the bridge of her nose and shook her head. "Thank you, but no. I have stacks of paperwork to file, relatives to contact, and Lily's personal effects to review. We'll be looking into her digital, financial, and medical history. I'll be eagerly awaiting the coroner's report."

"Did you hear she had a heart condition?"

Hal's bushy eyebrows shot up. "She did?"

Dr. Caldwell nodded. "According to those close to her, yes. Although apparently, it was controlled by medication. The first phase of my paperwork tonight will be establishing a need to access her medical records. Then I'll need to secure authorization and put in a formal request." She looked at me. "As you know, according to HIPAA, healthcare providers have up to thirty days to respond to requests. I'm counting on it not taking that long, but you never know."

One pervasive myth in the field was that investigations moved at a rapid speed. Nothing could be further from the truth. Autopsies, toxicology reports, and requests for records took weeks, if not months. It was only in the movies and television that police closed a case in a matter of hours.

"Receiving confirmation about Lily's medical history could certainly clear up some of my lingering questions, but I maintain that something about this case feels off."

"Off?" Hal asked, catching my eye and scowling.

Dr. Caldwell pressed her lips tightly together and formed her hands into a steeple, making strong eye contact with us. "I'm not a betting woman, but I would put my money on this being a murder."

# TEN

After Dr. Caldwell, Sugar, and Becca left, Hal, Fletcher, and I closed the store and gathered to regroup in the Foyer. The sun had long sunk into the Pacific Ocean, shrouding Redwood Grove in darkness. Light from the sparkling outside strands filtered in the bay windows like fireflies.

"You both continue to amaze me," Hal said, patting his heart. "Today was difficult, to say the very least. I wish I could take it away. If only we had a magic wand, but alas, Lily's death will leave an imprint on all of us."

I nodded, not trusting myself to speak. Hal always knew the words to say to pierce my heart.

"I'd like to take a moment to honor her. Is that all right with you?" Hal looked at each of us. The lines on his face deepened as he nodded solemnly.

Fletcher bowed his head.

Hal cleared his throat. "To Lily, who filled our store with gingerbread and happiness. May she rest in peace."

I felt hot tears begin to well. I hadn't realized how tightly I'd clenched in my emotions just to survive the day. Tears spilled from my eyes. I let them flow, keeping my eyes on the small tabletop Christmas tree like it was my own personal North Star. I'd learned over the years to lean into my grief. Now that the store was empty and we were alone, I let the emotions I'd been keeping inside come rushing to the surface.

Hal handed me a tissue, brushing a tear from his cheek. "My dearest Annie, your heart is huge. There's no making sense of this tragedy."

I dabbed my nose and tried to smile, but tears continued to fall. It wasn't just Lily. It was Scarlet. Lily's death had brought those emotions to the surface. Maybe it was a good thing to let myself have a bit of a release before meeting Mark Vincent on Monday.

"How are you both feeling about tomorrow?" Hal asked after we had taken a minute to recover.

Fletcher's voice was thick with emotion. "The idea is to proceed as normal? I saw Sugar and Becca livestreaming. That can't be right, but then again, it would be a big hit to our bottom line to have the store closed on a weekend."

That was one of the things I loved about him. He was equally practical and compassionate. I appreciated that he was concerned about glossing over the tragedy while equally focused on how we approached Lily's death from the perspective of managing the store.

I gave them a brief recap of what Becca had shared with me. "Personally, I would prefer to make some kind of a statement tomorrow, assuming Dr. Caldwell is able to contact Lily's family. Maybe we can dedicate the rest of the competition to her?"

"Excellent idea." Hal ran his fingers along his beard. "I agree that we need to mark the moment. Should we cancel the performers? Proceed with the closing party or forgo that, too? I defer to you. The Secret Bookcase isn't going to be mine forever, so you two should take the lead."

I glanced at Fletcher. "I'm inclined to continue with everything. What about you?"

"Same." He tapped a finger to his chin and nodded. "We can ask Becca to share some stories about Lily at the party. Again, acknowledge her and her contribution to Redwood Grove."

"That's decided, then." Hal pressed his hands together in gratitude. "Thank you for being the wonderful humans you both are. I'm due to meet Caroline for dinner and a viewing of *Elf* at the Royal Playhouse, so I'll see you both tomorrow. Try and enjoy the rest of the night."

Hal ambled to the stairs. He and Caroline, who owned a small boutique, Artifacts, in the village square, had been dating for months and were getting more serious.

"Hot date tonight, Annie?" Fletcher asked, his eyes gleaming playfully.

"If you call soup and a sandwich at the Stag Head a hot date, then sure." I winked. "What about you?"

"My Sherlockian society is watching *The Adventure of the Blue Carbuncle*. It's set two days after Christmas, which is as close to a holiday story as Sir Arthur Conan Doyle ever got."

"I love that." It was good to see Fletcher branching out. Shortly after Halloween, he started a Sherlockian society. They met once a month to view and discuss one of the many films in the Sherlock canon.

"I do want to discuss our next step with you. I've been working on a PowerPoint. I've got a new idea that could help generate additional revenue. Do you want to meet at the store before we open tomorrow morning?"

"Oooh, tell me more." I rubbed my hands together in anticipation.

"Patience, young Annie." He puffed out his chest like a peacock. "I have a few minor details to complete."

"Okay. Okay. I'm intrigued. What time tomorrow?"

Fletcher and I had been tossing around ideas for the store for the last few months, but if he was taking it to a PowerPoint level, that meant he was getting serious. PowerPoints and Excel spreadsheets were usually my domain.

"Never underestimate the element of surprise." He tapped the side of his cheek pensively. "Let's say nine."

"Perfect. See you then." I left out the front door for the short walk down the gravel drive to the Stag Head. Fletcher's Power-Points were the stuff of legend. I was curious to see what he had crafted for me. Usually, we teamed up to pitch Hal ideas for events and signings at the store.

Dark had fallen over Redwood Grove, but the village glowed with thousands of twinkling lights. There was no better place to live any time of the year, but the holidays were absolutely stunning. I rubbed my shoulders as I traipsed along the pathway, guided by gold and white sparkling lights. The air smelled like winter—crisp and fresh, tinged with a touch of salt and evergreen.

The Stag Head was at the end of the long drive. Liam had decorated the exterior of the rustic two-story building with retro holiday lights in primary colors. A jolly, plush Santa was propped on the porch, along with a bowl of candy canes and a note for anyone passing by to help themselves.

Inside, the pub was buzzing with activity. A large pine tree was decked out with strings of popcorn and cranberries and homemade sugar cookies cut out in the shapes of stars and decorated with colorful icing. The paper stag heads that lined the walls had been embellished with bright red noses to make them look like Rudolph the Red-Nosed Reindeer.

I smiled to myself. I never would have pegged Liam as the type to embrace the holiday spirit. There was a lot about him that I had to learn.

I scanned the crowded room. Nearly every table was taken. Miniature Christmas trees lined the bar, and paper stars hung from the exposed beam ceiling. The Pogues's "Fairytale of New York" blared from the speakers. People raised frothy pints and swayed to the haunting holiday ballad.

Liam was behind the bar mixing cranberry martinis.

"What's a girl gotta do for a cocktail around here?" I asked with a flirty wink, sliding up to greet him.

"Ask nicely," he bantered back, holding the silver cocktail shaker over his head and twirling it to the beat of the music.

Flirting has never been my forte, but I did my best to bat my lashes at him.

"Nice try, Murray." He rolled his eyes and chuckled. "Pri's waiting for you in the back booth. If you're lucky, I just might deliver a round of these cranberry orange martinis and some appetizers."

I was suddenly famished. With Lily's death, the subsequent investigation, and the gingerbread competition, I realized I hadn't eaten anything other than a handful of Christmas candy and some cake since breakfast. I was running on sugar, coffee, and fumes.

"Are you able to join us?" I asked hopefully. The line for drinks wasn't terribly long, and Liam's assistant bartender deftly poured beer orders from the taps.

Liam untwisted the lid on the shaker and poured gorgeous crimson liquid into two waiting martini glasses. He finished them with an orange slice and a skewer of sugared cranberries. "Duty calls. I have to deliver these, so I might as well follow you."

I hid a smile, feeling the familiar creep of heat spreading up my cheeks. One thing that worried me when Liam and I began dating was whether our banter would fade away, but so far, the opposite was true.

Liam waited for me, balancing the fancy martinis on a tray. "In all seriousness, Annie, I heard about Lily."

The fluttery feeling in my chest shifted. I swallowed hard,

trying to force down the memory of finding her lifeless on the floor.

"Sorry." Liam's voice was tender and husky. "We don't have to talk about it if you don't want to."

I was about to turn around and thank him when Pri spotted us. She jumped to her feet and wrapped me in a tight hug.

"Annie, oh my God, I can't believe it. Lily died after we left?"

I inhaled deeply, letting myself collapse into her arms.

She smelled of coffee and cinnamon. I breathed in the balmy scent and held her tight.

"Sorry, I'm more emotional than usual," I said, finally letting her go.

"A woman died at the bookstore. I would be seriously concerned if you *weren't* emotional." Pri scooted into the booth and patted the seat next to her.

"Maybe this will help take the edge off." Liam placed our drinks in front of us and took the spot across from me.

I picked up my martini. The jewel-toned cranberry juice and vodka was almost too pretty to drink. I popped one of the sugared cranberries into my mouth. "I think it's partially Scarlet. I'm in my head about meeting Mark on Monday and having Lily drop dead in the store resurfaced so many memories." The tart zing of the cranberry made my cheeks pucker.

"That's understandable." Pri patted my knee. "You know my offer still stands. If you want moral support, I'll come with you."

"Same here." Liam held my gaze, making my heart flop.

"Thanks. I appreciate it. I really do, but this is something I have to do on my own. I can't risk spooking him." I took another sip of the cocktail, letting the ice-cold liquid coat my throat. Telling Liam and Pri about Mark had been a major milestone for me. I'd spent so many years telling myself different stories about

Scarlet, fictionalizing her death, trying to rewrite her ending, and keeping her bottled up in my head. I was proud of my growth. Being vulnerable with my friends had allowed me to let go. I also wasn't taking any chances or risks in meeting Mark. Pri, Liam, Dr. Caldwell, Fletcher, and Hal knew every detail—when we were meeting, where, for how long I was expected to be gone, and what to do if I didn't check in at our agreed-upon time.

"I'm not sure that makes me feel any better about you meeting a stranger who could be connected to two murders," Liam said, his brow creasing with concern. "I think you should meet him here."

"I have a solid plan, I promise."

He looked like he wanted to say more but waved one of his waitstaff over. "Can we have a round of the holiday appetizers to start?"

The server agreed and headed toward the kitchen.

"What are the specials tonight?" I hadn't looked at the menu yet. The Stag Head featured comfort classics—shepherd's pie, burgers, mac and cheese, and California-style bowls and salads. What I hadn't realized when I first met Liam was that the vast majority of recipes were from his family's home kitchen.

Liam hadn't opened up much about his past, but he'd dropped a few subtle hints that told me he, too, had experienced grief. I wasn't pushing it. When he was ready, I would be here to listen.

"We're doing a Christmas pasty in a buttery crust with herbed chicken, red onions, and sweet potatoes," Liam replied. "Chef is also doing individual beef Wellingtons with a puff pastry shell. They're both incredible."

"Oooh, you had me at Wellington," Pri said, pretending to wipe drool from her chin. "Honestly, anything in a puff pastry and I'm sold."

"Good. You get that and I'll order the Christmas pasty and we can sample each other's." I lifted my glass in a toast.

She clinked hers to mine. "Done and done."

Liam smiled. "Wise choice."

"Are you up for talking about what happened, or do you just want to check out?" Pri asked. "We'll follow your lead."

"No, I'm fine. I'd like both of your input." I took another long sip of my drink before launching into a recap.

"So it could be natural causes, or it could be something much more nefarious." Pri dragged her teeth over her bottom lip. "What about Shane?"

"My thoughts exactly," Liam added.

"Yeah, but how? You saw him. He took off. I never saw him again." I wrinkled my nose. "Although it is a big store."

"Exactly. He could have snuck in through the Terrace," Pri suggested. "You keep those doors unlocked during the day, right?"

"Yeah. That's true," I agreed.

"He seemed unstable for sure," Liam said.

As the words escaped his mouth, the door burst open. Shane stumbled inside. He clutched the coat rack for support as his body swayed like he was out on choppy waters or very drunk. "What have I done? What have I done? She's dead," he wailed, and then released his grip on the coat rack and dropped to his knees.

# ELEVEN

We all raced over to help Shane. He rocked on his knees like he was trying to soothe himself. "What have I done? What have I done?"

"Shane, what's going on?" I asked while Liam kept people back.

"It's Lily. She's dead. She's dead. Haven't you heard? She's dead." He repeated it again and again like he was trying to believe it. His hair fell loose from his ponytail. He didn't bother to try and fix it.

"I know." I placed my hand on his shoulder. The question was, how did he know? Had Dr. Caldwell already finalized her contact with Lily's family members? Was it public news now?

"You know? How?" He rubbed the back of his neck and looked at me with a pained stare. The skin around his eyes bunched tight like he was trying to squeeze out the reality that Lily could be dead.

"I found her," I said, keeping my tone even. I wasn't sure what I was dealing with in terms of Shane's mental state, and I didn't want to make things worse by agitating him more.

"You found her? Oh no. This can't be real. Not Lily." He buried his face in his hands and sank farther onto the floor.

There was little I could offer him other than the truth. "I'm sorry. I know you cared for her deeply."

"It's my fault. I did this. I did this, and now she's dead."

I glanced at Pri and Liam. "Why would it be your fault?" I asked Shane. Even if news had broken about Lily's death, I knew it was highly unlikely Dr. Caldwell would have shared anything about her concerns foul play could have been involved.

"It's my fault," he repeated, sobbing loudly.

"Let's have you come sit, man," Liam suggested casually. "We've got a booth in the back." He offered Shane a hand and helped him to his feet.

I ignored the watchful eyes of other diners as we returned to the booth. A large tray of appetizers awaited us—Brie and honey crostini, pesto cheese balls, crab cakes, and sausage rolls.

Why had I bothered to order a main course?

There was enough food to satisfy even the hungriest of appetites.

Shane quivered as if he was on the brink of going into shock. Liam kept a firm arm around his shoulder and nudged him into the booth.

"I'm going to grab a glass of water," Liam said pointedly to me.

I nodded at him, loaded a plate with a variety of the appetizers, and passed it to Shane. "You should try and eat something. It will help."

His hands trembled uncontrollably. He held them out for us to see, staring at them with despair. "I don't think I can pick anything up. I can't stop shaking."

"Try this," Pri said, drinking in two small sips of air through her nose and then releasing them slowly through her mouth. "It's a breathing technique we use in my yoga class."

Shane followed her lead, sniffing and huffing the air out.

After a few attempts, it started to calm him. His breath became steadier, and the shaking subsided a bit.

Liam returned with a glass of ice water and thrust it at Shane. "Drink."

Shane trembled as he lifted the glass to his lips, and then he looked at me with eyes as wide as the ornaments hanging from the Christmas tree. "She had a heart attack, right?"

"The police don't know yet. They're waiting for the autopsy report." My internal radar dinged like a warning bell.

How had Shane already heard that, especially since Dr. Caldwell explicitly asked for discretion until she contacted Lily's family?

"Autopsy?" Water sloshed from Shane's glass when he set it down. "They're doing an autopsy?"

"It's standard procedure." I helped myself to a sausage roll.

"That's terrible." He gulped like he was having difficulty swallowing. "Who's doing the autopsy?"

"The county coroner," I answered truthfully.

"No." Shane shook his fork in protest. "They can't do an autopsy."

Why was he so concerned with the autopsy?

Was he worried the coroner would find something linking Lily's death to him?

I decided to try another tactic, circling back to his original statement. "You mentioned this was your fault. Why?"

"It's her heart." He thumped his hand against his chest to mimic his heartbeat. "She told me that she didn't want to take the medication because it made her feel weird. She said her doctor agreed. At least that's what Lily told me."

"Lily talked to you about her health?" I couldn't wrap my head around their relationship. If Shane was stalking her, why would she share such personal information with him? Did that mean he was telling the truth, and they had been in direct contact? I'd been operating under the assumption Becca had been their go-between, but maybe I was wrong.

"We talked about everything." He massaged Lily's face on his sweatshirt like it was his personal safety blanket. "Like I told you, she was one of my best friends."

I took a bite of the sausage roll.

Pri jumped in. "When did you and Lily discuss her health?"

"A few days ago. She knew that I have SVT, so she reached out to me in DMs. She had her annual checkup with her doctor, who told her she'd grown out of her heart murmur and she could stop the medication. I take similar medication and tried weaning myself off it a few years ago, so I told her about my experience. I shouldn't have given her medical advice. It's my fault she stopped taking the medication and is dead." He broke down.

Pri kicked me under the table.

There were so many things to unpack with Shane's confession. Taking a methodical approach was the only option.

"What's SVT?" I asked.

"Supraventricular tachycardia," Shane sniveled, using his napkin to mop up his tears. "It's a heart rhythm issue that makes my heart beat extremely fast sometimes. My heart rate can spike to over two hundred beats a minute when I'm sitting still."

"That sounds terrible," Pri said, biting into a crostini.

"It's not that bad. The medication keeps it under control. The only bummer is it makes my heart rate perpetually slow. I'd never win a running race, but I don't like to run anyway."

I savored the spicy sausage, buying another minute to quickly formulate a list of follow-up questions. "Lily's heart issue was different?"

"Yeah, she has—had—a heart murmur. She was diagnosed with it when she was young and has been on medication ever since." He reached for his water glass but decided against it. "The medication isn't bad, but it makes you feel slow. It's like walking with a weighted vest—that's how she described it. She didn't like it because she's so full of energy and life. She wants that to come across to her fans. And baking was physically taxing. She said stopping the medication was the best thing she's done in years. It made her feel ten years younger and like she was floating."

"But her doctor recommended she quit taking it?" I confirmed. I also noted Shane was speaking of Lily in the present tense.

"Yeah." Shane nodded, but then realization snuck back in. He hung his head. "That's why it's my fault she's dead."

# TWELVE

Shane burst into tears as our food arrived. "I should have told her to talk to her doctor again. What was I thinking? I'm not a medical expert. I just wanted her to be happy, and she seemed so good. She looked the best I've seen her look in months yesterday. She had so much color and energy. I could tell she was feeling great, which makes it even worse that she had a heart attack."

I looked at Pri and saw her whisper something that sounded remarkably like "unless she didn't" under her breath.

"How did you and Lily have these conversations?" I asked, giving Pri a warning look. Shane sounded sincere. There was no doubt he was devastated by Lily's death, but I wasn't willing to rule him out as a suspect yet. He could be fabricating his story. Maybe he overheard Becca and Lily discussing her health. Perhaps this was his attempt to shift suspicion away from himself.

"In DM," he replied without hesitation.

"Do you still have the messages?" My heart sped up. That could be a major breakthrough.

"Yeah." He perked up a little. "I save everything from Lily."

"Can we see them?" I asked.

Pri kicked me under the table. I squeezed her leg to signal to play it low-key. I didn't want to put Shane on edge. He was teetering there already, but if he really did have a thread of messages from Lily, that might be enough to cross him off my suspect list.

He reached into his pocket and took out his phone. He opened the app and tapped the screen with force. Then he threw his hand to his cheek and gasped. He leaned closer to his phone, squinting like he was struggling to see. "They're gone. They're not here." He tapped harder as if hoping that might somehow bring the messages up.

"Could I take a look?" I leaned across the booth.

He handed me his phone and ran his hands through his wild hair. "They were here. I swear. We exchanged at least ten messages back and forth. I don't understand. Where did they go?"

I reviewed his private messages. There wasn't a single thread from Lily regarding her health.

I handed him the phone back.

"You don't believe me, do you?" He searched the table, his eyes becoming more frantic. "How would I know all this? None of it is public information. Lily asked me to keep this between us, and I did. I would never betray her trust. I'm not making this up. Lily asked me for my input because she knew I struggle with heart issues, too."

"Have you shared this with the police?" I asked.

"The police? No. I haven't spoken with the police. You think they'll want to talk to me?" He sounded nervous again.

I was surprised Dr. Caldwell hadn't been in touch with him yet, but she was probably busy with the dozens of requests she had to submit. "They're taking statements from everyone who was at today's event, but your input will be highly valuable. I'll give you Dr. Caldwell's number. You can contact her directly."

"Okay, but where did the messages go?" Shane blinked and rubbed his eyes. "I don't understand how they just disappeared."

"The police might be able to trace your digital footprint," I said, not adding what I was thinking internally—*if the messages had ever existed*. Shane's demeanor matched someone struggling to grasp the finality of losing a loved one. He was also unstable and unreliable. He could be crafting a story to convince himself his relationship with Lily was more than a handful of comments and emojis.

"Yeah, that's a good point." Shane nudged Liam. "Can I get past you? I'm going to go to the police now. They'll get to the bottom of this."

Liam cleared his throat and looked at me, not budging.

"Don't you want Dr. Caldwell's number?" I asked Shane. "You can call her."

He pointed toward the front door. "I was going to go to the police station. Should I call?"

"It's probably a good idea to call first. I don't know if anyone will be in the building this late," I said, gesturing to the clock.

"No. No. I have to tell them what I know—now. This is too important to wait." He nudged Liam again. "Can I get out, man?"

Liam looked at me for approval as if making sure I was fine with letting Shane leave.

I bobbed my head.

Liam shrugged and moved for him.

Shane took off. He reminded me of the skittish rabbits that darted through the gardens in the spring.

"Well, well, well. That was interesting." Pri set her appetizer plate to the side and stabbed her beef Wellington. Steam puffed from the top like an erupting volcano. "Do we believe a word of that?"

I considered it for a minute. "Maybe. His body language

matched what he told us. I didn't pick up on any glaring cues he was lying, did you?"

They both shook their heads.

I ran my teeth on my bottom lip, trying to decide if I believed him. "The problem is, without evidence, it's going to be impossible for him to prove he and Lily actually discussed their health or anything else."

"It's convenient that the messages happen to be missing." Liam scooped walnut and pear salad onto his plate. "I wonder if they can recover direct messages that have been deleted."

"If Dr. Caldwell gets a search warrant for Shane's phone, there are advanced tools she can use to recover his deleted messages. Digital forensics is a rapidly growing field. It depends on the storage capacity of Shane's phone and how much time has elapsed since the messages were deleted, but it's possible."

"Detective Annie." Pri clapped, giving me a round of applause by making a circle with her hands.

Liam tipped an imaginary hat. "Who knew we had a digital forensics expert in our midst."

I felt heat creeping up my cheeks. I laughed. "Hey, I like to keep up on current trends."

"See, this is why you need to work for Dr. Caldwell, Annie," Pri said, blowing on her dinner. "I never knew any of this. How are you so up-to-date when you haven't worked in criminology in years?"

"I stay in the loop," I said, feeling my cheeks flame more. "I might spend a few hours every now and then on Forensic Focus, and I could have subscriptions to the FBI bulletin and the National Institute of Justice's newsletter."

"And she blushes." Liam wiggled his eyebrows.

This wasn't the time to bring up the topic, but I was nearly ready to make a decision about my next career path. In preparation I'd been doing my homework.

"I don't know why, but I feel sorry for the guy," Liam said, changing the subject much to my relief. "I understand that he could be stalking her or worse. If that turns out to be true, I'll eat my words, but he comes across as wholesome. That or he's totally pulling one over on us."

"I agree." I cut into my pasty, inhaling the aroma of sage and rosemary.

"Are we still on for the coffee demo tomorrow?" Pri asked. "I'm set, but I get it if Hal wants to cancel."

"No, we chatted about it and decided to proceed as planned. We're hoping Becca and Sugar can say a few words about Lily and dedicate the event to her. The contestants have worked so hard, so we want to make sure to honor them as well. Dayton will do a gingerbread baking demo, too, and there will be tastings."

"I like that." Pri handed me her Wellington to try. "Liam, I hate to inflate your ego even more, but this might be my favorite yet."

Liam puffed air into his cheeks. "Consider me inflated."

"You're the worst," Pri teased.

I passed her a bite of my dinner. "I don't know; this might be a contender for the best dish."

She took a bite, closed her eyes, and chewed with intention like a food critic. In fairness, her palate was quite refined. Her experience in the world of coffee flavored everything she touched. "It's good. I'd give it a nine and a half, but my Wellington is nearly a ten."

"Nearly a ten?" Liam scowled.

"I'll say nine point seven." Pri flashed him a devilish grin and ducked, anticipating Liam would toss his napkin at her.

"Watch your back, I'll tell Chef."

Pri finished the Wellington and gathered her things. "I'm getting out of here before this gets ugly." She blew me a kiss. "See you in the morning for Christmas coffee."

After she left, I helped Liam clear the table. "Can I walk

you home? I can't stay because I'm on closing duty tonight, but I wouldn't mind taking a break and having a moment to ourselves." His eyes lingered on me, turning my stomach into a blubbering mess.

"Sure, as long as you have time," I managed to squeak out. Why did he make me feel so jittery? We'd been dating—or at least hanging out—for over a month, and I still felt fluttery every time we were in close proximity. It was either a good sign that we had real chemistry or a sign that I was in over my head.

I hadn't felt like this about anyone in years—if ever. I'd dated in college and on and off once I moved to Redwood Grove, but nothing had stuck. It was different with Liam. We had started as friends, well technically, enemies. I'd known him long before anything sparked between us.

"Give me a minute to check in with my staff." He took the dishes to the kitchen.

I waited at the bar and texted Dr. Caldwell to give her a heads-up about Shane. He sounded sincere about getting in touch with her, but he could have said that just to get us off his back.

"Ready?" Liam asked, returning wearing a blue, yellow, and white striped puffy vest and a ski hat.

I zipped my coat and twisted my scarf around my neck.

He reached his hand out and laced his fingers through mine.

Outside, the crisp, cold air made my breath quicken. Or maybe it was Liam's warm grasp. We strolled along Cedar Avenue and crossed into Oceanside Park. The trees that flanked the park were decked out in dazzling twinkle lights. Garlands wrapped around the solar light posts. The pergola in the center of the park, which bloomed with fragrant wisteria during the summer, had been transformed into Santa's workshop with a temporary cottage, reindeer-feeding station, and North Pole photo booth.

"Are you okay?" Liam asked, squeezing my hand tighter. "I'm worried you're putting on a brave face."

"I won't lie, it was a rough afternoon, and like I said to you and Pri, Scarlet has been top of my mind the last few weeks as I've been preparing to meet with Mark, so that brought everything rushing back. I obviously didn't know Lily well, but she seemed genuinely excited about the event and engaged with fans both online and in person. It's just so sad that someone young and vibrant dropped dead." I shuddered at the memory.

Liam listened, waiting for me to continue.

"It's also shocking she just collapsed. My mind has been running through so many potential scenarios, especially since our conversation with Shane. I wonder if her cardiologist could be liable. Had she been given bad advice about stopping her heart medication? Or did she decide on her own because she was frustrated with the side effects?"

"Good questions."

We walked past benches tucked between redwood trees on the pressed bark path that cut through the park. Smoke wafted from nearby chimneys filling the air with a woody aroma.

"I wish there was more I could do."

"Does that mean you're leaning toward saying yes to Dr. Caldwell?"

Liam and I had talked at length about me potentially returning to the field.

"Honestly, maybe not. Lily's death is nudging me even closer to a new direction I've been ruminating on for a while."

We passed through the park, spilling out onto Woodland Terrace, the street that dead-ended at my cul-de-sac. My little private neighborhood comprised cute and cozy individual cottages with front porches and small fenced backyards. Most of my neighbors were retired and looked out for me. I was like their adopted granddaughter. Rarely did a day go by when I didn't have a plate of homemade cookies or sourdough bread waiting for me when I arrived home from the Secret Bookcase.

"Are you saying you're leaning toward staying at the store and taking over management with Fletcher?" Liam's voice held no judgment but a touch of surprise. "It's a big financial undertaking."

"There might be a way to do both. I've been mulling over some ideas, but I need to discuss them with Fletcher first." I smiled at the sight of the glowing cottages. As anticipated, a platter of Christmas cookies sat on the side table between the two rocking chairs on my porch, along with a handwritten note from my next-door neighbor.

"You're very intriguing and mysterious, Murray." Liam released my hand as we walked up the steps.

I picked up the plate of cookies. My neighbor must have been baking all day. There were chocolate pinwheels, peppermint meltaways, cranberry and white chocolate oatmeal cookies, and a variety of frosted cutouts. "Cookie?" I lifted the plastic wrap to offer one to Liam.

"And masterful at the art of changing the subject. Noted." He took a peppermint meltaway. "I never turn down a homemade cookie You know, we should do some holiday baking. I've been wanting to recreate my grandmother's recipe for a coffee cake crown. She was originally from Sweden and always baked her sweet breakfast bread shaped like a crown."

The idea of baking with Liam made my heart want to melt into a gooey puddle. "I'd love to bake with you. And listen, in terms of my next career move, I'm not trying to be coy; it's just that I don't want to jinx anything."

"It's fine. You don't owe me an explanation." Liam took a bite of the cookie.

Was it my imagination, or was there a touch of sadness in his voice? It wasn't that I didn't want his input or advice, but I needed to make this decision for me—and me alone. I'd spent so many years living in Scarlet's shadow. I needed to be intentional about me—what did I want? What did I need?

I unlocked the door. "I'll see you tomorrow at the store, right?"

"Count on it. If not before." He leaned close, his breath grazing my neck. "But not before I kiss you goodnight."

I grinned. "It's about time. I was wondering what you were waiting for."

He placed a hand on my cheek and leaned in, his voice grumbling with desire. "It takes every ounce of self-control, Murray. Every ounce."

I got swept into his kiss, letting him pull me so close that I could feel his heart beating against mine. Blood rushed through my head as our lips met. His kiss was gentle at first and then searching.

When we finally broke apart, sweat trickled down my neck, and my cheeks felt like they were on fire.

"Okay, yeah, well, on that note, see you tomorrow, Murray." He turned and sauntered away. I watched him go before heading inside. I was starting to fall for Liam—hard.

# THIRTEEN

The next morning, I woke to Professor Plum kneading my head. His soft paws massaged my shoulder, urging me out of bed to feed him.

"Good morning to you, sir." I petted his head and stretched, not wanting to leave the comfort of my bed. It was outfitted with snowflake flannel sheets and fluffy blankets. "Do we have to get up?"

He purred in response and nudged his head under my chin.

"I know, but it's chilly, and we're so cozy under all of these yummy layers." I pulled the covers higher.

He pawed at them. Professor Plum was nothing if not insistent about his feeding schedule.

"All right. All right." I threw the covers off. "Give me a minute to get ready."

Professor Plum had been my steadfast friend and supporter since Scarlet died. The least I could do to repay his kindness was to feed him on time. I pulled on a pair of leggings, knee-high boots, and an oversized sweater. I finished my look by tying my shoulder-length red hair into a ponytail, dusting my cheeks with blush, and adding a shimmery lip gloss.

I padded into the kitchen with Professor Plum at my ankles. Light spilled in through my bay windows. Buffalo plaid pillows were propped in my breakfast nook with a tabletop Christmas tree. Paper snowflakes that Pri, Penny, and I had cut out on a girls' night hung from the rounded windows. I filled Professor Plum's dish with salmon pâté and started a pot of coffee. Then I made a bowl of hot oatmeal and polished off two Christmas cookies. Once the coffee was ready, I savored a cup and let Professor Plum curl up on my lap.

I hoped that Dr. Caldwell might have new information on Lily's death today. We had a busy morning planned. Pri would be doing coffee tastings, and Dayton and his students would offer a gingerbread class. The high school choir would perform carols, and we hired Liam to provide small bites and sparkling cider and champagne for the closing party and announcement of the winners.

"What's your plan today, sir?" I asked Professor Plum, stroking his head. He turned his chin so I could scratch his favorite spot. "I'm meeting with Fletcher this morning. He's bringing a PowerPoint. Can you believe that? Our resident Sherlockian has something up his sleeve."

Professor Plum responded by stretching his paw toward my face to signal he'd like more petting.

"I'm nervous because I desperately want to keep the Secret Bookcase open, but I'm also sure that my path forward involves investigating. I didn't realize how much I missed this. How much I needed this. I've run my own numbers, but I'm not sure if I can make both work. Not without Fletcher's buy-in." I sighed. "I don't want to have to choose."

I'd spent the last couple of months making endless spreadsheets, forecasting future sales, staffing costs, and how many hours I would have to devote to the store. I had pulled out my old notebooks from college and reviewed Scarlet's and my vision for our detective agency, all while brushing up on my skills and researching the steps I would need to take if I said yes to Dr. Caldwell and pursued a career in law enforcement.

There were too many possibilities.

Hal was the other unknown. As much as he said he wanted Fletcher and I to take over, he'd been less than forthcoming about his future plans. Was he waiting on us?

Professor Plum flopped onto his back and stared at me with his knowing eyes. Some people might think talking to a cat like an old friend was odd. They would be wrong. There was no better companion or listener in the world than a loyal tabby.

I kissed his head and took another sip of my coffee.

I couldn't decide if the store would be busier than expected once news of Lily's death spread. Gossip tended to take root quickly in Redwood Grove. I just hoped that it wouldn't keep shoppers away from the store. There were only a couple of weeks left in the holiday season. If we could maintain yesterday's sales, we'd be in decent shape, but it wasn't as if the bookstore was flooded with cash. Every sale counted at this point.

Professor Plum purred contentedly while I caught up on email and poured myself a second cup of coffee. I considered everyone attached to Lily—Sugar, Becca, Shane, Dayton, and even Kari from Queen Mary Flour. They'd all wanted something from Lily, whether financial or personal. If natural causes were ruled out, could one of them have killed her?

Sugar had been distraught over her broken gingerbread display. Understandably so. Was there a nugget of truth that Lily had intentionally knocked it over? And if so, was that a strong enough motive for Sugar to want her dead? Was she envious of Lily's platform? Desperate for social media attention?

That was a huge stretch.

Becca was the closest to her. I was curious about the nature of their relationship. If an opportunity arose to speak with her alone today, I would try to press her for more information. She knew the most about Lily, not only about her medical history but her financial situation and her relationships with her fans. According to Sugar, she did all of Lily's grunt work. Maybe she finally got fed up with not getting any credit.

That led me to Shane. He was the most obvious suspect. But our conversation last night made me more inclined to believe his story. He seemed genuinely distraught. I supposed there was a chance he could be faking his emotional response to her death, but I doubted it. What I wasn't clear on was his claim that they had exchanged medical information. What happened to their private messages?

Dayton was a bit of an unknown. Lily's reaction to tasting his gingerbread had been odd, to say the very least. Why had she said it was "familiar" and then asked to speak with him "off-line"? I couldn't pinpoint exactly what bothered me about their exchange. But I had definitely picked up tension between them.

Lastly, there was Kari. Lily shut her down immediately when she attempted to publicly pitch her on partnering with Queen Mary Flour. Why? Had that been her first pitch? Or had she been hounding Lily like Shane?

I had more questions than answers, but I had to remind myself this was normal at this stage. Early in an investigation, everything was on the table. There were no wrong questions, and no one should be ruled out as a possible suspect.

I sighed and finished my coffee. Of course, I could also be jumping to conclusions. The more likely probability was that Lily died of natural causes.

"Are you going to sleep the day away?" I asked Professor Plum, moving him off my lap and tucking him between the throw pillows.

He meowed in response.

"Fair enough. Don't exert yourself too much." I kissed his head and took my dishes to the sink. My potted winter herbs resting on the windowsill flourished in the sun. I glanced out onto the cul-de-sac. Red, pink, and magenta cyclamens added a vibrant pop of color in the green space between the cottages. Ripe oranges and lemons clung to citrus trees in pots and in the ground. There was nothing like having a burst of freshness during the holiday season.

I left Professor Plum perched on the window seat and strolled down my lane and into the park. I loved the quiet of my morning walks to the bookstore. It was a chance to clear my head and center myself.

When I arrived at the bookstore, Fletcher was waiting impatiently for me. He was dressed in slacks, a long-sleeve black shirt, and a houndstooth holiday vest. He waved from the front windows and flung the door open when he spotted me. "Annie! You're here. Good. I was up all night putting the finishing touches on my magnum opus."

"Magnum opus? Uh-oh. Should I be concerned?" I shrugged off my coat and hung it on the rack. Fletcher had already brewed coffee and boiled water for tea. The front counter gleamed, and chocolate, almond, and raspberry short-bread cookies were fanned out on gold-rimmed plates near the drink station. "I thought we were going to chat about possibilities for the bookshop. We only have an hour before we open."

Fletcher pushed me toward the Conservatory. The small cleft in his long, angular chin deepened as he gave me a toothy smile. "Not to worry. I've timed my presentation twice. It won't take more than twenty minutes, leaving us ample time to discuss."

I smiled. Fletcher had a penchant for droning on about Sherlock facts and obscure details, but he had the sweetest heart. I could totally picture him practicing in front of the mirror for me. Completely unnecessary, and also the most wholesome gesture ever.

"This way. I have a holiday spice tea waiting for you." He

ushered me forward like a flight attendant directing passengers to their seats.

I was impressed, although not surprised, by his attention to detail. One of the wingback chairs had been pushed next to a side table where a steaming mug of tea and a notebook and pencil awaited me. "You're taking this pitch seriously."

"Is there any other way to approach a future business partnership?" He frowned. "Please sit. For your convenience, you'll find a notebook should you want to document anything during my presentation."

I chuckled internally at Fletcher's extreme professionalism but gave him a serious nod and opened the blank notebook.

"Thank you for your time this morning, Ms. Murray." He bowed and clicked on the projector, pushing another button to automatically roll the screen on the stage down. "Welcome to the Secret Bookcase, a bookstore with its own secret."

A photo of the exterior of the store flashed on the screen.

"Things are not always what they seem when you enter the Secret Bookcase," Fletcher continued in a mysterious tone, tapping into his inner Sherlock. A video played. It was shot from a first-person perspective, weaving through the hallways and between the bookshelves. "Is it a charming store packed with tomes for the ages? Yes. Is it also something else? Let's see."

I smiled, wondering where he was going with this.

"Your store owners, Annie Murray and Fletcher Hughes, welcome you to peruse our vast stacks of mystery novels. You'll find hidden treasure around every turn, and should we not happen to have the title you seek, we will go out of our way to find it for you because, after all, we are NOVEL DETECTIVES."

"Novel Detectives, clever." I laughed.

"Exactly, *Novel Detectives*." Fletcher tilted his head to the side and stared at me, giving me a hard look.

"What? Am I missing something?"

"Novel *Detectives*." He emphasized "detectives" again.

"Okay." I still wasn't getting it. Maybe it was too early. Maybe I needed more coffee. I took a sip of the spicy tea and waited for him to continue.

"You see, our staff isn't solely versed in fictional crime—not mere aficionados in the genre but also adept detectives in our own right." He clicked on the next slides, which showcased photos of me with Dr. Caldwell and him at his desk, wearing a pair of old-school spectacles and reviewing documents.

I was starting to grasp where he was going with this. I sat up taller. Was he suggesting what I thought he was suggesting?

"Our booksellers double as skilled investigators. We apply the insight and cunning we've gleaned from the literary world into the real world. No case is too big or small. Might it be a cryptic message written in a second-hand novel or piecing together a missing persons case, our crack team blends our love of detective literature with our genuine sleuthing prowess. Our vision of the Secret Bookcase is not only to make it Redwood Grove's most welcoming third space but also to make it a hub for local investigations. At the Secret Bookcase, no mystery goes unsolved. Our team will diligently ensure that every case that crosses our desk is closed with the same finality that comes with reading the last page of your favorite book."

That was a bold claim, but I loved Fletcher's pitch. I couldn't believe we were so aligned. I'd spent weeks running numbers and creating spreadsheets trying to figure out if there was a way I could combine my passion for crime-solving with my deep desire to keep the Secret Bookcase open. I never imagined that Fletcher would want to join me.

# FOURTEEN

"Wait, are you proposing what I think you're proposing?" I asked Fletcher, setting my tea down. Was this a dream? "You want to partner with me on the bookstore and opening a detective agency?"

How had we both been thinking the same thing and never said it aloud?

His smile stretched to his eyes as he smoothed his vest and looked at me with eager anticipation. "If you'll have me. I know you have official criminology training, and I think that's what makes us good partners. We have completely different skill sets that complement each other. You're professionally trained, astute, methodical, and have an uncanny ability to read people. I've studied Sherlock's methods for years, which might sound trite, but there's legitimacy to his ability to make deductions. It's no coincidence that Conan Doyle's work has passed the test of time. My research skills are stellar. My attention to detail is unparalleled. We can do this, Annie."

I took in a breath, overwhelmed by his pitch.

"Don't say anything yet." He held up a bony index finger to stop me. "Let me finish." He flipped to the next slide. "I've run the numbers. I believe the income we would garner from taking on cases will make a dent in operating costs. The math checks out; at least, I think it does. That's more your specialty."

I was impressed he had graphed out expenses, quarterly sales, and current inventory. Spreadsheets were more my department.

"We'll need to hire some part-time help, but if my estimates are correct, those costs should be offset by what we bring in with hosting more events and taking on private investigation clients. I'm sure we can recruit some Redwood Grove High students who want to make some extra cash. If you're on board with this idea, we can talk to Dayton today and see if he has a contact at the high school we can reach out to."

"I'm one hundred percent on board with this idea, Fletcher. I love it." A fuzzy, warm feeling spread from my head to my toes, and it wasn't from the tea or the cheerful holiday decorations in the ballroom.

"You do?" He mopped his brow with the back of his hand. "I've been a bundle of nerves getting this pitch ready. I thought for sure you'd turn me down immediately."

"Why?" That made me sad. Fletcher and I had been friends for years. I hated that his initial thought was that I would dismiss his idea. I hoped I hadn't done anything to give him the impression I wouldn't want to partner with him. He was more than a friend—he was family.

"Because technically speaking, I'm not qualified to be a private eye like you, but I have done my research, and I don't need a special degree to be your assistant. You, of course, will have to pass the private eye exam and get your license in order for us to operate out of the store, but that should be a walk in the park for you."

Scarlet and I had studied for the exam before she was killed. I was rusty and would need to read up on current procedures and any new laws and statutes, but with some studying, I felt confident I could pass the test. And knowing that Fletcher and I would be a team filled me with a new level of confidence and enthusiasm. We could do this. We could totally do this.

A happy hum spread through my body, like tiny little bees pollinating the winter flowers.

"My assistant?" I wrinkled my nose and stared at him through my glasses. "Uh, I don't think so. If we do this, we're going to be partners."

His smile grew wider. "I appreciate that, Annie, but the reality is that you will need to be the lead PI. Maybe you take the lead for our investigations, and I will take the lead at the store. That would balance the power dynamic."

I wasn't worried about our power dynamic. We already had divided roles and responsibilities at the Secret Bookcase. Fletcher managed inventory, whereas I handled events and author signings.

"We need to speak with Hal," Fletcher cautioned, holding up a finger as if to stop himself from getting too caught up in the excitement. "He's mentioned stepping back and selling the store, but we need to discuss hard numbers and what that really means in terms of how much time he wants to commit to the store."

"I agree." On numerous occasions, Hal casually tossed out the idea of passing the business down to us, but I wasn't going to accept a gift that generous. I knew he owned the estate, which in and of itself was of huge value. He lived at the store and had made it his life. Even if he wanted to scale back, I couldn't imagine a scenario where he wouldn't be involved in some capacity.

"Are you serious about doing this?" Fletcher reminded me of an eager kid.

Truthfully, I felt the same level of excitement. A surge of adrenaline pulsed through me like I'd downed a strong shot of Pri's espresso.

"Yes, one thousand percent."

I couldn't sit still. I stood up and walked to the window. Peachy morning light stretched across the opulent gardens, drenching the greenery in a soft radiance. This would be my view.

I wanted to pinch myself.

I wanted to throw my arms around Fletcher and hug him.

I wanted to run through the village square and Oceanside Park shouting for joy. Liam and Pri were going to flip out.

This was the best holiday gift I could ever ask for.

The longer I'd spent with the idea of leaving the Secret Bookcase to work for Dr. Caldwell, the harder it was to consider. The Secret Bookcase had been my home for a decade. I had grown up here. I had found myself here. I had created friends and family here. I couldn't give this up. I didn't want to give it up, but reconnecting with Dr. Caldwell had also reawakened a part of myself that I had stuffed away. I was made to solve crime. Piecing together the clues, like with Lily and Scarlet, lit me up from the inside. There was something almost addictive about being on a case and trying to line up the puzzle pieces until they fit together neatly. However, that didn't mean I wanted to work full-time on the police force. Fletcher was offering me a path to both and a partnership. It felt too good to be true, and yet it felt perfectly aligned. I could almost picture Scarlet cheering from the sidelines, pushing me forward, encouraging me to take a risk and a chance on myself.

"Fletcher, this is amazing! You're amazing." I turned away from the window, pressed my hands together, and grinned. "What's the next step? How do we do this?"

"I'll send you my documents. Look them over first and double-check my math. Then let's schedule a meeting with Hal this week."

"Okay, count me in. Thanks for doing so much legwork, Fletcher. I really appreciate how much thought you've put into this, and I think we can make a real difference in this community." I returned to the chairs. "I would guess that Dr. Caldwell will use us as consultants if she needs an extra set of eyes on cases."

"You think so?"

"Yeah, it happens all the time in police work. Detectives build relationships with private investigators and collaborate on cases. She'll probably be a bit disappointed when I turn down her offer, but I know she'll understand."

"How do you think Hal will react?"

"React to what?" Hal's throaty voice made us both jump. He padded into the Conservatory wrapped in a new Christmas cardigan, cradling a tea mug.

"Uh, um, I..." Fletcher stumbled over his words, looking at me to save him.

Now was as good a time as any. Sure, I could spend extra hours running the numbers, formulating spreadsheets and profit and loss statements, but before we went much farther down this road, it made the most sense to find out if Hal was actually on board with the idea.

"Go for it, Fletcher," I said, encouraging him to replay his presentation. I patted the chair next to me. "Have a seat, Hal. You're going to be in for quite a treat."

"A treat?" Hal stared at me quizzically. "I'm intrigued."

Fletcher's hands shook as he clicked his laptop to reset the slideshow. "I wasn't exactly prepared to give you our pitch. Annie was my guinea pig this morning. I'm not sure I'm ready."

"You're ready. Don't overthink it." I nodded, giving him my full attention.

"Should I be concerned?" Hal asked.

"Not at all," I said, patting his knee. "You're going to be impressed."

Fletcher tugged at his shirt. "Don't oversell it, Annie."

"I'm not."

"You two are pouring on the mystery," Hal said. "I have no idea what that's about, but please don't keep me in suspense much longer. My old ticker can't take it." He winked and tapped his chest. Then he gasped and shook his head as if scolding himself. "That just came out. I'm sorry. I shouldn't be making light of heart issues, given recent events."

"It's okay, Hal," I said. "We know what you meant."

Fletcher launched into his presentation. His voice was shaky and uncertain while he went through the first few slides, but then he found his groove, becoming more confident. "You see, Annie and I love the store, and we think there's a way to add another revenue stream and tap into Annie's tremendous talent for crime-solving."

"I wouldn't go that far," I interjected.

"I would," Hal said, catching my eye and beaming at me like a proud parent.

"Yeah, but you're biased."

"Guilty as charged." He tossed his hands up in surrender. "Only because I have the best two staff members on the planet."

Fletcher fumbled with the next slide. "See, so what I guess we're trying to say is that if your offer still stands, Annie and I would like to manage the store and run Novel Detectives from inside these hallowed halls. We'll obviously have to work out the financials of buying you out, discuss how much you want to be involved, and so forth."

Hal wrapped his arms around his chest and rubbed his shoulders like he was hugging himself. His eyes brimmed with tears. "What can I possibly say other than yes."

"We don't want to force you into anything," I said, suddenly worried that maybe we'd pushed too hard. If Hal didn't like the idea of running a detective agency out of the store or wasn't ready to scale back yet, I didn't want to force him.

"Force me? Force me?" Hal scoffed, throwing his head back in a chuckle and then dabbing his eyes with his sleeve.

"Nothing could be further from the truth. I'm overcome with emotion. I'm stunned in the best possible way. I had given up hope that either of you were actually interested in running the store, and I haven't wanted to pressure *you*."

"Pressure us? We love this place. You'd have to pull me from here kicking and screaming," Fletcher said with a funny grin. "We have to discuss the details of the arrangement. Obviously, neither Annie nor I can afford to buy the estate, but I think if my math checks out—and Annie is going to look at my numbers—we should be able to buy the business from you over time and lease the space. We'd like to offer to pay you back in installments, maybe in a three-to-five-year plan for the store. We're guessing you would want to continue to live here, which would be wonderful. We'd love to have you remain involved in operations in any capacity, but clearly, that's also up for discussion."

Hal blinked back tears. "I've been running some numbers, too, and I think all of this sounds reasonable, but I do want to warn you this business isn't for the faint of heart. Sometimes, seeing the balance in the store's bank account sends my heart racing. It hasn't been an easy path and, well, let's just say there's always room for improvement and growth. I'd like to help with that. I don't want to be a nuisance, but if you'll allow me to tinker around with my creaky knees, I'd love to remain involved and help if I can."

I leaned into him. "We'll take whatever amount of time you'll give us."

He put his arm around my shoulder in a show of solidarity. "Well, I will say that Caroline has a touch of the travel bug. She wants me to spend three weeks in Italy with her in February. I've hesitated to say yes because I didn't want to leave you high and dry, but maybe I'll have to reconsider. Plus, we can't forget our group trip to England next summer. Maybe Caroline and I will go early and meet up with you there."

"Yes, reconsider. You have to go to Italy with Caroline," I insisted, pulling away from him so I could look him in the eye. "The plan is for you to pop into the store whenever you like. You don't need to have set hours or an official role."

"Exactly." Fletcher nodded in agreement. "We figure you can ease into retirement."

"As long as we're clear on me supporting you. If you two own the bookshop, its future vision should be yours, not my stodgy, outdated Agatha obsessions taking over."

"Oh, we're not going to change anything in the store," I said. "We'll brainstorm more events like the gingerbread competition, but as long as Fletcher and I are in charge, nothing will change at the Secret Bookcase."

Hal's eyes misted again. "That's fine for now, but the store will ultimately belong to you. It's only fitting that you'll find a way to fully make it your own."

*Make the Secret Bookcase my own.*

I thought about that. For the moment, there was nothing I would change, but Hal was probably right. Once Fletcher and I created a new routine, opened the Novel Detectives Agency, and hired some part-time staff, things probably would shift. I didn't envision making any radical changes to the store I knew and loved, but sinking into the idea that the Secret Bookcase might be officially mine was beyond my wildest dreams.

# FIFTEEN

We spent the next few minutes hashing out potential plans but had to shift gears to prep the store for opening. Fletcher and I set up tables for Pri's coffee tasting and Dayton's cooking demonstration while Hal turned on the lights in each room and made sure tea service was set up in the Parlor.

A knock sounded at the front.

"Pri must be early," I said to Fletcher. "I'll let her in."

"Okay, I just need to hook up the microphone. Otherwise, we're ready for her." Fletcher positioned his laptop on the podium and took out the lapel mics. I was glad he was well-versed in AV equipment. I never had to worry about the technical aspects of hosting authors or events—another way our skill sets complemented one another.

Pri wasn't waiting at the door. It was Dr. Caldwell. She didn't look like she'd slept much. She was dressed in jeans and a fleece. Rarely did I see her in anything other than slacks or a skirt.

"Good morning, I wasn't expecting you," I said, propping it open and waiting for her to enter before locking it again.

"I have an update that I thought you'd want to hear," she said, observing the store with her eagle eye. "Are you in the middle of work?"

"Not really. We're waiting for Pri to set up her coffee tasting, but we don't open until ten."

"Excellent. Can we speak somewhere in private?" Her unwavering gaze scanned every inch of the Foyer.

"We can go to the Sitting Room." I motioned to the hallway.

"Excellent." Her short heels clicked on the floor as we walked to the cozy reading room. Hal had already turned on the lights and lit the gas fireplace. The room glowed with a warm radiance. Garlands wrapped around the bookcases, and fragrant herbed wreaths made from rosemary and pine adorned the bay windows.

"Can I pour you a cup of tea?" I asked, motioning to the tea cart.

"No, thank you. I'm tight for time." She glanced at the antique clock on the nearest bookshelf and sat down, tucking her bag on her lap.

"Did you speak with Shane last night?" I asked, sitting next to her.

"One of my officers took his statement." Her tone was matter-of-fact. Did that mean she was hinting at something?

"He sounded sincere when he told me about their shared medical history, but then he couldn't prove it. If he's telling the truth, where are the messages?" I propped one of the buffalo plaid pillows behind my back.

"That is the question, isn't it?" She removed her glasses and cleaned them with the sleeve of her silky blouse. "I was able to speak with Lily's family."

"I can't imagine that was an easy conversation," I said, feeling a rush of emotion. Breaking the news that a loved one had been killed must be the worst part of her job.

"It never is." She blew on the lenses and rubbed them again. "Her parents were very forthcoming in our conversation. This is preliminary information and will need to be confirmed by the medical experts, so I would appreciate it if this stays between you and me."

"Of course." I would never betray Dr. Caldwell's confidence.

"Her parents confirmed that she was diagnosed with a heart murmur when she was younger. It was well-controlled with medication for years, and her doctor told her she had grown out of it. According to them, she's been off the medication for months without having any issues or side effects. There was no hesitation on their part—they said that the murmur was gone. No one has been able to hear it with a stethoscope in years, and just to be safe, Lily's cardiologist ran several additional tests before advising her to discontinue the medication. She had an echocardiogram, an EGK, and a stress test. Her heart was in perfect condition."

"Really?" I blinked, letting my mouth fall ajar. This was a major reveal. That meant Lily's death wasn't natural.

She put her glasses back on, peering at me from behind their shiny lenses. "I researched heart murmurs last night, and it's quite common for them to be detected in youth. Many people outgrow them as adults. Lily's parents claim that's exactly what happened with her. Without access to her medical records, I can't confirm any of this, but there's little reason for them to lie, which makes me all the more inclined to believe that Lily's death was a homicide."

I took a second to process what she was saying. "And that matches Shane's statement."

"It does." Her eyes drifted toward the windows. The garden was illuminated by the rising sun. If I didn't know better from this view, I could pretend to be living in the pages of a Miss

Marple mystery—visiting a rich aunt's country estate for the weekend.

"Does this mean you're officially opening a homicide investigation?" I repositioned the pillow and crossed my legs.

"I'm unofficially calling this a homicide until I have further information from the medical examiner and Lily's personal physician, but between us, I'm ninety-nine percent positive Lily was murdered."

I sighed. I suspected as much, too, but hearing Dr. Caldwell confirm it sent my emotions swirling. "Do you have any idea how?"

"I'm not a betting woman, but I'd put my money on a poison that mimics a heart attack."

"Something she ate or drank, maybe?"

"Possibly. We're not ruling anything out, but *how* the poison was administered will be key in cracking this case." She reached into her bag and showed me a picture on her phone. "Do you recognize this?"

"Yeah, that's the pen Shane gave her." I immediately recognized the expensive pink pen.

"Did you see Lily with it?"

"Yes when she was about to start judging and then again when I found her. He tried to give it to her, but we kicked him out of the store before he had a chance."

"How did she end up with it?" Dr. Caldwell asked the obvious question.

"Sugar offered to give it to Lily. She went to make sure Lily had it to appease Shane. At that point, we were worried that he would cause even more disruption with the event, so Sugar promised she'd make sure Lily got it."

"She was true to her word." Dr. Caldwell put her phone in her bag.

"You think the poison was in the pen?" Images of Lily

chomping on the end of her ballpoint pen flashed through my head. "Shane knew about Lily's habit. He specifically mentioned getting her this pen because she couldn't chew through it."

"He relayed the same information to me," Dr. Caldwell said, raising one eyebrow ever so slightly.

"So Shane could have poisoned the pen, knowing that Lily's first instinct would be to put it in her mouth. That explains why it was lying next to her."

"We're having it analyzed at the lab. I've informed Shane that he's a person of interest, and he is not to leave Redwood Grove without my permission."

*Was it Shane?*

*Could his obsession with Lily have led him to do something so drastic?*

*It could be a case of if he couldn't have her—then no one could.*

"I can see you're puzzling through possibilities," Dr. Caldwell noted.

"Yeah. Shane is the most likely suspect for all the reasons we've discussed, but I don't know. I tended to believe him when we spoke last night. He seemed genuinely distraught about Lily's death and shocked that his messages were gone. Maybe he's more cunning than he comes across."

"Possibly. I have other people of interest as well. Were you aware that Lily sent Kari and Queen Mary Flour a cease-and-desist letter?"

"No."

"It came up in our public records search. Kari has been attempting to get Lily to sign a sponsorship deal with the company for nearly a year. Lily continued to decline every offer, and things turned nasty."

"Nasty how?" I sat up taller.

Dr. Caldwell flicked a piece of lint from her fleece. "Kari

posted threats on Lily's social media and emailed her and her family. She even mailed physical letters."

This was new.

"That's unexpected," I said, not trying to mask my surprise. "She did mention that she had come to Redwood Grove specifically to pitch Lily in person, but I didn't give it much thought at the time. When she asked about a sponsorship deal during the Q&A session, Lily shut her down instantly. No wonder. I had no idea that they had that kind of history."

"I'm bringing her in for additional questioning later. If she shows up here, I would appreciate it if you keep an eye out and let me know. The same goes for Shane."

"Of course. I'll text you right away if I see either of them."

"Excellent." She started to stand up.

"Do you have another few minutes?" I asked, ignoring the fluttering feeling in my stomach. I wasn't looking forward to telling her about my decision, but I couldn't drag it out any longer. It wasn't fair to her, and after my chat with Hal and Fletcher, I was eager to get to work sketching out a plan for the Novel Detectives.

"For you, always." She smiled kindly, making it even more difficult.

I blew out a long breath and stared at the woven throw rugs before meeting her gaze. "As you know, I've been seriously considering your offer, and I can't thank you enough not only for giving me time and space to make a decision but also for reigniting my love for criminology."

She smiled sadly.

I knew she was already ten steps ahead of me.

"I sense a 'but' coming," she said, leaning forward in her chair.

"It's more of an 'and.'"

Her smile was real this time.

"I love doing this kind of work, *and* I love the bookstore."

My eyes drifted around the room with its vintage wallpaper, stained-glassed lamps, and bowls filled with Christmas candies. It was impossible to feel bad when cocooned inside the Sitting Room. Spending even a few minutes in the warm room always made me feel like I was being wrapped in a hug.

She nodded.

"I want to do both. I think that's why it's taken me so long to figure out. I can't leave the store, at least not for a full-time position or even working for you part-time, because I know how invested I'd be in every case and the extra training I'd need."

"Don't forget the mountains of paperwork that are a bonus perk with this job." She chuckled, lightening the mood.

"Yeah, what a great perk. I mean, I'm tempted to say yes just for that." I laughed but then turned serious again. "In all honesty, I'm so grateful for our connection and your help and insight into Scarlet's case. I don't want to give that up and I also don't want to give up the Secret Bookcase. This past year has been the best year of my life. Hosting events and bringing new readers and tourists into Redwood Grove has sparked creative energy that I didn't even realize I had."

"It's a talent, Annie. A real talent." She dipped her chin, her lips tugging up in the corners.

"Thanks." A flush spread up my neck. "I've been going back and forth and making dozens of pro and con lists. You should see how many spreadsheets I've created. It's out of control."

She laughed again.

"The answer I've kept coming back to is both. I want to do both, and thanks to Fletcher I think I've now got a way how to make that happen."

"Oh, now I'm excited." She raised one eyebrow and waited for me to say more.

"I'm going to open a part-time private detective agency here at the bookstore. Fletcher and I are going to buy Hal out and continue to grow events and author readings. We're even talking about hosting an annual writing conference in addition to Mystery Fest each year, and then we'll open Novel Detectives and take on smaller cases, hopefully assist you if you're ever in need of contract work."

"Ever in need?" She gave her head a little shake. "I'd hire you today if you were ready."

Relief flooded my body. I let out a breath of air and placed my hand on my chest. "Really? Thanks. That means the world to me."

"That sounds like a wonderful balance, Annie. I'm truly happy for you. Would I love to have you on the force? Absolutely, but not if it's not right for you. I, too, am thrilled we've reconnected. As I've told you, you were always a standout student, and I have no doubt we'll continue collaborating. Congratulations." She paused for a minute, collecting her thoughts. "I do want you to be cautious about your meeting with Mark."

"Yeah, of course," I replied with all seriousness. "I have a plan."

"I'm aware." She stopped again and chose her words carefully. "I would advise you to meet him somewhere much more public."

"Okay."

"Good." She stood and looped her purse over her wrist. "I'll be around later, but please let me know if Kari or Shane make an appearance."

"Thanks for being so great." I walked to the front with her.

Now that we'd had a conversation, I could fully embrace the next steps. I was about to become a partial owner of a bookstore and open my own detective agency. Scarlet would be so proud of me. I was proud of me. I'd spent too much time making myself small and closing myself in in the early years after her death.

But that had changed.

I had changed.

I was ready for this. With the gift of distance, I could see how far I'd come. I'd built a world here in my beloved Redwood Grove. A world filled with friends who had become family, a new burgeoning relationship, and a future that involved manifesting my dreams.

...

...

# SIXTEEN

Pri had already arrived and was nearly set up when I finished my conversation with Dr. Caldwell.

"You ready for some serious caffeination?" She looked adorable with her long, dark hair tied into two braids with peppermint-striped ribbons. She wore a matching red and white long-sleeve T-shirt under her Cryptic apron. Her heart-shaped cheeks glowed underneath the incandescent lights.

"You're festive this morning," I said, greeting her with a hug.

"It's all part of my caffeinated Christmas theme." She spread her arm over the coffee-tasting display. Carafes of different holiday blends were intermixed with pitchers of cream, eggnog, oat milk, and various house-made syrups. Flickering tea lights and bundles of mistletoe gave the table an extra special touch.

"It looks like you brought the entire store with you." I wafted the scent of the strong cinnamon spice coffee closer to my nose. "That, or you're setting up Santa's own roastery here, which, by the way, I would *not* complain about."

"I sort of did. I couldn't skimp. We promised the people holiday coffee and holiday coffee they shall get." She filled a cup and handed it to me. "Try this. It's my Plum Pudding with notes of plums, cranberries, and warming spices. I've been drinking it nonstop the last few days."

Drinking her coffee was an otherworldly experience. I closed my eyes and drank in the bright notes of the jammy fruit. "I've never had plum pudding, but I would bet this is exactly how it tastes."

"We'll have to ask Hal. I got the recipe from him." Pri arranged tasting cups and pretty snowflake napkins. "How long do you want me to talk? You know me, once I get started on coffee, I can go forever, so rein me in. Rein me in."

I chuckled. "I have you slotted for thirty minutes. If you're up for it, we can open the floor for questions, and then Dayton will do his gingerbread demo after you."

"Is he actually baking live? How?" She shot a glance at the empty table nearby. "Is he bringing an Easy-Bake Oven?"

"No. He pre-baked everything. He'll go over techniques with a slideshow."

"Okay, that makes so much more sense." She poured herself a cup of the holiday blend. "Have you heard the fallout from him posting his recipe?"

"What fallout? No." I shook my head, my curiosity piquing.

"Yeah, I follow him on social because he's sent quite a few students our way for jobs. He did a collection of posts about the competition. There were a bunch of photos of the students prepping their gingerbread bakes in the high school culinary kitchen and pictures from yesterday. He also shared his recipe, but then he got a ton of backlash and ended up taking it down."

"What kind of backlash?"

"Backlash from Lily's fans." Pri knocked back her coffee like it was a shot. "They railed on him for stealing her recipe."

"Stealing her recipe?" I sipped my drink. The longer I tasted it, the more flavor came out on my tongue. I picked up a hint of honey and warming spices.

"One of her superfans screenshotted a photo from two years ago with the exact same recipe. I mean down to the quarter teaspoon of ground cloves. They lit Dayton up in the comment section—accusing him of stealing her original recipe."

Their exchange flashed in my mind. Was that why Lily cut him off and said she wanted to speak with him "offline" about his recipe?

"It got ugly," Pri continued. "I'm surprised Dayton didn't remove the entire post. He took down the recipe, but the comment section is still live. I'll show you." She set her coffee on the table and grabbed her phone from her oversized bag. Pri rotated handbags often. She had a huge assortment of embroidered and patchwork bags, many of which she had hand-sewn herself. "Take a look."

I scrolled through the comments. They were eviscerating, to say the very least with misspellings and inflammatory language.

FRAUD. YOU'RE A BAKING LEACH.

THIS IS LILY'S RECIPE—SO OBVIOUS. DIDN'T THEY TEACH YOU HOW TO PLAGERIZE IN SCHOOL. OH, WAIT, YOU'RE A TEACHER.

THOSE WHO CAN'T BAKE TEACH.

They went on and on. There were timestamped photos of Lily's holiday posts from two years ago with the same recipe ingredient for ingredient and measurement by measurement. Even Dayton's styling and presentation were a carbon copy of Lily's original bake.

"He's not even trying to fake it," Pri said when I returned her phone. "It's so obvious."

"I know, and now my head is spinning. Could the recipe be connected to her death?" Why would Dayton, a culinary high school instructor, steal the influencer's recipe and try to pass it off as his own? "Why wouldn't he have given her credit? Let's say he was trying to impress his students by being 'in the know' about the current baking influencers. Wouldn't it have been even better for him to have them do one of her bakes? Follow her recipe and break it down, or just post it on social in hopes that she would repost it?"

"That makes sense to me." She ran a finger along the edge of her coffee mug.

I savored the fruity coffee and considered what this new piece of information meant in terms of the case. "What if there's another possibility," I said to Pri. "What if it really is Dayton's recipe?"

"I'm not sure I'm following." She appraised me as she sipped her coffee.

"What if it's the other way around? Maybe Lily stole Dayton's recipe and passed it off as her own. We'll have to look into whether they had a previous connection. Nothing's connected them so far, but I can check with Dr. Caldwell. But let's imagine that Lily stole Dayton's recipe a couple of years ago. What if he's been angry and bitter? She shows up in Redwood Grove, and he exacts his revenge."

"Oh, juicy." Pri tapped her finger on the mug. "That makes sense to me, but I'm not an expert like you."

"I'm hardly an expert." I paced from the table to the stage. "The other possibility is that he *did* steal Lily's recipe, and she threatened to out him. Would that have impacted his job? Could he have been fired? But then again, if her fans have already called him out on social media, that theory doesn't quite work. Also, do we know if recipes fall under copyright? Can they be exclusive?"

"Uh, good question. I'm not sure."

"I'll look into it." I noticed Fletcher waving from the Foyer to signal it was time to open the store. "Thanks for the intel. This could be important."

"Hey, if you need coffee or criminal advice, I'm your girl." She winked and picked up her coffee, raising it in a toast.

"I have to run help Fletcher, but I have some big news: we're going to keep the store open together and start a private detective agency—Novel Detectives."

Pri gasped audibly and threw her hand over her mouth. "Oh my GAWD, Annie, that's perfect!"

"Right? It's good, yeah?" My cheeks hurt from smiling.

"It's brilliant. I can't wait to hear more and we're going to have to talk logo, stickers, design. I'll hook you up."

I blew her a kiss and left to help Fletcher welcome readers. Seeing Pri's reaction made me even more excited about Fletcher and my future endeavors. However, the more I learned about Lily and her connections with everyone involved in the gingerbread competition, the more I was coming to realize that multiple people could have wanted her dead.

## SEVENTEEN

After ensuring everyone got into the store smoothly and introducing Pri, I did a quick Google search on recipe copyrights. It turned out that a list of ingredients couldn't be copyrighted. I wasn't sure how that information impacted Dayton's gingerbread recipe, but I did intend to speak with him about it before his baking demo.

I didn't have to wait long because he showed up shortly into Pri's coffee talk carrying trays of gingerbread cut into holiday shapes. "Can I give you a hand?" I offered.

He motioned to the gravel drive. "I parked the van outside temporarily since the gate is open. I hope that's okay."

"We left it open for that very reason. Why don't you set those on the tables in the Conservatory? I'll help you unload."

"Wonderful. None of my students were eager to get up early on a Sunday morning. I can't imagine why." He smiled, looking like a true professional in his crisp black chef coat. The one difference was his mustache streaked with red and green hair dye. "You like the 'stache? I do it every holiday for my students. They get a kick out of it."

"I bet they do." I waited for him and we walked outside

together. "Rumor has it that your gingerbread recipe is quite coveted." I needed a way to bring up the topic of copyrights and who first posted the recipe—him or Lily.

"Is that so?" He adjusted the top button of his uniform. "Teaching high school has made me leery of paying much attention to rumors."

Was that his way of avoiding the topic?

I decided being direct was my best bet with him. Plus, we didn't have much time, so I wanted to take my shot at questioning him now. "Someone mentioned Lily had a similar recipe."

"You heard that?" He stopped at the back of the van and stared down the gravel drive like he was worried someone might be lurking nearby, eavesdropping on our conversation. "From who?"

I wasn't going to throw Pri under the bus. "You know what the rumor mill in Redwood Grove is like. Everyone's talking about it. I heard that your social media was flooded with angry comments."

He opened the back doors and reached inside for another tray. "Can you carry this, or do you want something lighter?"

"This is fine." I took the tray. I might be short and petite, but I was stronger than I looked. My walks through town and hikes in the surrounding redwood forest kept me fit, and there was rarely a day at the bookstore when we weren't unpacking heavy boxes of new shipments, which kept my "guns" tight, as Fletcher liked to tease. It was fun to watch big, burly guys like Dayton be shocked by how much I could carry.

"Damn, I didn't realize everyone in town had heard. I thought it was just online." He lifted another tray of the sweet cake slices from the van. "What have you heard?"

"Conflicting things—both that you stole the recipe from her and vice versa." Technically, that was a white lie, but Dayton didn't need to know that.

"Ha! That's classic." He laughed, but there was no happiness in his tone. "What if I told you neither was true."

"I'm not sure I follow."

He shut the door with his hip. We balanced the trays and turned toward the store. "I guess it's going to come out now. I can't stop it, so it's probably good to come clean."

Was he about to admit that he had stolen the recipe?

He kicked a pebble with his foot, sending it scattering into the side of the house. "Lily and I met a little over two years ago at an event in San Francisco. I was showcasing my sugar-pulling techniques, and she was already a star. She was headlining the weekend."

So they had met previously.

Why had he failed to mention such an important detail?

"Everyone wanted to meet her, take selfies, get an autograph, pitch her on a project, just like this weekend. She had her entourage around her the entire time. It was impossible to get a minute with her without standing in a two-hour line for a photo op or a headshot signing. I wanted to talk to her about the possibility of Zooming with my students or even doing something like this." He nodded toward the ivy-coated estate. "Have her judge a baking competition—anything to get them engaged. Teaching isn't what it used to be. We're constantly competing with phones and devices. I figured instead of battling it, I could embrace it. If an influencer were involved, they would get into any project I assigned."

"Did she agree?" I took the stairs carefully.

"No. I couldn't get close to her. Trust me, I tried, and usually, I'm fairly persuasive. I mean, look at me. I'm not your average teacher. I've got street cred—tats, piercings, and this cool mustache." He stopped and puffed out his chest like I was supposed to be impressed. "I spoke with Becca. She said she would pass on the request, but I never heard anything. That's why I was excited about this weekend. I figured it was a smaller event, so I would be able to speak with her about inspiring this next generation of bakers."

We paused our conversation while we put the trays on the table. Pri was in the middle of her coffee demo, and I didn't want to interrupt her. Once we were back outside, I pressed Dayton for more. "How does your first meeting Lily tie into the illustrious gingerbread recipe?" I pointed to the last two trays of dainty cakes.

"Because we both discovered our infamous recipe at that baking convention." Dayton hoisted another tray over one arm. His muscles bulged beneath his chef coat.

He certainly would have had the strength to overpower Lily, but that didn't seem to matter in this case. Not if she was poisoned.

"Discovered it?" I asked.

"Yes. A prestigious San Francisco Baking School culinary instructor demoed this very recipe. I've used it with every class during the holiday season. It's a winner, and it's failproof, which is great when you're teaching new chefs." He handed me the last tray and shut the van again. "Lily decided to co-opt the recipe and claim it as her own. It went viral online, but it's not her recipe."

"Why did you ask her to taste it?"

"Because I wanted her to be honest with my students about the recipe."

"I was under the impression that recipes can't be copyrighted." I tried to sound casual, knowing I had just researched the subject.

"They can't be. That's true. However, as chefs and bakers, we have a moral obligation. I try to impart the importance of collaboration to my students. My job is to foster deeper conversations. Can a recipe be copyrighted? No. But should you give the original chef credit? Yes. Other chefs have inspired me over the years. You can take a recipe and make it your own. You can pay homage to a great meal or the perfect pastry by recreating it, but Lily was operating in a murky space in the middle. Honestly, I'm not sure she can even bake."

"What?" My stomach knotted. This could be a critical piece of information. Was Lily's entire social media persona a ruse?

"I don't know, but I wouldn't put it past her. I've watched her videos dozens of times, and something is off about them." He balled up a fist and pounded it on the edge of the table like he was trying to force the answer.

"Off how?"

"I can't put my finger on it. Maybe it's the style—her shaky, choppy cuts, but I wouldn't be surprised to learn that she bought her cakes and pastries from a professional bakery and passed them off as her own."

That was a huge shocker.

A little part of me believed him. There had been a few hints that made me question at least how much involvement she had in the baking and designing process like Becca mentioning the hours and hours she'd devoted to building the gingerbread replica or the amount of time Lily devoted to being online. Did that mean she couldn't bake? Or was it that her career had shifted as her audience grew?

It could also be that Dayton was envious of Lily's fandom and was bitter.

"Who knows?" He sucked in a sharp breath and gave me a nervous smile as if I'd caught him in a lie. "Like I said, there was something off about her baking."

"So you never claimed that the gingerbread recipe is yours?"

He shook his head. "Never. Check out the QR code when we're inside. It tells the story of tasting this cake, falling head over heels for it, and teaching all of my students how to bake it. The link takes you to the San Francisco Baking School website. They love it. I've sent tons of students their way."

There went my theory that Dayton had killed Lily to protect his job.

We were almost back to the front steps. He waited for me to go first. "You know what's a really small world?"

"No, what?"

"Kari from Queen Mary Flour was at the same baking convention."

"She was?" This was another nugget of news. I was quickly learning Lily had a past with multiple suspects.

"Yeah, the baking world is smaller than you think. That's another thing I teach my students. You never want to burn a bridge because chefs move around. You might end up working with or for a former colleague."

"Do you happen to remember if Kari and Lily hung out at the convention?"

"Oh, I remember. Everyone in attendance probably remembers because they got in a wicked fight—like a knockdown, drag-out, bloody-your-knuckles fight. They hated each other."

# EIGHTEEN

Dayton made space on the skirted table for the last trays of gingerbread.

"Kari and Lily got in a fight at the baking convention?" I repeated.

"Yep. It was wild." He started to touch his mustache but stopped when he realized it was coated with temporary hair dye. "I remember it vividly because it was so strange. It's not every day you see professional bakers or industry people blowing up at each other. They had to be pulled apart. It was a *whole thing*, as my students would say."

Is that what students said today? I didn't think so, but I didn't bother to correct him. It felt like some of the pieces of the puzzle were starting to fall into place.

Why had Kari lied? She said she'd never met Lily. She told me she had come to Redwood Grove specifically to pitch Lily on a partnership deal. Could there be another reason for her visit?

Revenge?

Dayton wound sprigs of holly and mistletoe between the trays. Some of the miniature cakes were dusted with powdered sugar as if they'd been kissed by new fallen snow. Others were iced with a vanilla glaze and dotted with maraschino cherries. They looked too pretty to eat.

I noticed Pri wrapping up her presentation.

That was my cue to moderate the Q&A.

"I'll introduce you in a few minutes," I said to Dayton. "Flag me down if you need anything in the meantime. I'll be running back and forth with the microphone."

I joined Pri on the stage. "Thanks so much for sharing your coffee expertise with us," I said, taking the second microphone off its stand. Everyone applauded. "Pri has generously brought samples of Cryptic Coffee's holiday blends for you to sample, but before we get to the good stuff, do you have any burning questions for our resident barista?"

A few hands shot in the air.

I walked the room with the mic. People asked interesting questions, some highly specific, like the exact steaming temperature for milk and how to pull an espresso shot with a perfect layer of crema. My favorite question came from one of our youngest readers, who asked if Santa might prefer a latte instead of hot chocolate on Christmas Eve.

"My mommy says caffeine keeps her awake, and Santa has a lot of houses to deliver presents to," she said in a sweet voice.

Everyone cracked up.

"You know, I think Santa would appreciate a latte," Pri responded with the utmost seriousness. "You're right. Santa is a busy guy, and I bet he would love a latte. It's so thoughtful of you to think about him. Because of your kindness, I have a special gift for you. Stop by my table, okay?"

The crowd let out a collective "aww."

"Wonderful. Not only are you going to taste some of the most delicious holiday coffees, but now we've given Santa an extra-special reason to stop in Redwood Grove. Thanks, Pri."

I waited for the applause to die down.

"But what would a coffee tasting be without a slice of cake to go with it?" I waved Dayton to the stage. "Redwood Grove High School's culinary instructor, Dayton Coyle, will teach us how to bake his decadent gingerbread. You just might be inspired to add it to your holiday meal or at least grab a bite to pair with your coffee while you shop." I explained our special offers, reminded people to get their gingerbread votes in, and encouraged everyone to stick around for the closing party and announcements of the winners later.

I bumped into Sugar after handing the mic over to Dayton. She was slumped in a chair near the floor-to-ceiling arched windows. Instead of listening to Dayton's presentation, she had positioned the chair to look outside into the garden. I didn't blame her. The view was spectacular. The English-style garden gleamed under the morning sun. Boxwood shrubs created green pathways through the extensive grounds. Topiaries and fountains provided height and contrast among the winter blooms.

"I love this view," I said to Sugar.

She tossed her hand to her chest and gasped. "Oh God, Annie. Hi. You scared me."

"So sorry. I didn't mean to sneak up on you."

"It's okay." She scooted the chair so she didn't have to crane her neck and looked at me with dull eyes. "It's a nice turnout this morning. I wondered if people would stay away, but I guess not."

I pulled an empty chair closer to her and sat. Everyone was focused on Dayton's cooking presentation. This was my chance to speak with Sugar alone. "Have you heard any more from the police?"

Her face blanched. She gaped at me in shock. "How did you know? You already heard? Oh, great. Wonderful. That's just perfect and on par with the disaster that is my life. I'm screwed."

"What?" Something was clearly lost in translation.

"You heard about me and Lily, I take it." She blew air out of her lips like a motorboat.

"No. What about you and Lily?"

She gulped and ran her fingers through her hair. It frizzed out in every direction like she'd stuck her finger in an electrical socket. Her eyes were equally wild. "You don't know? Wait. You haven't heard?" She gave her head a shake and then exhaled slowly. "Okay, that's good. That's really good. Maybe the rumors haven't started to spread yet. Although I probably don't have much time. I'm sure people are already whispering."

"Whispering about what?" I didn't want to push too hard, but now that she'd slipped up, I needed to know what she was talking about.

She dug through her unruly curls again. "You're going to hear about it soon enough, and honestly, I could use a friend right now. Actually, maybe you can help. You're tight with Detective Caldwell."

"I don't know if I would say tight, but Dr. Caldwell was my college professor, and I'm always here to listen."

"She's intense." Sugar knotted a section of her hair. "Dr. Caldwell. Yikes. I wouldn't want to get on her bad side."

"What makes you say that?" My experience with Dr. Caldwell had been different. From the very first lecture I'd attended, I had been captivated by her intelligence, cunning, and kindness. She wasn't effusive, but she was deeply caring and opted for a career path in the field to bring peace and justice to the families and victims on her caseload.

"She came by the bakery early this morning." Sugar's eyebrows shot up, arching toward her hairline. "Why? I guess she realized that I keep baker's hours, but I was not expecting a crack of dawn shakedown. She interrogated me forever. I thought I was never going to make it here in time for Dayton's presentation."

"Why was she interrogating you?" I had a feeling I knew

the answer, but I wanted to hear it from her. I also couldn't picture Dr. Caldwell shaking anyone down. Her approach was much more methodical.

Sugar picked at an invisible piece of lint on her apron, flicking it away like an unwanted fly. "She saw the video of Lily knocking over my gingerbread replica. I already told her that it wasn't a big deal. I mean, yeah, I was upset. Who wouldn't be? Hours and hours of time and money went into that build, and I had expected to get some serious social media traction out of it, but it's not like I killed her because she tripped."

"Unless she didn't trip," I added.

"That's what Detective—sorry—Dr. Caldwell implied. Apparently, her team analyzed the footage and found some inconsistencies. She wouldn't expand on what she meant by inconsistencies, but basically, she thinks that shattering my gingerbread display wasn't an accident."

"How does that implicate you?"

"It's not just that. It's the financial fallout. You see, I paid Lily a huge amount of money to come to Redwood Grove for this event and specifically to promote Sweet Room. I needed a boost to business, and having tons of eyeballs on my bakery and product was going to give me the bump that I've been desperate for."

I was still lost.

"I swear they think I killed her." Sugar pounded her chest so hard it shook the chair.

"Why? Because she broke your gingerbread?"

"Yeah, that and more. They found a threatening note I left for Lily, but they've taken it completely out of context."

"What kind of note?"

"Lily didn't follow through on her end of our bargain. She was supposed to post on her accounts for weeks leading up to the event and then do a variety of posts and takeovers while she was in town. She didn't do any of it. I reached out to her kindly at first, but then I got angry. I paid for her promotional services. She came back with a lame excuse about 'not feeling the vibe.' That's not how business partnerships work. She was contractually obligated to post. The only things she did post were terrible —how I can't bake and I'm a fraud. That's the opposite of what I paid her for. The goal of our collaboration was to have her build my business up, not tear it down."

"Did you have a legal contract documenting the scope of the work?"

"Not officially." She lowered her head and nibbled on the inside of her cheek. Then she looked at me with a touch of desperation behind her eyes. "But I have our email exchanges and a breakdown of what she would do. That's proof, right? I paid her close to fifty thousand for promotion. I've barely seen any results in return. My social followers have grown by twenty. She promised I'd see at least a few thousand new followers. That's why I wrote the note. I told her in no uncertain terms that she needed to start posting and tagging me. The police have twisted my words. I told her I would take matters into my own hands if she didn't. They're claiming that is a direct threat. I don't know if you've heard this, but they're looking into the possibility she was killed."

I nodded but didn't say anything.

"They think I threatened her with the note." She threw her hands over her face and ran them along her jawline in an effort to wash away the thought.

"Did you?" I asked gently. I wanted to believe Sugar. I wanted to help her, but I had to know the truth.

"Yes! I did—but not to murder her." Sugar's voice turned shrill. "By taking matters into my own hands, I meant *legally*. I spoke with a lawyer to figure out what my options are. My lawyer believes we have a solid case. The email threads between me and Lily serve as written documentation of intended services. She failed her contractual obligations, and we were preparing documents to take her to small claims court."

"Did you explain this to Dr. Caldwell?"

"I'm not an idiot." She shook her head. "They don't believe me, though. I can tell. They searched the bakery. They didn't have a warrant. I gave them permission because I have nothing to hide, but they treated me like a common criminal."

Dr. Caldwell was always professional and empathetic. I couldn't imagine her treating Sugar like a criminal, but I waited for her to continue.

"I don't understand her logic anyway," Sugar said through pinched lips, like she tasted something sour. "Why would I kill Lily? I needed her alive to help promote my bakery."

"True," I replied with a small nod, although I wasn't sure that was factually correct. Lily's death had launched Sugar into the spotlight. She took over her social media accounts yesterday. She would be the star of the show today. Lily's death had benefited her. I wondered how many new followers she had amassed in the last twenty-four hours.

However, the idea of taking over Lily's social was entirely Becca's. Sugar had initially resisted. That made me more inclined to believe her.

Could Sugar have taken matters into her own hands? She was admittedly angry and upset about the lack of return on her investment. She also had ample opportunities alone with Lily. She could have slipped Lily something while they were working together at her bakery to prepare for the competition.

I didn't want Sugar to be the killer, but I understood why Dr. Caldwell was keeping a watchful eye on her.

# NINETEEN

Dayton wrapped up his baking demo. I had more I wanted to ask Sugar, but I couldn't shirk off my bookstore duties. "Let's chat later," I said to her, standing up and putting the chair back in its place.

Customers began to disperse, queuing for coffee and ginger-bread tastings and searching the bookshelves for the perfect holiday gift. I couldn't stop thinking about what I'd learned from Sugar and Dayton as I directed readers where to find hard-bound copies of *Hercule Poirot's Christmas* and packaged collections of stickers, holiday teas, and candles in our custom silver-and-gold boxes.

I wasn't convinced either of them were telling me the whole truth. It should be relatively easy to confirm Dayton's story. When I had a free minute, I could research the baking convention and try to trace the original recipe. I also intended to spend some time on the Redwood High culinary website and social media pages to see if Dayton had indeed given credit to the orig-inal chef.

As for Sugar, I was torn. She raised a valid point that having Lily's ongoing support benefited her bakery and raised her profile, but that didn't align with Lily's horrible comments online. And I still maintained that she had been suddenly thrust into the spotlight with the takeover yesterday. When Becca suggested it, she immediately declined. But was that an act? Could she have orchestrated that move? Planted the seed in Becca's head, knowing Becca would be hyper-focused on Lily's brand image and protecting her family from hearing news of her death from strangers online? Potentially.

Shane remained high on my suspect list, and I needed to speak with Kari and Becca. If Dayton's story checked out, that could mean Kari was the killer. I wanted to know more about their history and Lily's rise to fame, and Becca was the person who could provide me with the most insight.

Unfortunately, I didn't have a chance to speak with her as the morning wore on. We were slammed with sales and custom requests, which was not a bad thing.

Hal dropped off a stack of new kids' mysteries. "Annie, it's like a fire sale today. I had no idea we'd keep selling books like hotcakes. It must be a sign from the mystery gods and goddesses and my dearly departed Agatha that you and Fletcher are destined to take over the store."

I smiled. "Or maybe it's because half the town wants the scoop on Lily's murder."

"You make our village sound so macabre." Hal frowned. "But you're not wrong. You wouldn't believe how many times I've been stopped and asked about Lily. Word is certainly out about her death. Has anything been posted publicly?"

"That's a good question." In the morning rush, I hadn't had a chance to check her social media pages. "Let's pull up her sites," I said to Hal, turning the computer screen for him to see.

Sugar's face was front and center. The last ten posts were her "takeovers," none of which made any mention of Lily's death, which I knew was Becca's plan, but it still felt weird.

"Doesn't look like it." Out of curiosity, I clicked on Sugar's profile. I didn't know how many followers she had started with, but she was inching close to fifty thousand. That couldn't be a coincidence. It had to be a bump from taking over Lily's accounts.

Again, I was struck by the fact that Sugar had indeed benefited from Lily's death. I didn't know yet whether that meant she was the killer, but I intended to keep a close eye on her for the remainder of the day.

"I wonder how long they'll drag this out?" Hal asked, thinking out loud. "It feels wrong to me. I don't like this idea of Sugar acting as if all is normal when it most certainly is not."

"I agree." I closed the webpage. "I understand Dr. Caldwell's reasoning when it came to notifying Lily's family. It would be terrible to discover your loved one had died while scrolling online, but even yesterday, when she and Becca were brainstorming their approach, it felt gross, for lack of a better word."

"I believe *gross* does justice to the situation." Hal sighed. "Are we expecting an appearance from Dr. Caldwell?"

"Yes. She said she would be by at some point. She also asked us to keep an eye out for Shane and Kari."

"Kari? The flour woman?" Hal rubbed his temples. "You know I saw her and Lily yesterday. They didn't appear to be very, well, shall we say, cordial?"

"Really? Do you remember when?"

"Not specifically, but it was shortly after the livestream." Hal paused, trying to recall the details. "They were in the Dig Room. I passed by but didn't want to linger as it was clear they were having a private conversation."

A customer ready to check out brought a stop to our conversation.

"In case you're wondering, I did share that tidbit with Dr. Caldwell." Hal looked at me knowingly and restocked the cookies and tea.

I rang up the sale and spent the next hour gift-wrapping and chatting with customers. The ballot box was nearly over-flowing as the lunch hour neared. We were cutting off votes at three o'clock to give us time to count the tally before the closing party at four p.m.

Fletcher came to relieve me. "You ready for a break?"

"That would be great," I said, handing him a roll of tape. "My fingers are starting to go numb, and my stomach has been growling for the last twenty minutes."

"It doesn't help that we're in such close proximity to the ballroom. I'm going to be smelling gingerbread for days."

"It could be worse."

"No complaints." Fletcher shot a glance toward the Conservatory. "I just can't guarantee that I won't sneak another slice or ten before you return from your break."

I stuck out my tongue and made a funny face. "It's your stomach, my friend."

I left the cash register in his capable hands and went and grabbed my lunch, taking it outside to the Terrace. Although there was a chill in the air, we kept the patio open year-round with portable heaters and firepits for readers to gather around and warm up. LED rattan deer with candy apple red bows were strategically positioned throughout the gardens as if they were really nibbling on the grasses. Spheres of lights and snowflakes hung from the pergola, and brilliant red poinsettias lined the walkways.

There were only a handful of people scattered throughout the large brick space. I found a table with a garden view and unpacked my lunch.

I unwrapped a peanut butter, banana, and honey sandwich and apple slices and breathed in the crisp winter air.

*How lucky am I to get to live and work in such a beautiful place?*

*And now I am going to be a partial owner?*

I wanted to pinch myself.

There were so many good things happening, which made me all the more resolved to solve Lily's murder and restore Redwood Grove's peaceful winter bliss. Things like this weren't supposed to happen in our sleepy community. It felt good knowing Fletcher and I would be part of protecting our little town moving forward.

I enjoyed my sandwich and the view, allowing my thoughts to linger on happier ideas like seeing Liam in a few hours. He had an uncanny ability to make me feel like I was back in high school.

If I wasn't careful, I would probably start leaving him secret notes and doodling his name in my journal.

I laughed out loud at the thought.

With Christmas fast approaching, I had yet to decide on a gift. It wasn't an easy decision. We were newly dating. That was murky, uncharted territory for holiday gifts. Should I go for something benign like socks or a nice cashmere scarf? Or should I opt for something more personal, like a new stag head statue for the pub or a first-edition copy of one of his favorite historical fiction books?

Probably the latter.

But if I was going to track down rare or out-of-print nonfiction, it was time to get started.

Becca's voice pulled me out of my thoughts. I turned to see her storming toward me.

She looked more energized than she had yesterday. Her curly brown hair was tied in a high ponytail. She wore dark jeans, ankle boots, and a Lily Hawthorne hoodie. Her eyes were brighter and clearer. A night of sleep had done her good.

"Good. There you are." Her voice was breathless. Sweat pooled on her forehead. "I've been looking everywhere for you."

"For me?" I pointed to my chest and glanced around the Terrace, unsure if she was speaking to someone behind me.

"Yes. We need to put our heads together to figure out this PR crisis." She dabbed her cheek with the back of her palm, wiping sweat on her sweatshirt.

"What crisis?" I packed my leftovers into my lunch bag.

"Word has leaked about Lily. It's all over social. I've been getting calls and DMs from magazines and news stations." She showed me her home screen. "Look, I have forty-seven voice-mails, and that's just in the last hour. We have to announce the winner and make a statement, but Sugar is freaking out. She doesn't want to do it now. She's had a change of heart, whatever that means."

A change of heart?

"It's going to have to be you." Becca's speech was rushed like she had just chugged a triple shot of Pri's dark espresso. "There's no other option. I've been considering the optics. We can't leave Lily's followers hanging. You're the next woman up. You're going to have to announce the winner on the livestream."

"We could cancel the livestream."

"No. No." She shook her head with force. "It's absolutely out of the question. We have huge financial sponsorships. Part of their contract stipulates the exact number of times that Lily mentions their products or does official shoutouts. That's going to have to be you, too. I'll work on a new script."

"You want to do ads while announcing Lily's death?" A sour taste spread over my tongue.

"Of course I don't want to, but there's no other choice. I don't know what else to do." She sounded like she was on the edge of breaking down. "We're contractually obligated. I've been on the phone with our legal team. The reality is that our livestream numbers will probably be off the charts. Everyone is going to tune in to pay their respects."

"I don't feel comfortable advertising anything." There was no chance she could convince me to read any sort of advertisement. Talk about poor taste.

"Fine. I'll read the ads, but I need you to announce the contest winners and discuss Lily's impact on this event and the town in general. I don't think it's overstating things to say that she handily put Redwood Grove on the map."

I wasn't sure I would go that far.

"I'll write a speech honoring Lily's contribution to this event and town. You can tabulate the winners and announce the names. I'll take care of the rest, okay?"

"Are you sure this is the best approach?"

Panic—or maybe it was fear—flashed across her face. "I don't know. I'm barely hanging on by a thread. Lily is dead, and it's my job to try to hold it together. I'm inches away from having a full meltdown. Inches." She puffed air out of her mouth like she was breathing fire. "I'm going to salvage something from this disastrous weekend if it's the last thing I do."

# TWENTY

"Why don't you take a minute?" I suggested, trying to model slow, calm breathing for Becca. She was understandably upset, but was there more to her panic and outburst than just the stress of putting the right PR spin on Lily's death?

She hesitated. "I don't know."

"I've found I can operate better with a clear head," I said gently. "I lost someone dear to me, so I have some sense of what you're going through."

One of the things I'd come to realize in the wake of Scarlet's death is that the experts on grief and the process of grieving got it wrong. There weren't distinct stages. My grief was wild and untethered. Often, within the same moment, I could go from rage to utter despair. I recognized her almost feral behavior.

"Yeah, yeah, okay." She slunk into the chair and let her head lag to one side like it was too heavy for her to continue to hold up.

"How are you doing? This must be a lot of pressure and it seems like you and Lily were close."

"We were." She glanced over at me with glassy eyes,

blinking back tears. "She was like a sister to me. A more beautiful, composed, and popular sister."

I picked up a hint of jealousy as I reached out to touch her arm. "How long had you been working together?"

"It feels like forever, but technically, it's only been a few years." She flicked her forehead with her thumb and middle finger. "She hired me right out of culinary school."

"You attended culinary school?" This was news to me. It made sense that Lily would employ a personal assistant with baking knowledge, but I didn't realize Becca was classically trained.

"Yeah. I graduated from the pastry academy and thought I would go to work at a restaurant or bakery, but Lily and I met at an influencer event, and we hit it off instantly. She offered me a job right on the spot. Her social was just starting to take off, and she needed someone to run and manage the backend of her growing empire. Her talent was front-facing. The camera loves her. So do her fans. I did the heavy lifting with the baking and designing behind the scenes; she tied on an apron and flashed her dazzling smile—everyone ate it up. We were a dream team."

*She baked and handled the design.*

*This is exactly what Dayton had alluded to earlier.*

"Lily didn't bake?" I wanted to hear her response.

"Oh, well, yeah, she could bake, but not like me, no." Becca's tone shifted. She sounded almost patronizing. She scrunched her ponytail like she was trying to give it body. "If you scroll back through her feed to the very beginning, you'll be able to see the evolution and pinpoint when she hired me. In fact, we discussed taking down all of her original posts, but she insisted on keeping them up. She felt like they were aspirational. They would give her fans at home something to aspire to. They could see her journey over the years. Only the truth is it would be much harder for them to parallel her growth because it wasn't her, it was me."

I kept my expression passive.

How did this fact play into Lily's death? There had to be a connection.

"Was that hard for you?" I asked.

"Hard for me?" Becca's lip curled as she pointed to her chest where Lily's name and logo were embroidered on her hoodie. "Why?"

"Moonlighting for Lily. It must have been strange to have her take the credit for your baking and artistry."

"No." She blew me off with a flick of her thin wrist. "It happens all the time in the industry. Every celebrity chef has a team of people who do everything for them—the prep, the presentation, all of it. They show up in hair and makeup and stir something on the stove for a minute or two."

"Really?"

"One hundred percent." She rolled her eyes and nodded emphatically. "Name a celebrity baker, and I'll give you twenty of their staff members who make it look like they've effortlessly whipped up the most spectacular ten-tiered wedding cake in a matter of minutes. It's all smoke and mirrors. None of it is real. Social media influencers are our modern version of Hollywood starlets. We're just making a different kind of movie magic these days."

It made sense. I understood why Lily, or other bakers of her caliber, needed support teams, but I wasn't convinced that Becca was as chill about her role in their working relationship as she was pretending to be.

I decided to switch topics slightly and see if I could extrapolate any additional information from her. "I heard from Dayton that his gingerbread recipe originated from a chef at the San Francisco Baking School. He mentioned he met Lily there and they both received a copy of the recipe."

"Yep. That's true," Becca said. "It's another little dirty secret in our industry. Influencers, um, let's just say—*borrow*—

recipes from each other. They pass them off as their own and then get pissed when they see the same recipe on someone else's social profile or blog a week later. There's nothing that can be done about it. Lily had me research it years ago when one of her competitors poached my recipe for raspberry rolls. Our legal team informed me recipes can't be copyrighted."

"I learned the same thing this weekend."

"Yeah, it's a bummer when you're the one creating the recipe," she admitted, rocking from one foot to the other. "But on the flip side, when you stumble upon something great like the gingerbread, it can work to your advantage."

"Right." I was getting a much clearer picture of the influencer world. "How did sponsorships work?"

"Sponsorships?" She leaned in like she hadn't heard me.

"Yeah. Did you handle that part of the business for Lily?"

"Why do you ask?" She folded her arms across her chest in a protective stance.

Had I touched a nerve?

What made her suddenly look like she was on the defensive?

"I'm curious because I heard a rumor that Kari has been trying to ink out a deal with Lily for a while now. It sounds like they may have even gotten into an argument at a baking show?"

"Oh yeah, that. That's true." She loosened her grip on her shoulders and rubbed her hands together. "Kari has been relentless. You should see how many messages I receive on my private channels from her."

"Do you think there was bad blood between them? It seems odd she would show up out of the blue here in Redwood Grove." The afternoon light drenched the garden in sunshine, giving everything an ethereal glow.

"There was definitely bad blood between them. She's like Shane. She's a glorified stalker. She shows up whenever Lily has —had—a public appearance."

"This wasn't the first time?"

"No. It's not even close. She's always around, and like with Shane, I constantly have to tell her that Lily isn't interested. We already have much bigger flour sponsorships. Lily wasn't about to give up the kind of money she was pulling in from them to go with an unknown mom-and-pop shop. No chance. I give Kari credit for her persistence, though. She doesn't take no for an answer. Every few months, she appears out of thin air with a new pitch and a new attempt to sweeten her deal. Sadly for her, it pales in comparison to the kind of money we're bringing in with our other corporate sponsorships. Maybe five or six years ago, she could have convinced Lily to partner with them, but Lily's brand is in the stratosphere. She's at an entirely different level."

I noticed Becca kept slipping into the present tense when referring to Lily. That was another tendency I understood. There were still days, even a decade later, when I would start to text Scarlet or make an internal note of something funny I wanted to tell her, and then I'd have to remind myself that she was dead. It was like losing a little piece of her over and over again.

"You know, I've been thinking about Kari a lot," Becca said with a pensive glare. "Why did she show up here? She pitched us on this idea via email about three weeks ago. I already turned her down."

"You did?"

"Yep. It's another example of her stalker-ish persistence. It makes me worried that she might have done something drastic this time."

"Drastic like what?" I knew what she was hinting at, but I wanted to hear it from her.

"Like kill Lily."

# TWENTY-ONE

"You think Kari could have killed Lily? Why?" I studied Becca's face. Her pupils were wide, and her cheeks pinched like she was trying to contain her emotions. I couldn't tell if she was nervous or lying.

Maybe both.

"Not at first, but the more I've thought about it, the more I think she could have done something. She's become incrementally more upset every time we decline her pitches. She had to have known that Lily would say no. You saw what went down. Lily didn't even blink. Kari tried to use the live audience, maybe hoping she'd embarrass Lily into saying yes. She was furious after the Q&A. She went on a rampage."

"A rampage?" I asked. That was quite the word choice.

"Did you not see it?" Becca reached toward one of the poinsettias resting on the railing and yanked off a dead leaf.

"See what?"

"Their fight," Becca said, tugging on her hoodie strings. "Kari tracked Lily down while Lily was shooting B-roll around the bookstore. Lily told her to back off and threatened to get the police involved if Kari wouldn't stop harassing her."

"Was she harassing her?" That was a strong accusation, but it also matched what Hal had witnessed. Maybe not the harassment or rampage, but he had definitely seen them arguing, too.

"Yes. I don't know what else you'd call it." She picked up the poinsettia and held it to the light.

"Did you get involved?"

"What do you mean?" She set it back down, but not before fluffing up the leaves like an interior decorator. She probably couldn't escape her need to style and frame the perfect shot.

"I was under the impression that you acted as a bit of a referee between Lily and her fans."

"That's true, but Lily told me she could handle Kari. She said—" She stopped and clasped her hand over her mouth. "This is my fault. I should have stepped in. I should have called the police about both Shane and Kari. If I had, maybe Lily would be here today."

I recognized her guilt and bargaining. I had spent more hours than I'd like to count playing out scenarios where I could have saved Scarlet. It simply wasn't true.

I was about to console her, but she jumped to her feet.

"Oh no! I just remembered something. Kari gave Lily a cup of tea right before she died."

"What? When?" This was a huge revelation. Kari could have spiked Lily's tea with something lethal.

She pointed behind us. "In the kids' room, what's it called, the Dig?"

"The Dig Room," I said with a nod. Again, she was confirming exactly what Hal had witnessed, but why hadn't she said anything sooner?

"She brought Lily a cup of tea and a cookie when she launched into her pitch. I saw Lily take a long sip. It's all so clear now. I can't believe it's taken me this long to figure it out. Lily had a strange look on her face after she tasted the tea, like it was too strong. Lily preferred her tea and coffee with a gallon of sugar and cream, so I didn't give it much thought at the time. I figured she just didn't like it, but now I realize it had to be Kari —she must have spiked the tea with poison. That's why it tasted bad."

"When exactly was this?" I shifted into interrogation mode, making mental notes to share with Dr. Caldwell.

She danced from one foot to the other like she couldn't stand still. Her body hummed with energy as she rocked from side to side. "I'm not sure, but probably ten or fifteen minutes before Lily died."

"So Lily drank the tea, then what happened?"

"Um, what did happen? Uh." She pounded her forehead like she was trying to force the memories forward. "We both told her no. Lily tried to let her down easy. She explained that her contract with the national flour company doesn't end for another two years. I don't know why, but she told Kari to try again then. Her words were something like, 'You never know. I might be in the market for a new partnership by then.'"

"How did Kari respond?"

"She got angry. Really angry. She knocked books off the shelf and kicked sand in the sandbox. It was like she had a temper tantrum. She must have thought she had a shot, but again, I don't know how she could be that delusional."

"How much tea did Lily drink?" A shiver came over me. I wasn't sure if it was from the breeze or the dawning realization that Kari could have poisoned Lily.

"I don't know—a few sips, maybe?" She tugged one side of her hoodie string and then the other in rhythm, marking the beats of her anxiety as she swayed and stared out into the garden.

"And then did they stay in the Dig Room?" I kept my tone even and steady. I needed to get as many facts and details from her as possible.

"No. Lily left first. She said she had to film more before the store got too crowded and she took off and left me with Kari. I was used to having to clean up her messes, but I didn't want to keep going round and round with Kari. There was nothing more to say. It was a no. A solid no."

"How long did you and Kari keep talking?" I maintained eye contact, hoping to encourage her to stay engaged.

"Not long." She ripped another leaf from a poinsettia and gazed out to the garden. "I had a ton of stuff to do. I didn't have time to keep saying no. I told her as much and left her there."

"Did you see Lily after that?"

She shook her head. "No. I went back to the Conservatory to take pictures and check in with some of the contestants. I should have looked for her. What if I had? Maybe we could have gotten her help sooner. I wonder how long she lay there, passed out, before you found her?"

"I know it's hard, but try not to play the 'what if' game with yourself. I've been there, and it does you no good other than to cause yourself unnecessary agony."

"You're probably right." She hung her head. "I just can't believe I didn't see it all until now. I feel like I should tell the police. What do you think?"

"Absolutely. You didn't share any of this with them when you gave them your original statement?" That struck me as odd.

"I shared the big picture, but at that point, we didn't know that Lily had been killed. I thought it was her heart condition, so it didn't even cross my mind to consider Kari might have spiked her tea."

That reminded me of what I'd learned earlier. "Did you hear Lily's family said her heart was fine?"

"That's a relief. I've been feeling guilty about that, too." She glanced at the doors. "I should probably go call the police and get started on working out this new script."

"One more quick question before you go." I lifted my finger to stop her.

"Uh-huh?"

"Do you really think Lily broke Sugar's display on purpose?" I leaned in to get a good look at her facial expression.

"Zero doubts." She shook her head emphatically. "Lily intentionally ruined it. I'm sure of that."

She sounded convinced.

"Lily was an actress of sorts. She knew how to put on a good show. She could butter up her fans and have them eat out of the palm of her hand, but she did not like *not* being the star of the show. She craved the spotlight. You couldn't show her up in any way, especially when it came to baking. It was a point of contention with us because she'd bring me outlandish designs and ideas for cakes and pastries, and I had to figure out a way to execute them because she always wanted to lead the trend. She was desperate to stay relevant and on the cutting edge. Sugar threatened her. She's really talented."

"Why would she have agreed to the event and the competition?"

"Because she thought Sugar was a small-town, no-name baker. She figured she could look like she was imparting her wisdom and helping to bring attention to a new era of bakers, but when we arrived, she realized Sugar is incredibly skilled. She hadn't counted on that. She might have had an outward aura of sweetness, but she could be cruel and cunning. If you were on her good side, she was a delight, but if you weren't—watch out."

# TWENTY-TWO

"Annie, you're needed in the Conservatory." Fletcher gestured to the ballroom. "Your *boyfriend* is here." He batted his eyes and fanned his face like a character in a Jane Austen novel.

"What are we, twelve?" I reached out to swat him.

His reflexes were too quick. He ducked out of range. "Sorry, I should have been more on point with my book eras. 'Your *suitor* is here.'" He winked and hid behind the counter.

I rolled my eyes. "You're terrible."

Liam was already here? I wasn't expecting him for another hour.

"Don't leave him hanging." Fletcher blew a kiss. "And remember, no making out on the clock. If we're going to be business partners, I can't have you bringing down the level of professionalism in the store."

It was a good thing there was a counter between us because otherwise, I would have given him a soft punch in the shoulder. "Uh, in what world would I bring down the level of professionalism? I think you need a mirror, my Lego-building friend."

"Don't bring Legos into this, Annie. That's low. Really low."

I tightened my lips, pinched my nose, and went to check in with Liam. He was chatting with Sugar near the stage.

"Have you heard anything more about Lily's case?" Sugar asked me. She'd changed into a crisp Sweet Room apron and her unruly hair had been tamed into two braids with candy cane bows.

"Not lately. Why?" I glanced around half expecting to see Dr. Caldwell waiting in the ballroom.

"People are saying the police are close to making an arrest. They were at the bakery again an hour ago. I'm starting to get worried that I'm on the top of their suspect list. Why do they keep coming back to the bakery? What could they be looking for?" She gnawed on her fingernail.

I wanted to say, *For about a thousand reasons*. They were probably searching for additional evidence. Lily had used Sugar's kitchen for her prep work; she could have left physical evidence behind, or Dr. Caldwell might suspect that whatever substance had killed Lily was still in the kitchen.

"It's a good question," I replied, catching Liam's eye. He looked as handsome as ever in his well-fitting jeans and cream pullover sweater that brought out the deep ebony tones in his eyes.

He returned my gaze, causing my heart to flip. I placed my hand over my chest to try to steady the sensation.

"Have they told you why they're searching your space?" Liam asked Sugar pointedly.

"No, not specifically." She shook her head slowly. "They say it's related to the case, but I'm starting to think I might need a lawyer. I mean, technically, I could probably refuse, right? Don't they need a search warrant?"

"Do you have anything to hide?" Liam challenged.

I was glad he had said it. I was thinking the same thing. She was well within her rights to hire a lawyer, but I agreed with

Liam's perspective. Why was she suddenly so concerned with the police searching the bakery?

"What would I possibly have to hide?" She threw her head to the side and glared at Liam, her demeanor shifting dramatically.

"I don't know—kitchen knives?" His smile grew wide as he shrugged.

He tried to make a joke, but Sugar wasn't biting. "This isn't funny. This is my life and my livelihood we're talking about. For some reason, the police are targeting me."

"Targeting you?" That was a leap from where our conversation had started.

"Yes. I have no idea what I've done to warrant this, but they've turned all their attention on me, and it's quite unnerving." She tugged on her apron strings. "I've done nothing wrong. I've been helpful. I've complied with their requests. Now it feels personal, like they're attacking me. They're looking for a scapegoat, and I'm the easy answer."

I wasn't sure about that. Dr. Caldwell would never make an arrest without doing her due diligence, and even if she didn't, Shane was a much more likely scapegoat than Sugar.

"It must have something to do with my baking supplies. They've searched every square inch of my bakery. This morning, they were going through my huge bags of sugar and flour. It's all wasted now. That's another reason I think it's probably time for me to speak with a lawyer. They need to reimburse me for the product they've ruined. That flour is Queen Mary. It's not cheap. I paid for the premium because I want my customers to have the very best, but I can't bake with any of it. It's unusable."

"The police opened bags of flour?" I clarified. "Did they open any other products? Sugar, spices, your other baking supplies."

"Yep—everything. It looks like a tornado tore apart the

bakery. Fifty-pound bags of flour, sliced open and spilled all over the floor. These aren't the bags of flour you find at the grocery store. They're wholesale for professional bakers. I should be due compensation for that, right?"

Different states had different laws regarding compensation. Unlike the way legal searches were portrayed in the movies, I knew that Dr. Caldwell and her team were methodical when it came to searching private property. There were strict protocols officers would follow—going room to room, starting in one corner and working around the perimeter, checking furniture, under rugs, behind paintings hanging on the walls. Drawers would be taken out individually, the contents sorted through and then returned. The same went for cupboards, closets, and furniture. Damage was usually very minimal and most often happened when something was locked, and the owner refused to open it. Sometimes, damage was unavoidable. In those cases, the team would document, note, and explain how items were broken or damaged. As to whether or not the police would pay for said damages varied wildly.

"You'll have to speak with Dr. Caldwell about that. You're sure they didn't have a warrant?" I found it hard to believe Dr. Caldwell wouldn't have secured a warrant.

She shrugged, sounding distracted. "I don't know. I don't think so. I wasn't paying attention. They flashed something at me, but it all happened so fast I didn't have time to blink or consider whether I should let them in or not."

"If they had a warrant, it wouldn't have mattered anyway." I understood that Sugar might not share my interest in criminology and police procedures, but how warrants worked was surely common knowledge.

"Dr. Caldwell is by the book. I can't imagine her not securing a warrant before entering your property," Liam added, rolling up the sleeves on his cable-knit sweater to reveal his muscular forearms.

I felt a bit dizzy, imagining those solid, sturdy arms wrapped around my body. I wouldn't mind escaping to the comfort of my couch, lighting a fire, and curling up with a hot toddy and Liam for the rest of the afternoon.

"Look, fine, maybe that's what the police officer flashed at me before they barged in right as I was in the middle of baking cinnamon rolls," Sugar said, pulling back into the moment. "All I'm saying is that it's extremely unprofessional for them to destroy my product—expensive product—and not even bother to offer to pay for it."

"You should bring it up with Dr. Caldwell," Liam suggested. "She's very reasonable. I'm sure if you plead your case directly to her, she'll at least hear you out."

"I'm going to do that right now." Sugar yanked out her phone and swiveled in the direction of the Foyer.

"She's fired up," Liam said, watching her go.

"I don't blame her, but her attitude does raise some questions."

"Like, how could she not know whether they had a warrant?" Liam winced. "No chance Dr. Caldwell entered her property without a warrant or permission."

"Exactly. That was my first thought." I made sure Sugar was out of earshot and stepped closer to Liam, catching a faint hint of his rustic wood and bourbon-scented cologne. "I am curious about the flour."

"Why?"

"She said it was Queen Mary Flour—that's significant, especially with everything I've learned about Kari Harris. Speaking of things I've learned, I've been waiting impatiently all day to see you because I have some news."

He stood taller and tilted his head, narrowing one eye. "Oh yeah?"

"Fletcher and I are going to buy the store from Hal and run our own detective agency here." My words smashed together as

I bounced like I was warming up for a run. "Isn't that amazing?"

"That's great, Annie." Liam started to say more but stopped himself. "Hal's on board with this idea?"

"Yeah, of course." Why was he acting weird? "What is it?"

"Nothing." He didn't meet my eyes. "That's perfect for both of you. Congratulations. But how are you going to keep Fletch in check? You know him; he'll have a magnifying glass tethered to his hand and start running around the village with his plastic pipe. Also, where do you want me to set up?"

"Right over here." I motioned to the tables Dayton had used for his gingerbread demo. Was I reading too much into his response, or did he seem a little subdued? "I have fresh table-cloths and supplies stored underneath them."

"Great." He lifted a box from the floor. "Back to the investigation, what's significant about Queen Mary Flour?"

"Are you sure you're okay with us keeping the store?" I met his eyes. "I know you were interested in buying the estate from Hal a while back. Is this going to make things weird between us?"

"No. Hal and I both decided on other directions." He scowled and scooped me into a side hug. "It's great for you. I promise."

"Well, this is feeling like our first unofficial case. I've been ruminating on everything all day." I squeezed his waist and let him go. "The flour is significant. I'm sure of it. I just don't know why yet. Why are the police focused on the bakery? Why did they open her flour? I get going through her supplies. I'm wondering if Dr. Caldwell believes the flour could have been tainted. Kari has a motive for killing Lily. What if that's how she got Lily to consume the poison?"

"What's her motive?" Liam waited for me to remove the tablecloths.

"She's been trying to get Lily to sign a contract with Queen

Mary Flour for years. She didn't just show up in Redwood Grove on a whim. Everything she's done has been calculated. There's evidence of prior physical violence between them, and it sounds like she was pretty much stalking Lily. Not in a superfan way like Shane, but in an unrelenting-pressure way. She's on a singular mission to get Lily to sign a deal with them, and she won't take no for an answer." I folded the tablecloths and swapped them for fresh, new red linens with a white poinsettia design.

"Wouldn't that be a dangerous method?" Liam set the box by his feet to help me spread the tablecloths. "She would risk everyone getting ill or dying if she contaminated the flour."

"True, and it would be nearly impossible for her to guarantee that Lily consumed the product she altered, but still, I feel like there's something there. I can't quite grasp it, but it's at the tip of my brain."

"The tip of your brain, that's pretty cute, Murray." He tapped the top of my head with one finger like he was anointing me with a wand.

"What, you've never heard that?" I smirked, holding back a full grin.

"Oh, I've heard it. But I don't think that phrase is in my vocabulary wheelhouse. That's distinctly an Annie Murrayism." He smoothed the edge of the tablecloth. "Could Kari have done it when Lily and Sugar were prepping for the competition?"

"Yes, but how? She didn't have access to the bakery. I can't imagine they would have just let her in, not with the history between the two of them. Maybe I'm wrong. Maybe I'm grasping."

"Doubtful." Liam gave me a side eye and lifted the box. "Your brain works in mysterious ways, but it rarely fails."

"Thanks for the vote of confidence." I pretended to be injured.

"I'm serious, Annie." He stared at me with a tenderness that made my breath catch. "If you think you're close to an idea or theory, you are. Don't second-guess yourself."

"You're right." I smiled and reached for another tablecloth. "This phase of an investigation is always frustrating because it's like we're close but not close enough."

"Give it time. Don't force it."

That was exactly Dr. Caldwell's advice. "I will. Let's talk appetizers and the closing party. That will take my head out of murder. What do you need from me?"

"Your witty banter never hurts." He ducked, anticipating me taking a swing at him.

"If it's witty banter you want, witty banter you shall get." I pressed my hands under my chin to pose.

"I could actually use a hand taking a few trips to the pub if you're not too busy. I have a few more of these to cart over."

"A short walk and some fresh air sounds like a dream. I'm your girl."

"Yeah, you are." He ran his eyes over my body, making me flush.

"What's in box one?" I changed the subject and peered into the tub, willing my cheeks not to turn into bright cherries.

"I went with appetizers that travel well. These are antipasto kabobs." He lifted a tray of skewered kabobs out of the tub. "Black olives, green olives, cheese tortellini, salami, and pepperoni. They don't need to be heated, and they're easy to eat while wandering through the store."

"You forgot to mention festive."

"You said Christmas and I followed your brief to the letter."

We unpacked the skewers. Getting to help Liam set up was an unexpected bonus. The more time we spent together the more comfortable and easygoing our relationship was becoming. That had to be a good sign.

I just wished I could come up with what was bugging me about Sugar and her bakery.

# TWENTY-THREE

Setup with Liam was a breeze. It was a nice brain break to flirt as we placed cherry tarts, bite-sized pizzas, and spiced popcorn onto the draped tables, lit the flameless electric candles and twinkle lights in the Conservatory, and added a touch of color in the form of evergreen swags.

"Not bad, Murray. Not bad for a pub owner and a book slinger."

"A book slinger? That's a new one. You make me sound like something out of the Wild West."

"We do happen to reside in former gold country. We just traded our guns for books and brews." He pretended to pull a finger gun out of a holster.

"Oh no, are you saying I'm going to have to tell Fletcher that we might need to consider a rebranding for the Secret Bookcase? Maybe we should go with something more in line with the Wild, Wild West." I gave him a cheeky smile.

"It might draw people in." He slowly withdrew his gun from his imaginary holster again. "Get it, *draw* them in?"

"I thought you hated puns."

"I do, but only when other people use them." He cracked a

smile so wide it made my cheeks ache, and I reached for a handful of popcorn. "If I use a pun, I'm enlightening you with my sharp wit and impressive imagination."

"You really are a pompous ass sometimes, aren't you?" I shook my head slowly, narrowing my eyes into a frown, trying to convey that I was less than impressed.

"Did I ever claim not to be?" He shot his eyebrows up and stared me down with a challenging gaze that sent little flutters soaring through my stomach.

"Whatever, I happen to know you have a sweet and fluffy side. I've seen the way you snuggle with Professor Plum. You can't fool me, Donovan."

"As long as I keep you on your toes." He leaned close like he was going to kiss me on the cheek but, at the last minute, swerved for the popcorn bowl and scooped up a handful of the spicy treat.

Becca raced up to us, breathless and flushed. "Okay, here you go, Annie." She thrust sheets of paper at me held together with a large clip. "I rewrote everything. Take a look and make sure you're good with it. Fletcher is tallying the last of the votes. Like I mentioned, I'll read the ads and do the introduction. Sugar is going to help announce the winners with you."

I skimmed her talking points. There were two lengthy paragraphs about Lily and the lasting effect she would have on our community. It was a bit of a stretch, but at least the sentiment was in the right tone.

"No problem." I glanced at the typewriter clock on the far wall. "We're still planning to announce the winners at four?"

"Yes. That only gives us fifteen minutes. We should probably practice. Do you want to do a full run-through?"

She was running on pure adrenaline. I wanted to pour her a cup of tea and tell her to sit and breathe for a few minutes. It was the opposite energy from yesterday when I'd worried that she might pass out from sheer exhaustion.

"A full run-through? I thought I was reading this." I thumbed through the papers.

"Oh no. You can't read it. You need to memorize it. Word for word."

Liam scoffed and muttered something under his breath I couldn't make out.

"Wait, what? You want me to memorize this word for word?" I tapped on the stack of paper. "No chance."

"Yes, obviously. Lily was a professional. She never used a teleprompter or notes."

"That's fine." I looked at Liam for help. He shrugged and chomped on more popcorn like he was taking a bit too much amusement from the situation. "She was an influencer. It was her job. I'm a bookseller."

"Slinger," Liam interrupted.

I tried to hide my grin. "Right. Slinger. Whatever. I can't memorize this in fifteen minutes. I'm happy to say a few words and help Sugar announce the winners, but there's no chance I'm going to get this script perfect in that amount of time."

She hit her forehead with her palm. "The entire goal is for the livestream to feel real and authentic and unscripted. It's supposed to feel heartfelt. This is a tribute to Lily, after all."

"I understand, but it's not going to be authentic if I stumble over my words and try to cram memorizing this statement. If you want me to speak from the heart, I can do that in my own words."

She sighed and considered my offer like she was mulling over an important life decision. "Okay, I guess that's our best option if you really don't think you can get this nailed down in the next few minutes. It's not that much to memorize."

"I'm sure. I'll speak on my own and try to weave in some of the points you've listed. If you want authenticity, that's how we'll get it."

"Fine. Can we at least block this out?" She motioned to the

stage. "Where is Sugar by the way? I've been looking every-where for her."

"I saw her a few minutes ago. I'm sure she'll show up. Maybe she's counting the final votes with Fletcher." I looked toward the Foyer. Hal was ringing up sales. Fletcher wasn't anywhere to be seen. He probably took the score sheets to our office to tally them in private.

"Well, she better show." Becca tapped her wrist. "I've already posted that we're going live at four. It's non-negotiable now."

It was painful to watch how much pressure she put on herself. Was this what it had been like the entire time? Had the intensity come from Lily, or was it self-imposed?

"I'm good here, Murray." Liam swept his palm over the spread. "I'll keep the readers fed and pop open a few bottles of bubbly."

Hal had requested we serve sips of champagne to commemorate our first gingerbread competition. I thought it was a great idea at the time, but now I wasn't sure if it was in poor taste.

"Do you think we should skip that?" I asked Liam.

Becca cut me off. "No, champagne is a go. Nothing gets canceled at this point. We need to maintain a semblance of normalcy if we're going to control this narrative."

"But, with Lily's death, doesn't it feel odd to be cele-brating?"

"We're celebrating her life," she snapped, her tone going pitchy. "Don't stray from the script."

For someone who wanted this tribute to feel unscripted, she was strangely obsessed with following her plan to the letter.

"Bubbly it is," Liam said.

Becca practically dragged me to the stage. "I want you front and center with Lily's final creation behind you. I think it will be a poignant reminder of her talent. The camera will be right here." She pointed next to the microphone stand where she had positioned a tripod. "Speak directly into the camera and imagine you're talking to a friend."

"Got it." I gave her a thumbs-up.

"Are you sure?" She looked at me with such a deep level of skepticism that it made me wonder if I was underestimating my talk. "Do you want to do a practice run?"

"I'm good," I assured her. "I speak in public all the time at the bookstore. I'm not worried about it."

"Yes, but this is different. Hundreds of thousands of people will be joining the livestream."

Was she trying to make me nervous?

"I thought you said to pretend like I'm talking to one person."

"I did." She clenched her teeth, sounding like she was losing patience with me. "I need you to understand the magnitude of what's happening. There might be a few hundred people here in the store, but that is going to pale in comparison with how many people will be watching online."

People had begun to gather. I needed to make an announcement.

"I'm fine. I promise," I said to Becca. "Let me round up people in the store and remind them we're about to name the winners."

"Find Sugar while you're at it," she demanded.

I gave her a little leeway because I understood she was stressed, but there was no need for her to be short with me.

She must have realized her tone because she held out her hand to stop me. "Sorry. That didn't come across the way I intended. I appreciate your help and everything you've done this weekend. I'm just trying to hold an entire empire together with dental floss at the moment, so I apologize for my behavior. I'm not trying to be rude. We just have a lot riding on this going well. If we play our cards right, we can really turn Lily's brand into a lasting legacy. I've received so many calls and DMs from new and existing companies interested in partnering to preserve her memory."

"I understand. We're all still in shock."

"Yeah, exactly." She massaged the base of her neck. "It's the shock."

I couldn't tell if she was being truthful. "What kind of partnerships? Wasn't Lily the brand?"

"Yes, and there's an opportunity to capitalize on that. I've already spoken with her family about the possibilities. We could do some serious good with the funds we generate from any legacy partnerships. They're interested in funding baking scholarships and maybe even opening a school under her name." She checked her phone. "The thing is, I know it sounds callous, and I don't mean it this way at all, but there's a short window to garner these opportunities. If we don't act now, Lily will be forgotten. I don't want to see that happen. It's my job to see that she lives on."

I could relate to what she was saying. I felt the same about Scarlet, so much so that I wanted to brainstorm with Fletcher about ways we might honor her with our new venture.

"Kari and I chatted at length earlier about Queen Mary doing an entire Lily line. It's a shame that Lily won't be around to see it, but it's fitting to find a way to finally bring this partnership to fruition."

Why was she dropping this on me now?

Kari and Becca were partnering, too?

Everyone seemed to be benefiting financially from Lily's death.

I had so many questions, but time was running out. I left to make an announcement, my mind spinning with new considerations. Kari had finally gotten what she wanted—a partnership with Lily. The question was, had she killed to make that happen?

# TWENTY-FOUR

I found Fletcher and Sugar coming down the private stairwell after making the announcement. Readers crowded into the Conservatory. I spotted lots of familiar faces from Redwood Grove and Dayton and his entire high school culinary class were squeezed into the front row.

"Do we have winners?" I asked.

Fletcher patted the ballot box. "Counted, tabulated, double- and triple-checked."

"I'm shocked. Absolutely shocked." I let my mouth hang open as I teased him.

"I told him twice was probably fine," Sugar said with a small smile.

"Hey, no gingerbread scandals shall occur on my watch," Fletcher responded, clutching the box tighter to his body. "Our fellow Redwood Grove residents have baked their holiday hearts out, and I refuse to be the reason for any sugary, spicy drama."

"I appreciate your brevity." I nodded solemnly. "We have a room of eager participants waiting for the results."

"And a social media manager on the warpath, right?" Sugar asked, peering around me to get a glimpse of Becca. "I had to take a break from her. She's so intense. I get it, but it's a lot."

"Yeah. I was just chatting with her," I agreed. "I heard about the Queen Mary Flour deal."

"You did?" Sugar stopped in mid-stride and stared at me. "What? How?"

"Becca mentioned it. Sorry, is it a secret?"

Why was she acting so surprised?

"I haven't signed the contract yet. Kari said not to mention anything until the contract is fully signed. I guess I'm surprised Becca would tell you. It's not that I don't trust you, Annie, but I would really appreciate it if you could keep this under wraps. It's a huge deal for me."

"I won't say a word, but I'm confused. Why would you need to sign the contract?"

She tipped her head to the side and narrowed her eyes. "Because it's *my* contract."

"Oh, okay, we're talking about two different things. Becca told me that Queen Mary is doing a legacy partnership and creating an entire line of products with Lily's name and brand."

"What?" She shook her head. "No, Kari and I put together a deal. I'm going to be the new face of the flour company. It's a giant step forward for my business."

Fletcher tapped the top of the box. "I think we should continue this conversation later. The crowd is growing restless."

He was right. I didn't want to be late for Becca's livestream either, but now I had to wonder about Sugar's motives. She had inked out a deal with Kari. I had little doubt that the partnership would be a financial boon for her, which suddenly thrust her back to the top of my suspect list.

The high school jazz band serenaded everyone with upbeat renditions of "Winter Wonderland" and "It's Beginning to Look a Lot Like Christmas."

Becca took the stage. She grasped the microphone like it was a lifeline. Sweat was beading on her forehead. Her voice cracked as she timidly cleared her throat and spoke into the mic. "Thank you all for coming. We're here at the Secret Bookcase to crown a gingerbread winner. Many of you are joining us from around the globe and I want to take minute to thank our gracious sponsors."

She went through a laundry list of companies, taking a minute to acknowledge each of them with little quips about their products. "As I'm sure some of you are aware there have been rumors circulating about our dear friend and pastry queen Lily Hawthorne. It is with the deepest sadness that I must confirm the rumors. Lily is dead."

The audience went silent. Although it wasn't news to anyone in the room, Becca speaking it out loud served as a solemn reminder that a life had been lost.

Comments flooded her phone screen as the shockwaves reverberated out across the internet.

"I hate to have to be the bearer of this awful news," she continued with a quaky voice and quivering knees. "Lily was a friend, a business partner, a mentor, and a sister to me. I'm shattered, but I refuse to let her death be in vain. I intend to do everything in my power to keep her name alive and have her legacy live on in this amazing community."

I couldn't process the speed at which emojis and messages flew over the screen. It was a constant barrage.

"Bake It Till You Make 47, yes, thank you for that shoutout. Lily was one of a kind and we do owe it to her to preserve her aesthetic. That's why I'm pleased to announce a new partnership with Queen Mary Flour. We'll be launching a tribute line of products in Lily's name early next year. You'll be able to bake like her. I'll be sharing recipes, like her gingerbread cake and her structural building plans for her spectacular creations. I have many more ideas and I'd love to hear from you. She adored you. Everything she did was for you, so let's brainstorm together how we can honor her as we move forward without her." She closed her eyes. "Let's take a moment to send love and light and pastries to our dearest Lily."

The crowd went still.

A heaviness hung in the air.

After a long silence, Becca motioned me forward. "Now I'd like to introduce you to Annie Murray from the Secret Bookcase. She has a few words to say about Lily."

I took the mic and shared my heartfelt perspective on my short time with Lily. My speech might not have been rehearsed and I may have missed a few of the key points Becca wanted me to highlight, but I spoke from a place of authenticity. Lily's presence in Redwood Grove had given our little village a much-needed holiday boost. The gingerbread competition brought the community together and gave us a collective project, so that was my focus.

When I was done, Becca frowned in disappointment, like I'd let her down.

"Our superstar Sugar has a few words to share with you before the big reveal, which is what I know you're all waiting for," Becca said, taking the mic from me and passing it over to Sugar.

I stepped to the side, watching Becca and Sugar intently as Sugar addressed the crowd. "As Annie mentioned big things are brewing for Redwood Grove. We're obviously heartbroken about what happened to Lily." She made eye contact with the phone, staring at it like it was a person standing in front of her. "That heartbreak is leading us to action. We're not going to sit by idly. We're finding opportunities now to preserve and expand Lily's empire and we want you to be part of it."

Was she speaking for herself, or had Becca scripted this?

Fletcher handed Sugar the ballot box when she finished her impassioned speech. "And now what we're all here for—the votes have been counted. We had seventy-five gingerbread entries this inaugural year, which is much more than we ever anticipated. We ran some numbers for fun. We had to make our estimates based on the variety of sizes of each of the gingerbread structures, but we feel confident that over two hundred and sixty-five pounds of sugar, one hundred and thirty-five pounds of flour, and sixty-six pounds of butter were used in this week-end's bakes."

Everyone oohed.

"That's a hearty amount of sugar, flour, and butter." She applauded, making sure to clap so that the phone camera could see. "We need a drumroll."

I cued the band.

The snare drum rattled as Fletcher handed Sugar the results.

She read them slowly and with intention to heighten the drama. The high school students huddled around Dayton. He crossed his fingers as Sugar read the name of the first winner—it was a six-year-old girl who had designed a sugarplum fairy princess gingerbread castle adorned with pink and purple gumdrops.

"This one has a special place in my heart. Since I'm Sugar, how could I not love a sugarplum fairy castle, but it wasn't just me—you voted this your favorite of all of the youth entries."

Cheers broke out as the girl and her family took the stage to receive her ribbon and pose in front of her castle.

None of the winning entries were surprising. The crowd favorites mirrored my own and proved that Redwood Grove had great taste.

Once all of the winners had been announced, Sugar invited Hal to join her on the stage. "A special round of applause for a Redwood Grove legend—Hal Christie."

People cheered louder.

Fletcher and I were right there with them.

"Hal's name is synonymous with everything good about Redwood Grove," Sugar continued. "He's practically an institution in this town, and without his vision for this gorgeous estate and bookstore, we wouldn't be here today. Thank you for your generosity and for always putting Redwood Grove first."

My throat tightened at her words. I swallowed the lump as hot tears threatened to spill. Sugar was right. Hal had done so much for our community and me personally. I don't know how I would have survived Scarlet's death without him and the Secret Bookcase. It was my safe haven, and I had come to see and appreciate how Hal had wisely given me space to heal while gently nudging me out of my shell in the early years by assigning me special projects like unboxing videos for social media and creating themed kids' story time activities. His generosity was unmatched. He had established so many community partnerships and outreach opportunities over the years, from donations to local schools and shelters, fundraisers, free library boxes, book recycling programs, hosting ESL tutors and support groups at the store, and so much more.

Thunderous applause broke out.

Hal's cheeks warmed as he shuffled up to the microphone.

He deserved every second of it.

I brushed a tear from my eye and sniffed as he took the stage with a look of utter awe and amazement.

"I'm not one for speeches, but I would like to say as a long-time Redwood Grove resident and business owner, I am confident that we have the best small town on the West Coast, perhaps in the entire United States. Could I be biased, probably? Do I care? Absolutely not." He removed a bottle of champagne from behind his back. "A toast to you. A toast to the warm and welcoming spirit that makes living here feel like a fairy tale."

People whooped and hollered.

I was glad to see Hal receiving much-deserved praise. He

popped the champagne, filled a glass, and lifted it to the crowd. "To our wonderful Redwood Grove, happy, happy holidays."

"Happy holidays," everyone replied.

His sentiment was spot-on. Despite the ugly turn of events this weekend, it was lovely to see our community come together.

## TWENTY-FIVE

The winners gathered on stage for group photos and to be recognized by the crowd. I took pictures for our social media and to post in the store. The atmosphere lightened as the champagne flowed and people nibbled on Liam's appetizers. It was a relief to see so many smiling faces and happy customers. I chatted with some of our regulars about making this an annual event while sipping the effervescent bubbly that tasted like tart apples and fresh pears.

The champagne went to my head.

I found myself breathlessly laughing at a customer's punny dad joke.

"Did you hear the one about the gingerbread man?" the customer asked, biting off the head of a frosted spiced cookie.

I slowly sipped the remainder of my champagne. "No, but I'm dying to hear it."

The customer was one of my favorites. He came in once a week to buy a new stack of cozy mysteries for his retired wife. "I can't keep her in books, Annie," he would say with a wink, passing me a handwritten note with titles of new releases. "I'll take all of these and any of your recommendations, but she'll breeze through them by the end of the week."

"Why did the gingerbread man go to the doctor?" he asked, giving me a sheepish grin.

"I don't know, why?" I waited for the punchline.

"Because he was feeling crummy." His aging eyes twinkled with merriment as he watched me crack up.

"Oh, that's so bad, it's good. I'm going to have to use that on our sandwich board. I'll give you credit."

"I don't need any credit, but I do need more holiday cozies. I'll be in later this week." He took another bite of the gingerbread cookie and sauntered off.

I finished off the last sips of my champagne, feeling slightly off-balance. Or maybe it was the dizzying array of everything that happened since the start of the gingerbread competition.

I took my time picking up discarded plates and cups once everyone began to filter out. After locking up, we lingered in the Conservatory to help Liam clean up and start the process of restoring the bookshop. We closed the evening with another banner day of sales.

"Next week is going to feel like a breeze," Hal said with a soft smile. "No major events; what are you going to do with yourself, Annie?"

"Prepare for my major meeting tomorrow night." I realized my muscles seized up whenever I thought about meeting Mark face-to-face. I'd been waiting for this moment for so long it was nearly impossible to believe it was finally happening. But as it got closer, my nerves started to skyrocket. I didn't want to blow this opportunity, and I was also starting to second-guess whether meeting him out of town was a good idea. With Lily's murder fresh, I was leaning toward changing the plan and having him meet me in Redwood Grove. It was probably the smarter idea.

"That's right." Hal tapped his chin thoughtfully. "I nearly

forgot with all of the activity and frenzy. Do you need anything from us?"

"No, I'm fine." I thought back to my conversation with Dr. Caldwell.

"She needs to share her location with all of us and have a clear exit plan," Liam said, squinting with concern.

"Yeah, about that. I changed my mind. I'm going to meet him at the Stag Head," I said. "I decided it on my own," I clarified. "I didn't cave to pressure, but this will be good. You'll be there, and I don't think he's the killer. I think he's scared, too. That's why he's changed our meeting time twice and has been so adamant about not sharing any information via email or text. I'm not putting myself in danger."

"You're meeting with a source connected to the brutal murder of two young women," Hal responded, mirroring Liam. "Regardless of who is or isn't nearby, you are undoubtedly putting yourself at some risk."

"Okay, I know. I get it, and I appreciate your concern. But my point is I'm going to be extremely careful. I'm not naïve. I've trained for situations like this. I've done hours and hours of research into Silicon Summit Partners and Mark's work history. All of you know what's happening, as does Dr. Caldwell and Pri."

"I don't understand why you won't let us have dinner at a table nearby," Fletcher said, wiping down a table with a pine-scented mix of vinegar and water.

"Because I don't want to spook him. He's been clear that he'll only speak with me. That's another reason I think he's worried."

"He doesn't know us," Fletcher interrupted. "We'll play it casual."

"Fletcher, I love you, but no part of you can play it casual."

He grumbled and tossed his arms up. "This is the thanks I get for letting you be my Watson."

I didn't have the time or energy to debate who Watson and Sherlock were in our friendship. "Look, I'm not brushing any of this off. I'm so grateful that you all are worried about me. I really do appreciate it." I made eye contact with each of them. "I'm an adult woman. I've done my homework, but I'm not going to take any chances, I promise."

"Nothing is stopping us from having a casual dinner at the pub, though, correct?" Hal looked at Liam. "There aren't any special events tomorrow night, are there?"

"Actually, it's trivia night." Liam made a clicking sound with his tongue. "We're doing a special historical holiday trivia. Chef has put together a three-course dinner with a shaved Brussels sprouts salad, turkey and smashed rosemary potatoes, and a slice of chocolate peppermint cake. He's got other holiday stuff on the menu, too. If you want me to reserve a table for you, there are a few seats left."

"You know, Caroline has mentioned how fun it would be to try our hand at trivia." Hal looked at me pensively as if trying to determine how upset I might be with his idea. "I think that sounds quite lovely. Don't you agree, Fletcher? We could use your historical knowledge, and perhaps we could invite Pri to round out our team."

"Count me in." Fletcher glanced at me in triumph. "You can't stop us from a friendly game of trivia, Annie."

I rolled my eyes. "Fine. Fine. But you have to promise to be discreet. This is a huge break for me, and I don't want to do anything to jeopardize Mark's trust. If he has information about Natalie's disappearance, it could finally lead to finding Scarlet's killer."

"I will swear a blood oath. Let me find a knife." Fletcher dropped the rag and scrounged through the bucket of cleaning supplies.

"Blood isn't necessary." Hal wiggled his bushy eyebrows. "Annie, we will stay true to our word and stay out of your way. I admit I'm old-fashioned, but I'll feel better if we're at least in the same space as you."

I appreciated how much they cared. It warmed my heart to know they were not only worried about me but willing to drop whatever plans they may have had to tag along as my undercover bodyguard team.

"We should have a signal," Fletcher suggested. "A tell. Something to alert us that you need intervention."

"I'm not sure that's necessary." I started to protest, but Liam cut me off.

"He's right." Liam ran his finger along his chin, considering the possibilities. Then he tapped the side of his cheek twice.

"You want me to tap my chin like that? It seems kind of obvious." I squinted. "I feel like if we were playing poker, that would be an automatic tell."

"No, I'm thinking." He furrowed his brow. "It could be a safe word. I'm planning to cover your table. You could request something as a cue."

"Yeah, a glass of water." Fletcher sprayed the table again.

"But I'll probably want water," I said, stating the obvious.

"True." He scrubbed a sticky spot of melted peppermint. "We need to think like Sherlock. What would our perceptive and eccentric Mr. Holmes suggest?"

"What if you ask for something you know you wouldn't be in the mood for?" Liam packed empty platters and served utensils. "I've never seen you drink a Coke. You don't like it, right? If you get bad vibes from the guy or have even the tiniest flash of concern, order a Coke, and then I'll know it's time for us to swoop in."

He knew I didn't like Coke? We'd never discussed it. Liam often surprised me by how much attention he paid to small details.

"It's true. I can't stand Coke—it's too sweet and all those

chemicals." I stuck out my tongue. "Consider it done. If things go south, I'll order a Coke."

"What about us, though?" Fletcher asked. "You'll be busy running the bar. We should be the backup, which means we still need a signal. You can't exactly ask a table nearby to grab you a Coke. That will break our cover."

"Your cover?" I raised my eyebrows.

"This is a sting operation, isn't it? Our first assignment for the Novel Detectives."

"I wouldn't go that far," I cautioned.

"Annie, I always go too far. You should know that about me by now." Fletcher winked and intentionally dropped the rag on the table. "What if you do this? Drop your napkin."

"Right, but what if I accidentally drop my napkin? You'll all come running and scare away Mark for good."

"Yes, it has to be deliberate and obvious to us," Hal said.

Fletcher flicked his forehead. "True. I'm giving my fellow Sherlockians a bad name. What else would Sherlock do?"

"Chew on his pipe," Liam laughed. "I'd like to see you with a pipe, Annie."

"You all are too much." I shook my head and laughed, enjoying the lightness and ridiculousness of the moment. "This is getting out of control. If I feel like I need help, I can simply excuse myself to go to the bathroom and stop at your table."

"Why do you have to be so practical? You're taking the fun out of this." Fletcher pretended to pout. "My fingers are seconds away from ordering a deerstalker cap and trench coat."

"Sorry to ruin your fun," I said with a snort. "I'd love to see you blend in at the pub in that."

Hal swooped in, giving my shoulders a squeeze. "Annie, we're making light of this and forcing our way in because we care about you. We understand how important this is, and we will not do anything to jeopardize your meeting other than being on standby to jump in if necessary." He tipped his head to the side. "Well, these old knees aren't jumping, but metaphorically speaking."

"You're the best." I leaned into him. "I'm so lucky to have all of you."

"I'll continue pondering potential signals," Fletcher said.

"You do that." I grinned.

Hal left to do a final walkthrough. Fletcher returned the cleaning supplies to the cabinet in the Foyer.

"Dinner?" Liam asked, stacking the boxes onto a cart. "The holiday spread at the Stag is not to be missed, or I could make you a pot of soup and talk through the meeting."

"I'd love to, but I'll take a raincheck. I want to review my notes one last time before tomorrow." A tingling spread through my limbs like an electrical current. His support warmed my entire body—inside and out. I'd been so insular after Scarlet's death. I didn't realize quite how much I had closed myself off. I understood it was a protective measure, but knowing Liam was looking out for me felt wonderful. He was on my side. I could count on him. I could trust him. I could let myself be vulnerable.

I'd never had a relationship like this.

"Sure." He cinched everything together with a bungee cord. "I know how wrapped up you get. Don't forget to eat, or text me for a late-night pasta delivery."

"Thanks." I kissed him on the cheek and touched his arm lightly. "Before I go, I just want to say how much I appreciate your support. I know I said it earlier to everyone, but this is new for me, and I guess I'm fumbling my way through trying to say thanks. Thanks for being here for me. Thanks for caring and listening and for homemade scones and late-night gingerbread decorating. I really care about you, and want you to know I'm here for you, too."

A brief flash of sadness crossed his face.

I didn't push it. Like me, Liam had his own demons. I

trusted when he was ready he would share them with me and let me help lighten his burden.

He twitched ever so slightly and leaned closer, reaching for my hand. "I feel the same, Murray." His voice was thick with emotion.

We kissed. It was long and slow as if our lips could speak the words we weren't quite ready to say.

"See you tomorrow," I said, hearing the quiver in my voice as we broke apart. Part of me didn't want to go. The easiest path would be to curl up with him and forget about everything, but I owed it to Scarlet and myself to see this through and the only way I could do that was with a clear head.

I walked home, thinking about how the day had turned out and the taste of Liam's soft, sultry lips. There were still so many unanswered questions about Lily's murder, but I had to put them on hold for the next twenty-four hours. At this time tomorrow, I'd be meeting with Mark, and I intended to show up overprepared and ready to have some—if not all—of my questions answered.

# TWENTY-SIX

Professor Plum kept me company as I scanned pages and pages of notes about Natalie Thompson and Silicon Summit Partners. I made myself a bowl of chicken noodle soup and poured a small glass of buttery chardonnay. Professor Plum took his usual spot on the cashmere blanket tucked over my feet.

I had practically memorized Natalie's and Scarlet's case files word for word. The odds of suddenly uncovering something new were small, but I had to give it one last shot. I sipped the soup and studied the police officer's report from searching Natalie's apartment. The one thing that struck me when I first read the report after Dr. Caldwell shared the files with me, and now again, was that not a single fingerprint had been recovered on her desk. Not even Natalie's. That had to mean that her workspace had been wiped clean.

Her fingerprints were found in other places throughout the apartment—on cupboard doors in the kitchen, the bathroom door handle, her closet, but none of her desk drawers, her laptop, or her notebooks or pens had a single print.

That was impossible.

Dr. Caldwell and I discussed it at length, and she agreed.

But why had the police overlooked such an important detail?

Silicon Summit Partners was a powerful corporation. Could they have paid off the police? Were they involved?

The other thing that continued to haunt me was Scarlet's secret. She'd been almost giddy before going to meet with her source, "Bob," and had promised that she had "exciting" news to share with me when she returned.

Sure, maybe it was semantics, but I was stuck on her word choice. Why would she use "exciting" to describe her news? Yes, we were both obsessed with solving Natalie's case, and she seemed to think that she was on the brink of a breakthrough, but "exciting" didn't fit. It was like she had two secrets—one involving her source and the other about something else. But what?

Or was I reaching?

I sighed as I finished my soup and closed my laptop.

I was no closer to answers to either question by the time I finally headed upstairs to bed. Getting restful sleep was my best move. I wanted to be in top form for the meeting. Fortunately I was exhausted from the weekend and fell into a deep sleep the minute my head hit the pillow.

The next day passed painfully slow. As Hal had predicted, the store wasn't busy since it was a workday and there were no scheduled events. We used it to get caught up on inventory and online orders.

I checked the clock every twenty minutes, willing it to move faster. That wasn't typical for me. I loved the rhythm of the store—the rush of Saturday morning after our kids' story hour and the downtime on a Monday morning, but time seemed to move like molasses.

I busied myself with as many projects as I could—writing a newsletter to send to our subscribers with last-minute holiday gifts, reaching out to publicists about author events in the new year, and rearranging the front of store display with a shipment of Agatha Christie box sets that had been on backorder for months.

"Annie, you seem distracted. Are you sure you want to be here?" Hal asked shortly before lunch, coming into the Foyer with a small box of book ornaments. "I found these in storage. I thought maybe you or Fletcher could find a spot for them."

"These are adorable," I replied, taking the box from him and looking through it. Dozens of one-inch ornaments painted with real book covers glimmered in a shiny bunch.

"I'm afraid I'm such a pack rat I forgot I had them. I moved some things around downstairs and came across them. They were hand-painted by an artist in San Francisco."

"I'll find a place to showcase them for sure." I set the box on the counter and checked the clock. I could have sworn it was nearly five, but there were still six hours to go before I needed to be at the pub. "You're right, by the way. I am not fully present. Sorry. But it will be even worse if I just sit at home and wait for the clock to strike five."

"Fair enough." Hal looked like he wanted to say more but didn't. "Why don't you take a long lunch break? Maybe a walk through Oceanside Park to clear your head?"

"Are you trying to get rid of me?"

"Never. I'm concerned about your headspace, that's all. What I've learned over the years is that there's nothing like a slow stroll through the redwoods to clear out the cobwebs and center yourself."

"I could use some cobweb clearing and some centering," I said, pretending to pull an imaginary string from my ear.

"Excellent. Then go." He swished his hands like he was shooing away a fly. "Enjoy. The store will be waiting when you're ready to return."

"How did I get so lucky to have you as a boss and friend?"

"The feeling is entirely mutual, my dear." He smiled kindly and nudged me toward the door.

I took the long way through the English garden. The pathway was illuminated with buttery sunshine. It was too late in the season for pollinators, but birds flitted between the shrubbery and ground, pecking at seeds and gathering tiny sticks.

I exhaled slowly as the trail spilled out into the park. It was nearly deserted. December wasn't a popular time for tourists to visit. Kids were still in school, so aside from the casual lunchtime runner and a group of preschoolers having lunch in the pavilion, I had the wide-open space to myself.

I turned my attention to Lily's murder in hopes of releasing some of the nervous anticipatory energy pulsing through my body.

I wondered if Dr. Caldwell had made any further progress. It was odd that she never made an appearance at the closing event yesterday, but then again it was likely a sign that she was wrapped up in the investigation.

The most critical piece of information I was missing was the delivery method of whatever had poisoned Lily. There were multiple possibilities—something she ate, like Dayton's cake, or something she drank, like the tea Kari had given her. I hadn't seen any visible puncture wounds when I'd administered CPR but maybe the killer stuck her with something. Shane's pen was still a viable possibility. Or I was missing another delivery method.

I sighed. It felt like the answer was right in front of me, but I couldn't reach out and grasp it.

Sugar remained high on my suspect list. I didn't want to believe she could be the killer, but all signs seemed to be pointing in her direction. Which gave me a thought.

I could swing by Sweet Room now. It wasn't far. Maybe another two or three miles out of town, but Hal wouldn't mind if I took a longer break. In fact, if I showed up too soon, he might kick me out again.

I made the decision on a split second and veered out of the park. The main village square housed most of Redwood Grove's retail businesses and restaurants. Sweet Room was down the highway on the way to Penny's farmhouse. I turned off Cedar Avenue once I reached the end of the main pathway in the park and turned onto the highway.

There wasn't a sidewalk, but I should be fine if I stayed close to the edge of the two-lane road. Traffic wasn't heavy at this time of day. A few cars zoomed past as I trudged next to clumps of weeds, stepping over debris from recent rainstorms and making sure to watch my footing.

Eucalyptus and bay trees lined the road, making everything smell herbaceous and fresh.

Hal was right; being outside was exactly what I needed.

My body felt lighter, my head felt clearer, and I wasn't stuck on a spinning loop thinking about the exact phrasing I wanted to use in my conversation with Mark to put him at ease enough to allow him to open up.

I didn't even notice the car barreling toward me until my senses went on high alert.

It was a white Tesla coming straight at me.

Was the driver distracted?

Were they texting?

Why were they driving on the side of the road?

Didn't Teslas have lane-sensitivity warnings?

It was getting close.

Too close.

It was as if the driver had locked in on me and was intentionally trying to mow me down.

No.

That couldn't be the case.

I must be imagining things.

*Whatever you're imagining, Annie, you need to focus—now!*
My rational brain kicked into high gear.
I needed to get out of the way.
Fast.
But where?
The road dropped off to my left.
There was a deep ditch a good four or five feet down.
The fall would probably hurt. If not break something.
But there was no other choice.
The Tesla sped up, as if the driver were holding the pedal down.
*Jump, Annie.*
*Jump, now.*

# TWENTY-SEVEN

I jumped.

My body felt like it was sailing through the air.

I closed my eyes and tried not to clench too tight.

Oh, no, this is bad!

I don't want to die.

*Not like this.*

It felt like forever until I hit the ground.

I tried not to panic.

Blood rushed to my head so loudly I could hear my heartbeat thudding against my ears, whooshing around like a turbulent river.

*It's going to be okay, just keep breathing.*

I heard the Tesla fly past.

They didn't bother to stop.

That meant one of two things. They were either a distracted driver who had no clue they had nearly hit me. Or they were intentionally trying to run me down.

I didn't like either option.

Nor did I like the way my shoulder made contact with the ground.

The impact sent me rolling down the hillside.

I heard the screech of tires and a car skidding to a stop.

Had the driver of the Tesla realized what happened and turned around to come help me? Or had they failed at their mission and they were returning to finish the job?

Panic welled in my throat.

My entire body trembled and quivered like the ground was shaking.

It wasn't.

*Who would want to hurt me?*

I thought I might throw up.

*Breathe, Annie.*

*Keep it together.*

I exhaled slowly and closed my eyes.

Pain seared down my shoulder and all the way through my spine. I was afraid to move. Everything hurt.

I yanked a huge splinter from my left palm. Blood oozed from the wound.

*You have to get out of here, Annie.*

*You have to move.*

I couldn't risk lying in the ditch. I was a sitting duck.

I sat up partway, brushing off pine needles and debris and wiping my bloody hands on my jeans. My fingers quivered and my knees felt like they were about to buckle.

I recognized the early signs of shock.

*Use your training.*

I felt like I was giving myself a Star Wars pep talk, but it was true. Shock was normal in any crisis.

I needed to move and get help.

Another car tore down the highway at a breakneck speed as if they were competing in the Grand Prix.

Mud was matted to my hands and my hair. I tugged a stick from my curls and pushed myself to standing.

My legs felt wobbly.

My head throbbed.

Nothing seemed to be broken.

I was bruised and banged up, but I could probably hobble back.

Or was that a smart plan?

I was halfway between the village square and Sugar's bakery. Should I continue with my mission?

Or what if it had been Sugar who ran me off the road?

*That had to be intentional, right?*

*Or am I blowing things out of proportion?*

I checked my watch.

There was still plenty of time before I was due to meet Mark.

Maybe I should keep going.

I could call Pri or Liam once I got to the bakery safely and have them come pick me up. I wanted to see this through.

I scrambled up the ditch until I made it back to the median. There was no sign of the white Tesla, except for skid marks on the highway. That gave me a thought. I stopped to take pictures of the skid marks and texted them to Dr. Caldwell, along with a quick explanation of what had happened.

Looping her in brought me extra peace of mind.

I limped along the side of the road until I arrived at the bakery.

Sweet Room was a sweet sight for the eyes. Sugar had updated an old Victorian in multiple shades of pale pink with chocolate brown accents on the shutters and trim. She had decked her baking halls with more pink garlands, lights, and glowing lanterns. Pink cupcakes painted on the driveway pointed the way to the retail shop.

I followed them, feeling a touch like Hansel and Gretel. I was either being led to a delectable pastry tasting room or to the witch's den.

I inched along slowly, acutely aware of the pain in my knee.

I must have tweaked it in the fall. Every step felt like glass shattering against my joints.

I used the handrailing to support myself and took the stairs slowly.

The front porch was decorated with multiple cotton candy-colored Christmas trees and pink cookies hanging from the eaves.

If there wasn't a possibility that Sugar was the killer, I might have found the décor whimsical and charming. At the moment, I couldn't tell if it leaned more toward the deranged side.

I knocked on the door before trying the handle.

The sign, aptly in pink lettering, read OPEN, so when Sugar didn't answer, I went inside on my own.

"Hello, Sugar?" I called.

The lights were on in the small tasting area, but there was no sign of Sugar. Glass cases displayed Christmas petit fours, cranberry cream pies, and hazelnut chocolate cakes decorated in dark chocolate buttercream with edible gold glitter.

Four small tables and chairs, a self-serve coffee and tea station, and additional bar seating along the windows allowed customers to enjoy their treats on the premises. A stack of pink boxes with the Sweet Room logo sat beside the cash register for takeaway orders.

"Sugar, it's Annie," I shouted loudly, peering around the pastry case toward a swinging door that I assumed must connect to the kitchen.

No one answered.

I dinged the bell on the counter for help.

Still nothing.

Where was Sugar?

Had she forgotten to switch the OPEN sign to CLOSED?

Was she baking?

Maybe she had headphones on.

I leaned on the counter to hear better.

There was no sound of a whirling mixer or any baking equipment.

I didn't hear music or so much as a whisper of movement.

Sugar wouldn't desert her bakery and leave it unattended. Would she?

Something was off.

Was it my near miss? Could it have been her?

Maybe she caught wind of my suspicions about her after our conversation about her new contract with Queen Mary Flour. Perhaps she realized her flub.

What if she had left in a rush, looking for me, and fate had intervened?

Maybe it was pure luck on her part (misfortune on mine) that she spotted me walking along the highway.

She could have reacted in a split second.

It was possible that she hadn't meant to hurt me. Maybe she wanted to scare me. Or maybe she really hadn't seen me, and she'd been speeding away because she knew an arrest was imminent.

Another thought crept into my mind. This one was darker.

What if Sugar wasn't my assailant or the killer?

What if I'd just missed the killer and Sugar was lying in the bakery dead?

# TWENTY-EIGHT

*There's one way to find out, Annie.*

I took in a deep breath. Before I made even a single move toward the kitchen to see if Sugar was okay, I called Dr. Caldwell. She didn't answer so I left her a detailed message. Then I texted Pri.

> Can you pick me up? I'm at Sweet Room. Had a fall.

> Be right there. Don't move a muscle.

Should I text Liam, too?

I didn't want to send the cavalry, but then again, I didn't want to leave him out of the loop. I tried to imagine how I would feel if I were in his shoes. Without question, I would want him to call me.

> Don't freak out. I fell, but I'm okay. Pri is coming to get me.

I figured I could fill him in on the specific gory details later.

I'll come. Where are you? How did you fall?

At Sugar's. Had a little run-in with a car, but I promise I'm good.

A car?!? Annie, wth? I'm on my way.

I knew there was no stopping him, and honestly, that was fine. If something had happened to Sugar, it would be all the better that Liam and Pri were en route to the bakery.

I inhaled slowly, working up the courage to check the kitchen.

There was little chance that anyone else was around. There were no other cars in the small parking lot. We were a good few miles from town, which made it unlikely that anyone else had walked here.

I was on my own.

I walked behind the pastry case, trying to will my heart rate to slow. I wasn't going to take any chances, so I scanned the counter for anything I could use as a weapon.

Fortunately, a long cake knife rested near the cash register.

*This should do the trick*, I said to myself, grabbing the knife.

I took another quick sip of air.

*You can do this, Annie.*

First aid and self-defense classes had been mandatory in my criminology training. I'd kept my first aid and CPR certifications up to date. It was important working in retail to have staff prepared and equipped to handle emergencies. However, my self-defense training was rusty at best.

I made a mental note to sign up for a new round of classes in preparation for opening Novel Detectives.

If Fletcher and I were going to open a private detective agency, that was a top priority.

I gripped the knife tight and kicked the door open with my

foot, hoping the element of surprise would be on my side on the off chance the killer was hiding out in Sugar's kitchen.

Blood rushed to my head as I stepped into the commercial kitchen.

Stainless steel counters and polished epoxy floors greeted me. Bright, fluorescent overhead lights shined onto Sugar's workspace, forcing me to squint.

Trays of unfrosted cupcakes and mini pies sat on the counter along with ingredients, already measured. The bags of flour and sugar that had been opened by the police were pushed up against the far end of her workspace.

I let out a breath of relief when I realized that Sugar wasn't there.

She wasn't dead on the floor or slumped up against the stove.

That was good.

But where was she?

Seeing her supplies and ingredients made me more convinced she'd abandoned her baking.

*But why?*

Had she fled the scene because she knew the police were on to her? Or had she rushed out because she was in danger?

*What if I was wrong?*

*What if she isn't the killer?*

*Maybe the killer came to confront her?*

I tried to make sense of every possibility, but I came up with nothing until my eyes landed on another box of supplies filled with expensive baking gadgets.

I gasped.

An assortment of Sugar's cheap plastic pastry bags was packed tightly together. Something shiny was tucked in with them. Upon closer inspection I realized it was Becca's cake gun.

*That's it!*

*That's what I've been missing.*

It was like the world stopped spinning for a minute. I froze, gaping at the stainless steel tool.

*How did I miss it?*

*How was I so wrong?*

"Annie, Annie, where are you?" Pri's voice echoed in the tasting area.

I shook my head, forcing myself back into reality.

That was fast.

*How am I so lucky to have such good friends?*

I could feel the relief flood through my body. My shoulders sagged as I let out another long slow, breath.

"I'm okay. I'm here." I pushed the door open with my foot.

Pri jumped back. "Damn, that's quite the knife, girl."

I glanced at my hand, not even realizing I still had a death grip on the cake cutter. I returned it to its spot. "Precautionary."

Pri wrapped me in a giant hug once I put the knife down. "You look terrible. Tell me everything."

"I'm so glad you're here, Pri. Thanks for coming." I sank into her grasp and hugged her tight.

"Oh my God. I was so worried about you." She rubbed my back. "What happened? You fell?"

I clung to her for a minute, grateful to have a friend like her and grateful to be alive. I pulled away and squeezed her hands. "I'm going to gush, but I have to say I appreciate you so much for coming and coming so fast."

"Uh, yeah, duh. You never have to ask, Annie. You call. You text. I come." Pri's mouth hung open as she looked at me for the first time. "Did you fall off a cliff? You're a mess, geez. How can I help? Do you want to sit?" She pointed to the nearest table.

"My adrenaline has been running on high for the last hour. I don't think I can sit still. I need to burn some of it off, and I need to think for a minute." My mouth felt gummy. I was close to forming a theory, and every cell in my body buzzed in response to the frenetic connections bombarding my brain.

"Should we clean your wound?" She motioned to my hand. "You want me to get some water? Paper towels?"

Before I could answer, Liam burst into the bakery with wild eyes. They landed on me. He threw his hand to his chest and closed his eyes. "Annie, thank God. I think I broke every speeding record getting here."

"Me too," Pri said, holding out her palms to show us how shaky she was.

Liam assessed me with concern. His tight scowl made his jawline look even more rigid and defined. "Is that blood?"

"Only from my hand." I showed him the cut and then glanced at my stained jeans. "It looks worse than it is."

He shook his head and joined us at the table, placing a protective arm around my shoulder. "Don't do that to me again, Murray. I was terrified."

"I'm sorry." I let out a long sigh, allowing my body to release the tension it had been holding.

"It's a shocker that I'm going to say this, but I'm with the vampire here. What happened, Annie?" Pri studied the pastry case. "Where's Sugar?"

"I have no idea." I launched into the full story, starting from when Hal suggested I take a walk to getting run off the road and finding the bakery empty. "My mind is racing, but I'm think I'm close to figuring out who killed Lily."

"What?" Liam asked, gently massaging my shoulder.

Images flashed through my mind like cut scenes from a movie. "I can't believe I didn't put it together sooner. I think Becca's the killer."

"Becca, the assistant?" Pri asked.

"It all makes sense. I've been stuck on how the killer did it. That's why Sugar has been my top suspect. I figured Dr. Caldwell was focused on the bakery for a reason. Why else would she search here multiple times and cut open bags of flour? I assumed—wrongly—that the killer must have slipped poison into the cake Lily ate or the tea she drank, but they didn't. They were much cleverer. The cake gun. I think the poison was in the cake gun."

Liam raised his hands in surrender. "Hold up, you think she was shot with a cake gun? How do the physics of that work?"

"No." I lifted my finger and walked from the window to the pastry case and back. "I think Becca hid the poison in the cake gun. It's called that, but you can't shoot anyone with it. It's basically a giant syringe for piping frosting or filling donuts with jelly. Becca was adamant that no one touched her tools, weirdly so. Now that I'm piecing it together it all makes sense. She had access to Lily. She had motive. She admitted to me that she was the baker and cake designer. She did the work. Lily took the credit." I was on a roll and gaining steam. The connections were coming fast and furious. "She took Shane's phone and deleted a bunch of photos, but I bet she wasn't deleting photos. She was deleting his DMs with Lily."

"It sounds like a good theory." Pri motioned to the pastry case. "But what about Sugar? And how did Becca poison Lily with the pastry syringe?"

"She had to put it on something she knew Lily would ingest. But she's smart. She probably figured that the police would look at the obvious first, like Dayton's cake slice. Everyone saw Lily eat the cake. The same goes for the tea. In fact, I think she wanted the police to assume that Kari had slipped the poison into Lily's drink. All the while, she had come up with a masterful plan. Shane gave her the dream setup. He made such a huge scene about the pen. If the police traced the poison to the pen, he would be the likely suspect—her perfect scapegoat. *She* injected the pen with the poison, knowing Lily's habit of constantly chewing on her pens. It's brilliant. Twisted, but brilliant."

"I'm sold," Liam said. "We need Dr. Caldwell."

"I'm surprised Dr. Caldwell isn't already here," Pri said, reaching for her phone to check her texts.

"Me too." I peered through the frosted windows, hoping that Dr. Caldwell might appear. "Unless she's tracking the white Tesla down as we speak."

"That could be." Liam appraised the pastry case and began pacing. "I don't know, I can't stop thinking that there might be a different explanation and that the Tesla has nothing to do with Lily's murder."

"Like what?" I asked.

"Your meeting, Annie." He grew still, giving my shoulder a light squeeze. "Don't you find it odd that you were nearly run over by a car a couple of hours before meeting with this mysterious source?"

"Oh God." Pri stuck out her tongue and shook her head like she didn't want to believe his words. "Liam could be right. I never thought about that, but it is very coincidental timing, Annie."

My stomach dropped. "What?"

"Yeah." Liam nodded vigorously, encouraging me to catch up. "Think about it. Out of the two possibilities, what's more likely? Becca suddenly set her sights on you? Why? Have you been asking a few questions? Sure. But is that enough to try and kill you? Not in my book. How did she know you were out here anyway?" He paused and ran his fingers through his hair. "No, I don't think this was an accident or coincidence—I think this is entirely about Scarlet. I think Mark must be her killer and he's come to Redwood Grove for one reason and one reason alone—to kill you."

# TWENTY-NINE

Liam's suggestion made me physically sick. I placed my hand on my stomach and tried to swallow down the bile in the back of my throat.

"Annie, Liam's right. This is bad." Pri frowned and reached for my non-injured hand. "Maybe you need to reconsider going through with the meeting tonight."

"No way." I shook my head. "I can't. I'm so close. You both know how many years I've put into trying to get a break like this. I have to talk to Mark."

"But what if he's the guy, Annie? What if he tried to kill you? What's going to stop him from trying again tonight?" Pri asked.

Liam paced back and forth in front of the pastry case again. The dazzling holiday pastries seemed like a surreal backdrop for this serious conversation. "Agreed. I think you should cancel."

"I can't. We already covered this. You're all going to be there. If Mark is the killer, he's not going to attempt to hurt me in a packed restaurant in front of dozens of people. Plus, I *have* to go. Think about it. If he's the killer or involved in any way, he already knows that I've tracked him down. If I don't meet him for dinner, odds are good that he'll find me at home later tonight."

"Damn, that's also a solid point," Pri said, vacillating between us.

"We've already worked out a plan and a signal with Fletcher and Hal. You're all going to have eyes on me. I'll be safer at the pub than I would be alone at home."

Liam tilted his head from side to side, considering this. "Fair enough, but you have to watch your food and drink like a hawk. Don't take your eyes off it. In fact, maybe just don't eat anything."

"I'm so jittery I doubt I can eat anyway." The cakes and pastries in Sugar's display case were drool-worthy, but the thought of eating made me nauseous.

"Good." Liam bobbed his head.

Sirens sounded nearby.

Was it Dr. Caldwell?

Was she on her way to the bakery?

"But what about Becca?" Pri asked. "Do you think there's any chance it was her? Maybe she's been following you."

"I doubt it. Liam's right. How would she even know I was here? It doesn't make sense." I sighed. "It had to be someone else. I wish I had gotten a better look. I was too far away to see the driver's face, and then once I realized they were barreling toward me with no intention of stopping, I bailed. I didn't wait. I just launched my body down the ditch. There was nowhere else to go."

The sirens were growing closer.

"Sounds like Dr. Caldwell is coming," Pri said.

A minute later, blue and red flashing lights danced off the windows. The piercing sound of the sirens came to a stop.

Dr. Caldwell hurried into the bakery, her sharp eyes not missing a detail. "You're all here. Excellent."

She studied me first. "I received your text and your voicemail, Annie. Sorry, it took us longer than anticipated to get here. We were in pursuit of a suspect. I assume you're okay, all things considered."

I nodded. I was happy to see Dr. Caldwell and eager to hear what she could share about the case. If my theory was right, it would give me even more confidence to move forward with Fletcher.

"Are you in need of medical attention?" She scanned me like a trained emergency responder.

I held out my arm to show her. "No, it's just some cuts and bruises."

"In that case, you may go," she said to the police officer accompanying her. "Alert me immediately if the suspect is apprehended."

They nodded and left.

Dr. Caldwell pulled up a chair. "We've put out an APB for the killer."

"You know who did it?" I asked, sitting on a pink bistro chair across from her. "It's Becca, isn't it?"

Her thin lips pulled into a circle. She pulled her glasses to the tip of her nose and looked at me with a touch of pride. "Yes. And Sugar is the reason we're in pursuit."

"Does she drive a white Tesla?"

"No. We're looking for a black sedan," Dr. Caldwell replied.

Was Liam right? Could that mean the driver wasn't connected to Lily's murder? I gulped and ignored the tingling in my extremities.

"I'm not surprised in the least with what you've pieced together. Let me brief you." Dr. Caldwell got comfortable. "Sugar is at the station right now. She's fairly shaken up, but she's safe."

I was glad to hear her confirm Sugar wasn't the killer and that she was safe.

"Ironically, we were already gearing up to make an arrest when Sugar arrived. Our digital team recovered deleted files from Lily's phone. We found Shane's original exchanges with her. Everything he claimed was true. Unfortunately for him, the killer used him as a scapegoat." She paused and reached for her phone to show us the private message exchanges between Lily and Shane.

I nodded. "I'm kicking myself for not realizing it sooner. I saw Becca take Shane's phone when he was trying to make sure Lily got his gift. She's adept at social media. It wouldn't have taken her more than a couple of seconds to delete their message thread."

"Exactly."

"So, it seems like Shane was right about Lily having authentic connections with her fans?" I asked.

"To her potential detriment," Dr. Caldwell said with a nod. "We believe Becca intentionally fanned the flames of her friendship with Shane, leaning into the narrative that he was a stalker and dangerous. Nothing could be further from the truth. Shane and Lily appear to have connected over their shared health issues and stayed in regular contact. Becca painted him as obsessed and unhinged. She took advantage of their friendship to spin a different story in hopes of pinning the murder on him."

"That's cold," Pri added. "Her personal assistant."

"Her personal assistant who's been skimming off her financially for years," Dr. Caldwell added. "We've traced her bank records. She's been stealing from Lily, profiting large chunks of Lily's sponsorship deals for herself. Becca inked out a side deal with Kari, unbeknownst to Lily. We believe she intended to embezzle those profits, too. Lily was extremely skilled and savvy when it came to marketing and clearly had an infectious personality that built her a loyal following. However, she put her complete trust in Becca's hands when it came to her personal finances. We suspect Lily must have learned what Becca was doing and intended to stop it. We recovered email exchanges between her and a fraud investigator and tax attorney. Her mistake was not realizing Becca had access to her email and social media. She probably realized the gig was up and had to silence Lily."

"How did Becca do it?" Liam asked, looking at me. "Annie has an idea."

Dr. Caldwell waited.

"Was it in the cake gun?"

"Say more." She nodded encouragingly.

"Becca's cake gun is stashed here in the bakery along with Sugar's tools," I said, gesturing toward the back of the bakery. "I've been thinking about the method of delivery ever since our conversation, and she's so protective of her tools, like a helicopter parent. It didn't make sense until I started to think about *how* the poison was delivered. If her goal was to implicate Shane, she could have injected the pen he gave Lily with poison."

"Cyanide." Dr. Caldwell lifted her finger. "The toxicology report shows traces of cyanide all over the pen. Lily must have not only injected the pen with the poison but coated the outside for good measure. If you'll recall from your studies, cyanide resembles a massive heart attack within thirty minutes of ingesting a small amount."

"Do you think it could have been in the pen?" I asked, feeling hopeful that I was onto something.

"As always, Annie, you astound me. That certainly could be a possibility." She paused momentarily and considered my theory. "Yes, well done. Everything else has come back clean from the toxicology reports—the cake sample, the tea, the gingerbread pieces. Yes, if there's still cyanide in the syringe we'll have firm evidence to make an arrest. I need to text my team and get them out here again."

After she had sent the message, she returned her attention to me, shaking her head in mild disbelief. "The pen. The cake gun, yes, that's excellent work."

My cheeks warmed from her praise. It was a little ego boost for thinking about my future endeavors with Fletcher.

"Here's what we know from our end," Dr. Caldwell continued. "Sugar received an alert on her security camera that someone was attempting to break in. She raced to the bakery, but the alarms scared whoever was trying to get in away. When she checked the cameras, she spotted Becca. Instead of calling us, she made a rash decision to come to the station. I'm guessing that's why you found the bakery like this. She couldn't pinpoint what or why she felt 'spooked,' in her words, but she didn't hesitate. She said Becca looked desperate and wild on the footage."

"I wonder if Becca realized that Sugar accidentally grabbed her cake gun when she gathered supplies at the bookstore. The evidence has been right here in the bakery all along." My eyes drifted toward the kitchen.

"And she was trying to break in to grab it before anyone realized it," Pri added, pounding her palm on the table twice. "Annie cracks the case again."

Dr. Caldwell gave her a small smile. "Financial records back up this theory. As I said, Becca has been profiting off Lily for years. She's pocketed close to two million dollars. If you're correct, Annie, that aligns with what we've discovered."

"I can't believe it was Becca. They seemed so close," Pri said, shaking her head like she didn't want it to be true.

"Too close," Dr. Caldwell agreed. "Lily put her entire trust and fortune into Becca's hands. There was no oversight. She believed they were more than colleagues. She trusted Becca like a friend, which ultimately led to her demise."

"That's terrible." Pri reached for my hand again. "I swear I'll never do that to you, Annie. Unless you and Fletcher start pulling in big cash at the bookstore. Then, watch out."

I chuckled. So did Liam.

I appreciated Pri breaking the tension.

Everything made sense. I just wished I had pieced it together sooner.

"Do you think you'll be able to find her?" I asked.

"I'm confident we'll apprehend her shortly." She tapped her phone. "I've alerted my team about this new development, and as soon as we're done here, I'll retrieve the cake gun and send it to the lab for analysis."

"That's a relief."

"And the ultimate smoking gun," Liam said with a cheeky wink.

"Liam freaking Donovan is dropping puns?" Priya gasped and fanned her face, looking at Dr. Caldwell and me in disbelief. "What is happening?"

"If it gets served up to you on a plate like that..." He trailed off and shrugged.

I laughed. Even Dr. Caldwell broke into a full smile.

"Now, about this near hit-and-run," Dr. Caldwell said, shifting gears. "I have the photos you texted and will go observe the scene. Is there any more you can tell me? Did you see the driver?"

"No. It happened too fast." I shook my head. "I don't think there's anything else I'm missing, I just wish I had gotten a better look."

The truth was, if it hadn't been Becca in the Tesla, then I had a terrible feeling Liam was right. And if he was, I was in serious danger.

# THIRTY

"Do you think it's wise for Annie to go through with the meeting tonight?" Liam asked Dr. Caldwell directly. "It doesn't seem out of the realm of possibility that whoever ran her off the road could be connected to the cold case."

Dr. Caldwell appraised me with new interest. "You're sure you didn't see the driver?"

"Positive." I blew out a breath, wishing I had been more composed in the moment.

She tried another tactic. "What about a plate? Did you happen to catch a glimpse of the license? Even the first few numbers?"

I was kicking myself internally. In the heat of the moment, my rational brain had shut off. I knew the importance of staying sharp in a crisis, but I'd been so concerned with my personal safety that I didn't glance at the license plate.

In fairness, though, it had taken a while for me to process that the car was coming for *me*. If I had realized that sooner, I would have done a better job of gleaning more information that Dr. Caldwell could use to track down the car.

"No, sorry," I said.

"There's absolutely no need to apologize." Dr. Caldwell removed her glasses and tucked them on her head. "I'm just happy you got out of the incident with minor injuries. As for the danger of meeting Mark tonight, the plan is to connect with him at Stag Head, correct?"

"Right." I nodded.

"Then, I don't see a reason to call it off. Unless you're not up for it. I'm in the loop. You'll be in a public place, and I trust your instincts."

Her trust in me made me swell with pride. She also echoed exactly what I had said to Pri and Liam. "Thanks. I want to meet with him. You know how important this is."

"I do." A brief flash of worry crossed her face. Her lips turned down into a frown. "I'm fine with you proceeding. However, I would like to place a squad car at your house. I think it's a good idea to keep an extra set of eyes on you this evening."

"I think that's a great idea," Liam interjected before Dr. Caldwell had barely finished her sentence.

"Me too." Pri patted my knee. "We can't be too careful with our Annie. Do you want me to stay over tonight? We can do masks and watch *The Holiday* for the millionth time."

"That's also a good idea," Liam said, looking at me as if daring me to turn Pri down.

"Sure, okay." Honestly, having someone else in the house and an officer posted outside sounded fine to me. Two women had died because of whatever was going on at Silicon Summit Partners. I didn't want to take any undue chances, especially not after my near miss with the Tesla.

"Excellent. I'll arrange it." Dr. Caldwell reached for her phone.

"We should get you home to change and clean up your cuts," Pri suggested.

"Yeah." I glanced at the clock above the pastry counter. My

meeting with Mark was in less than an hour. It was suddenly starting to feel real.

"I'll see you there shortly." Liam helped me to my feet.

Everything ached more as I stood. My back seized up, and my knee had developed a new popping sound that reminded me of making popcorn on the stove.

I forced a smile and limped to Pri's car.

Liam hung back with Dr. Caldwell, probably to instruct her to surround my cottage with a SWAT team. I had to admit his concern made my cheeks warm and sent little butterflies flitting through my stomach. It was sweet that he cared.

"Annie, you don't look so good," Pri said, opening the passenger door for me and buckling me in like I was a kid.

"I swear, I'm good. I'm a bit shaken and sore, but I'll be fine. I'll take a quick hot shower and wash off the dirt and grime."

"Okay, but I'm not leaving your side." She tossed a bag of candy and a box of coffee beans in the backseat. "This is messed up. Someone tried to kill you."

"Maybe," I corrected her. "There's also a chance the driver was distracted and had no idea they nearly hit me."

"You don't believe that, Annie." She steered the car down the driveway and turned onto the highway. "It's me. You don't have to put on a brave face."

I pressed my hands together to stop them from shaking. "Thanks, Pri, you're the best, and you're right. But the reason I'm putting on a brave face is for me."

"Are you worried about meeting Mark?"

"Are you asking because my hands are like Jell-O?" I held my trembling fingers and winked. "Sure, I'm nervous, but that's the job. Dr. Caldwell used to tell us that if we weren't nervous, that's when we were in the most danger. It's about harnessing that energy. I'm not worried he's going to hurt me. I mean, I wasn't lying, I will be super careful, I swear. It's more that after all these years, I finally feel like I might be close, and if Mark turns out to be another dead end, I'm worried it's going to send me into a slump—or put me back in a dark place."

"I get that." She kept her eyes on the road and her hands gripping the wheel as if she anticipated another run-in with the Tesla. "You're a different person now, Annie. You've done so much work on yourself and had such tremendous personal growth since we met. I'm not concerned about that. You're going to be fine no matter what you learn or don't learn from Mark."

Tears spilled from my eyes and streaked down my cheeks. "I know I've said this like a dozen times already, but I'm so lucky to have a friend like you."

"The feeling is entirely mutual." She peeled her eyes from the road briefly and smiled at me in solidarity. "We're a team. You're not doing this alone."

"I know." I brushed a tear from my face, smiled, and squeezed her knee. "Having your support gives me that extra boost of courage. I'm ready. I'm going to do this. I'm more determined than ever. This is my future. If Novel Detectives is going to be successful—which I'm confident it is—it starts tonight. I'm not backing down because of my near miss or anything that's happened this weekend with Lily's murder. I'm meeting Mark, and I'm getting to the bottom of Scarlet's murder once and for all."

"Damn. Go, Annie." Pri lifted her hand from the wheel to reach for a fist pump. "I love it—big Annie energy. I'm here for it. Let's do this."

"Yes, let's do this." I tapped her fist, feeling excitement begin to build. This afternoon had tested my resolve and I had come out with flying colors. Nothing could stop me now, especially being bolstered by Pri, Liam, Fletcher, Hal, and Dr. Caldwell.

"When is Penny back?" I asked, changing the subject.

"Two more days." She grinned. "They can't come fast enough. I miss her face."

"Her face." I chuckled.

"She is a stunner." Pri ran her tongue over her bottom lip.

"You're not wrong." We drove past the skid marks and the spot where I'd rolled into the ditch. From this angle, I realized my fall could have been much worse. I easily could have broken a bone—or every bone in my body.

"What do you think of doing a friend holiday dinner next weekend? You, me, Penny, Liam, Fletcher, maybe Hal and Caroline would want to join in?"

"Oh, I love it. Should we do it at the store?" I was glad for a happy distraction. Seeing how close I'd come to a much more serious injury made me slightly jittery again.

"Do you think Hal would mind?" Pri kept her eyes on the road.

"Not at all. He's game for just about anything."

"Okay, cool. I'll chat with everyone at trivia tonight. We could do a potluck dinner to make it easy. Maybe everyone brings their favorite holiday dish to share."

"And a book swap?" I suggested hopefully.

"A book swap, and I've been working on a secret holiday coffee blend. No one needs to go over-the-top with gifts, but this is my passion project."

"Yes, that sounds like so much fun."

We were back to the village square in a matter of minutes. Pri turned onto my street. There was no sign of any police presence yet. Nor was there a white Tesla parked anywhere nearby.

That was a relief.

Pri accompanied me like my own personal bodyguard. She fed Professor Plum while I showered and tended to my wounds. I was glad to have something positive to focus on—a friend holiday potluck at the bookstore sounded like perfection. Now I just needed to get through tonight and maybe, just maybe, finally be in a position to track down Scarlet's killer.

# THIRTY-ONE

After a hot shower and a change of clothes, I felt like a new person.

"You look adorable as always, Annie," Pri said. Professor Plum purred contentedly on her lap. "I love you in green."

"Thanks." I did a little twirl. My emerald green sweater dress was a favorite. I paired it with leggings and knee-high boots. I dried my hair and wore it loose with a silver barrette. My cuts and scrapes were covered in bravery patches—cute floral Band-Aids cut in the shape of butterflies and stars. "I feel so much better."

"Good, shall we do this, then? You're bringing the girl boss energy." She set Professor Plum on his window seat pillow and reached for my hand. "The squad car showed up while you were in the shower, so I think it's safe for us to walk to the pub."

"Great." I placed my hand on my chest to try and slow my breathing as we cut through the park.

Pri and I were both on high alert as we passed a group of carolers and families waiting in line for pictures with Santa, Mrs. Claus, and the reindeer.

"How are you holding up?" She laced her fingers through mine.

"I can't remember a time I was this nervous, and also strangely excited," I admitted. "It's kind of like Christmas Eve. I was also super excited for presents and slightly terrified of actually seeing Santa Claus."

"Totally normal. It's a strange dude coming down the chimney. Think about the lyrics to 'Santa Claus Is Comin' to Town.' They're super creepy. He's watching you while you're sleeping and tracking while you're awake. Shudder. Stalker much?" She laughed and squeezed my hand tighter as the pathway spilled out onto the village square.

It looked like a scene from a postcard. Everything glowed under the dazzling lights. People mingled as they strolled along Cedar Avenue, taking in the elaborate window displays and stopping in shops.

The pub came into view.

I gulped.

*This is it.*

*This is my chance to take a step forward in bringing Scarlet's killer to justice.*

*You've got this, Annie.*

I sucked in a long breath and rounded my shoulders.

"You're going to be great," Pri whispered. "And remember, we'll all be nearby."

"Right."

She waited for me to go in first so as not to be obvious.

It felt like any other trivia night. The bar hummed with energy. There was a line of people waiting for drinks, and teams gathered at nearly every table, waiting for the host to kick off the game.

White poinsettias and tapered candles adorned each table and the bar. Wham!'s "Last Christmas" played overhead.

I shot a quick glance at a large six-person distressed wood

table where Fletcher, Hal, and Caroline were gathered. Then I scanned the crowded dining room, looking for Mark.

He told me he'd be wearing a San Francisco Giants hat. I spotted him in the farthest booth. He was different than I expected. I'm not entirely sure what I had expected. I guess maybe someone more formal. A suit. A finance bro.

He was about ten years older than me, and he had tattoos, a scruffy beard, and a baseball hat that I suspected concealed his receding hairline.

"Annie?" He gave me a tentative wave when he caught me looking at him.

"Mark?"

He nodded and motioned for me to join him.

*Stay calm.*

*Stay centered.*

*Remember your mission.*

*This is for Scarlet.*

I smiled and slid into the booth across from him. "It's nice to finally meet you."

"You too." His light blue eyes drifted toward the doors like he was worried someone had followed me in.

"Did you find the place okay?" I ignored the way his gaze flitted around the bar. He was obviously checking to make sure we weren't being watched. I hoped that everyone was playing it cool. Mark was skittish. If Fletcher or any of my friends were less than subtle with their surveillance, he was going to get spooked.

"No problem. It was a nice drive from San Francisco. I forgot how wonderful California winters are. At home in New York, it's sleeting and barely above freezing."

"What made you leave?" I figured if I could steer the conversation toward Mark's work, it would be a natural segue into the reason we were here.

"I was burned out." He gripped the edge of the table, his

knuckles turning white. "The pay was great, but the hours and the stress not so much. It was the textbook definition of a toxic work environment."

"That's interesting. I always assume the East Coast is more high pressure than the West Coast." A waiter came by with water and menus. As promised, I kept my glass close to my side of the table.

"It is. Well, it's different. The pace is, anyway." He studied the menu. "Silicon Valley is its own beast, if you know what I mean?"

Redwood Grove was close enough to the tech mecca to have some tourist spillover, but that was about all our little town had in common.

"Was that true working at Silicon Summit Partners?"

"You just jump right to it, huh?" He set the menu down.

"Sorry. It's been a long time coming. I guess I'm eager."

"That's fair." He checked around us again to make sure no one was listening and then rested his elbows on the table. "They were the main reason I left. There was some serious stuff going down there, and I wanted to get out before I caught any backlash."

"Serious in what way?"

He lowered his voice. "I can't go into too much detail for your sake or mine. It's better if we don't."

"Okay, what can you tell me?"

"That you don't want to mess with these guys. You're in way over your head. It's not just the company—it's their clients. We're talking powerful, powerful people."

I took a drink of water, trying to read his body language. He was nervous, that much I was sure about.

"Is that why you didn't want a digital trail of our conversations."

"Exactly." He picked up his glass but didn't take a drink. "I almost didn't come. Are you sure you want to re-open this can of worms?"

"Positive."

Our waiter came back to take our order.

This time it was Liam.

I tried to remain passive as he told us about the specials and recommended a beer for Mark.

*We're just getting to the good part.* I wanted to shoo him away, but instead, I ordered a bowl of chicken tortilla soup and a ginger ale.

When Liam finally left, I pressed Mark for more information. "Scarlet was my best friend. She didn't deserve to die young. She was meeting with someone named Bob the day she died. I know the reason she was killed is connected to Natalie Thompson."

"I don't know anyone named Bob who worked at the firm." He flipped his hat backward, momentarily revealing a shiny balding head. "I don't doubt it. That's why I got out of there. That's why I've never shared what I know, and I'm still not convinced it's the right move tonight. I signed an iron-clad NDA. That's one of the ways they make sure you don't talk."

"What's the other?" I was pretty sure I already knew what he was going to say.

"Brute force." He blinked.

I could see a visible pulse beneath his skin. He was scared.

I swallowed a large sip, forcing the cold water to open my throat.

"That's why I have to warn you that this is dangerous territory. I can't be part of this, okay? Whatever I shared with you tonight, you didn't hear from me. I'll claim I never met you."

What did he know?

My heart sped up, and my breath quickened.

"I understand. Whatever you share is between us."

"You realize you're putting yourself in danger if you keep

digging, though?" He clenched his hands into tight fists, causing the vein in his neck to bulge.

"I do." I nodded seriously. "It's a risk I'm willing to take."

Liam interrupted us. "Here are your drinks." He handed me a ginger ale and placed a beer in front of Mark. "Can I get you anything else?"

"No. We're good." I gave him a look to let him know I was fine and to leave us alone.

Mark lifted his pint in a toast. "Thanks, man." He waited until Liam was out of earshot to continue. "You're sure about this?"

"I've never been more sure of anything." I nodded with a confidence I didn't feel. Mark was spooked. I wasn't sure what that meant in terms of my own physical danger, but I did know that meant he had information that could lead to a break.

"All right." He sighed and held his beer as he started into his story. "I didn't know Natalie well. She was nice, friendly, and upbeat, but our paths didn't cross much. She was an assistant. I worked on the finance side. But shortly before everything blew up, she asked if we could meet. I didn't think much of it at the time. We met for a coffee at a shop nearby, and she was really freaked out."

"Freaked out how?" I wished I could take notes, but I knew that would put him on the defensive.

"I thought she was on something. She was paranoid—convinced she was being watched. She couldn't sit still. She was cryptic and outright deranged. At least that was my first impression."

"What did she want from you?"

"She asked a bunch of questions about reporting and taxes. She refused to say why, but it was obvious she didn't trust her boss."

Our food arrived. We paused the conversation again.

"She got in my head, so I did some digging based on the

questions she asked and realized that she wasn't paranoid. She had found a money trail that led nowhere good."

"What did you do?"

"I tried to meet with her again, but she vanished. I got spooked. I knew too much. I talked to the local police, but they weren't much help, so I made a plan then and there to bide my time. I didn't want to leave immediately. It would be too obvious. I used the next few months to gather evidence, but the company was smarter. They were twenty steps ahead of Natalie and me, so I gave my notice and took the first job in New York."

I tried to summarize everything he'd shared. It all lined up with my research. "So you think Natalie was killed because of what she uncovered."

"I didn't say that."

He took me by surprise.

"Sorry, I guess I misunderstood. I thought you said that you got spooked after she vanished."

"I did." He gulped down two big sips of beer. "I didn't say killed. I said *vanished*."

## THIRTY-TWO

I nearly spilled my ginger ale. "Wait, you don't think Natalie's dead?"

He shook his head. "She's been in hiding."

"Have you been in touch?" I couldn't believe it. This was a bigger break than I ever could have dreamed of.

"Very infrequently." He pressed his lips together and shook his head.

"Do you know where she is now?"

"No. It behooves her to lay low." He took another drink of his beer.

My mind was spinning wildly with possibilities. "But you're sure she's still alive?"

Was that Scarlet's secret?

He reached into his jeans pocket.

For a second, I wondered if I should call for backup, but nothing about Mark's demeanor made me worried that he would harm me. If anything, I got the feeling he was the one with more to lose.

He pulled up a picture and handed me his phone. "This is from August. It was uncanny timing when you reached out. I was worried you were a company plant. That's why I wanted to take extra precautions with this meeting. I don't want to be responsible for anything happening to Natalie. I'm really sorry about your friend."

I stared at the woman in the picture. She was so familiar, like an old friend. I'd seen her face dozens of times in police reports and internet searches. She was older, obviously, but it was clearly Natalie.

Blood rushed to my head. I felt like I was drunk. Never in my wildest dreams would I have imagined this outcome. Natalie was alive. This changed everything.

"Do you think she'll talk to me?"

"I don't know. I haven't told her about you." He finished off his beer. "We have a system in place if we ever want to get in touch. I wanted to meet you first and make sure you're legit."

"Could you arrange a meeting?" I asked again, this time with a bit more force.

"Maybe." He wavered. "I can try. I'm not sure if she'll agree, but I can ask."

I handed him back his phone. "That would be incredible. She might be the key to finally bringing Scarlet's killer to justice."

"I wouldn't get your hopes up. Like I said, these are powerful people. People in government and politics with a lot to lose if the truth comes out. Natalie is safe. I'm not sure she'll want to jeopardize her safety."

I tried to put myself in her position. If she felt like it was futile and there was no help, I could understand, but then again, Scarlet had died in vain. We had time, distance, and Dr. Caldwell on our side.

"I would appreciate it if you would at least ask," I said to Mark.

"I'm not making any promises, but I'll ask." He lifted his

empty glass like he was trying to decide if he wanted to order another.

"This is huge, Mark. I can't thank you enough. I've been studying this case for ten years and this changes everything. Scarlet and I were inseparable. We were like twins. We were going to open our detective agency, and then she got caught up in this case and killed. It's like a part of me died then, too. You've given me hope."

He stared at his glass, frowning and avoiding my gaze. "Um, about that. There's something else you should know."

I didn't like his tone.

He scrolled through his phone and passed it to me again. "Take a look at this. You probably need to zoom in to see it."

I studied the grainy picture. It looked like an old photocopy of a contract. The Silicon Summit Partners logo was at the top of the page. As he directed, I zoomed in to read the fine print. A wave of nausea came over me as I realized what I was seeing.

It was a contract with Silicon Summit Partners and Scarlet. She had signed an employment contract with them the day she died.

"I don't understand," I said to Mark, trying to keep my emotions in check.

"I don't either." He shrugged. "I found this when I was compiling information to bring to the police before I realized how deep the cover-up went. I'm not sure what your friend was involved with or how much she knew, but it looks like she was planning to come to work for the company."

That couldn't be true.

Unless she was forced into signing a contract.

Scarlet wouldn't lie to me, would she?

I thought back to our last conversation. She had mentioned she had a secret to share. Was it this?

I felt sick.

I wanted to get out of the bar as fast as possible.

*Was everything about our friendship a lie?*

I couldn't breathe.

My throat tightened like a noose was being scrunched over my neck.

*Scarlet, what were you thinking?*

*Was it her cover?*

Could she have pretended to be interested in a job with the firm as a way in to get more information about Natalie?

None of it made sense.

"I can see I've rattled you," Mark said gently.

"No, it's okay. It's another lead, but I guess I'm just shocked."

"I don't have any other answers about her employment. I just know this was an offer from the CEO, so she was being courted by the higher-ups."

"Right." I had to stay in the moment until our conversation was done.

"I would send you a copy, but I don't trust email or text. It's too traceable. If you want to give me your address, I can mail you a physical copy." Something about his demeanor shifted.

"Sure. Yeah." I felt dizzy. Was the room spinning?

How had I gotten things so wrong?

"Do you want a ride home?" Mark asked, pulling me back into my body. "You look a little pale."

"Oh, no thanks." I waved him off. "I can walk."

"Are you sure?"

"Yeah, it's no problem."

He handed me a copy of the receipt for the dinner bill and a pen. "If you write your address here, I'll mail you a copy. We can keep in touch about a potential meeting with Natalie. They can't trace snail mail."

"Right. Yeah." I couldn't put together more than a word or two. I scribbled my address on the back of the receipt. "Thanks again for meeting me. I have a lot to process, but I really appreciate it."

"I'm glad you pushed me. This case has been eating away at me, too. If this helps, then I'll feel better."

I started to gather my things.

"Oh, sorry, one more thing," he said, signaling with one finger to stop me. "Do you happen to know where the nearest charging station is?"

"Charging station?" I repeated.

"The rental company gave me a Tesla. I want to charge it tonight before I drive back to the city, just in case."

Now I really thought I might vomit.

Everything went blurry.

My throat seized. I tried to swallow, but it was like something was lodged in my larynx.

Mark was driving a Tesla. I'd just given him my address.

"Yeah, there's one a few blocks away at the high school." I grabbed my purse and coat. "I really need to get going. Thanks again for your time. This was super helpful."

I raced out of the bar, making eye contact with Fletcher and Pri to signal them to meet me outside.

Was this a complete setup?

Had Liam been right about my brush with the Tesla?

It had nothing to do with Lily's death and everything to do with Scarlet?

Did that mean Mark had been watching me?

For how long?

I gulped as my hand clasped the door.

Suddenly I was desperate for fresh air.

My body felt almost numb and tingly as a new thought invaded.

Had I just dined with Scarlet's killer? And was I next?

# THIRTY-THREE

Dr. Caldwell was waiting for me at my cottage. "How did it go, Annie?"

"Can we talk inside?" My body hummed with nerves as every shadow seemed to jump out at me.

"Of course." She motioned the squad car parked at the end of the cul-de-sac to alert them.

I flopped onto the couch.

"Are you up for talking about it?" she asked without judgment, sitting down next to me. "I understand if you need a minute."

"No, not at all." I sucked air in through my nose in a big gulp, feeling anger boiling inside me like a tea kettle on the verge of exploding.

How dare he? How dare Mark show up in Redwood Grove, in my hometown, claiming to have information for me?

"Let's talk through everything I learned while it's fresh." I stared at my hands, which were still shaky. I balled them up into fists and started at the beginning.

She took copious notes, interrupting every once in a while for clarification.

"It's too soon to jump to any conclusions," she said, trying to reassure me. "We need to proceed with caution. We don't want to give Mark any indication we suspect he could be involved. I know it's overwhelming, and I don't know what to tell you about Scarlet yet, but this is a giant leap forward, Annie. You did great. I'm confident we're going to be able to finally bring Scarlet's family and both of us some closure, but we'll need to work together as a team and take our time coming up with a strategy."

I unclenched my fists and nodded. "You're right. I just never imagined Scarlet would consider working for them."

"We don't know if that's true," she said. "This is a brand-new case now. We need to treat it as such. Remember, in the early stages, nothing is off the table. So let's not leap to conclusions or make any rash moves."

"Yes, of course."

"I'm going to keep my officer stationed here at least for tonight. I'll run some background on Mark, and then I suggest we regroup and start a methodical approach to piecing together what we already know with this new information."

I nodded again.

"Good." She closed her notebook. "Pri is staying with you tonight, yes?"

I checked my texts. "She's on her way now."

"Excellent." She stood. "Call me if you need anything."

"Okay."

Pri arrived as Dr. Caldwell was leaving. I went through the conversation with her again, letting my anger steam up again, until she finally suggested we make hot chocolate and popcorn and curl up with a movie.

We did just that.

The next few days passed in a blur. Dr. Caldwell and I met daily to review old case notes and begin to formulate our next steps. She wisely suggested that we take our time. If Silicon Summit Partners caught wind that there was renewed interest in the case, that could put us and Natalie in danger. We agreed that we'd tackle preliminary research through the end of the year and begin our investigation in earnest in the new year.

We also rehashed Lily's murder. Becca had been arrested and confessed to everything. Dr. Caldwell had put Shane in touch with Lily's family, and there was discussion about him continuing a fan site in her honor. Kari and Sugar were moving forward with a sponsorship, and Dayton announced that the high school would be offering a full tuition and board scholarship in Lily's name to a graduating culinary student.

"This is the reason I do this work, Annie," Dr. Caldwell said at the end of our conversation. "Providing closure to families is the best part of the job. I'm confident you'll experience the same thing when you and Fletcher solve your first case. I hope you'll keep me in the loop when you do."

"Always." I invited her to join our upcoming dinner, but she was flying home to Maryland to visit family for the holidays.

By the time our friend holiday potluck rolled around, I felt more settled and committed to seeing the case through to the end come January.

We gathered at the Secret Bookcase on a Sunday evening. The Conservatory was bathed in dazzling golden lights from the Christmas tree and the dozens of lanterns Fletcher and I had arranged around one long table in the center of the room. I draped it with a bright red tablecloth and dug Hal's grandmother's china from the attic. Fletcher made ornaments as place cards. We put sprigs of holly and chocolate truffles I special ordered from Sugar on everyone's plate. Fletcher dressed for the occasion in black slacks and a forest green button-up shirt with a bright red carnation pinned to the chest pocket.

"You look quite dashing," I said, placing the last truffle on Caroline's plate.

"As do you, my partner in crime. We're matching." He tugged the edge of his shirt and held it out to my dress. "Green is our color. We should take headshots for Novel Detectives tonight."

I laughed and gave him my best serious librarian pose. "Not a bad idea. We can set it up in the Parlor to play up the noir vibe."

"Did I hear you mention noir?" Hal interrupted, sweeping into the ballroom with Caroline, his girlfriend, on his arm. They looked like they belonged in one of Hercule Poirot's lavish parties. Hal wore a gray suit with a red-and-green bowtie, and Caroline's silver cocktail dress accented her silky white locks.

Hal turned on a Michael Bublé playlist and gave Caroline a little twirl. "I believe dancing is in order after dinner."

Pri and Penny arrived arm in arm, loaded with pretty packages wrapped in craft paper and tied with gingham ribbons. Liam came shortly after them with his own box of goodies.

We set out the food and poured wine.

Happy laughter reverberated through the room while we dished up servings of Pri's roasted pumpkin curry and vindaloo turkey and Liam's walnut-and-blue-cheese-stuffed mushrooms and cranberry meatballs. Caroline passed baskets of her homemade garlic and butter rolls and cheesy pretzel bread. Hal and Fletcher's contribution was made-to-order chocolate, crème brûlée, or pomegranate martinis. And I'd baked my mom's skillet lasagna packed with garden-fresh veggies and spicy sausage.

"It is an absolute delight to have all of my favorite people in my favorite place," Hal said, holding his martini in a toast as his eyes twinkled with happy tears. "Wishing us the happiest of holidays."

We clinked glasses and enjoyed the eclectic and hearty meal. After we'd stuffed ourselves, Penny revealed a dessert that was almost too gorgeous to eat—a pavlova with caramelized white chocolate bark, fresh raspberries, and chopped pistachios.

"Is anyone up for presents?" I asked while Pri poured coffee and Penny sliced into the pavlova.

"I thought you'd never ask." Fletcher clapped twice. "Presents, please."

I was eager to share my gifts. Finding the perfect present for someone I loved filled me with the holiday spirit, and I was delighted with what I'd found for everyone this year. For Hal, I arranged a video greeting from David Suchet inviting him to visit the English countryside and meet up for a cocktail at the Harrogate Festival. Penny's gift was an original blueprint of the Wentworth farm I found at the Redwood Grove Historical Museum. I packaged dozens of temporary literary tattoos for Pri. Fletcher was getting an autographed copy of the Sherlockian series I'd managed to score from one of my publishing contacts. I gifted Caroline Jane Austen coloring books and pastel pencils.

I'd found a first-edition copy of Liam's favorite history book that I wrapped in peppermint-striped paper and tied with green ribbon and cardboard coasters printed with fun historical facts.

His smile spread to his eyes as he opened his gift. He leaned in to kiss my cheek. "Thanks, Murray. Open yours."

I was impressed with his wrapping—vintage Nancy Drew with spyglasses and lanterns. "Is this what I think it is?" I asked him.

"Open it." He circled his hand. "Just rip the paper."

"Never," I gasped. Then I took my time, meticulously peeling tape from the edges and smoothing the wrapping. It was a watercolor map of landmarks from the first seven books in the famous novels. I'd had it in my Etsy cart for months, but I'd never mentioned it to Liam. "How did you know?"

He shrugged and gave me a sly, mysterious grin. "I have my sources."

The next hour was a frenzy of flying paper and oohs and aahs as everyone unwrapped their gifts.

I couldn't contain my smile as I watched my friends. The food was delectable, and the company was even better. I soaked in the evening, grateful for my friends and our bookish community.

Hal pulled me aside to thank me while Penny and Pri kicked off the dancing.

"I'll be watching this video on repeat," he said, cradling his phone against his chest like a newborn baby. "Imagine martinis with the Hercule Poirot. I don't believe I'll sleep for months in anticipation of next summer's festival."

"I'm so glad you like it." I patted his sleeve. "I wanted to ask you about the estate again. Are you sure it makes sense for Fletcher and me to buy the store financially?"

"The estate is in good shape. Fine shape." His response was too quick and too chipper. And he didn't exactly answer my question.

"Hal, is there something you're not telling me?"

"No, dear, everything is fine. Look at how happy we all are. Nothing pleases me more than seeing this." He shooed me toward the dance floor. "Go enjoy the party. We'll talk numbers and boring details in the new year."

I could tell he wasn't going to budge. Not tonight. But we weren't done with the conversation.

I joined the dancing.

The merriment lasted well into the night and when I couldn't dance any longer, Liam walked me home. We took the long way through the village square, soaking in the Christmas lights and the crisp night air.

"What do you say, Murray? A Christmas Eve feast—you, me, and Professor Plum?"

"That would be lovely." My pace quickened at the thought of spending the holiday with Liam. That was a big step. A sign that things were getting serious. "I promised my parents I would drive down on Christmas and be there in time for dinner, so Christmas Eve sounds perfect."

"Good. I'll make my famous eggnog. We used to drink copious amounts on Christmas Eve and go door-to-door, leaving baskets of breakfast scones on our neighbors' porches."

"That was your family tradition? How sweet."

He stiffened and froze for a minute. "Uh, yeah, I guess. It was a long time ago."

Soft lighting from the streetlamps cast a halo on his face. He looked like he'd seen a ghost.

"Liam, are you okay?" I reached for his hand. I could tell we had hit a nerve.

His palm was clammy and cold. He latched onto me tight as if my hand was his lifeline. "Yeah. I'm good. With you, I'm perfect."

I didn't push him. Whatever sadness lingered from Liam's past belonged to him. I knew that when he was ready to share, he would. I'd learned that on my grief journey. No one could have forced me out of my sorrow. I had to sit with it and let it slowly transform.

"I agree." I leaned into his shoulder, letting my head fall into the little gap that felt like it was made just for me. "You know I'm always here and willing to listen."

He kissed the top of my head, his lips lingering for a moment. "I know. That's one of the many things I love about you, Murray."

My heart pounded so fast that I was sure he could feel it.

"So, eggnog and a cozy Christmas Eve?" He massaged my thumb as we continued along Cedar Avenue.

"I couldn't ask for anything better."

We stopped again when we reached the giant redwood in

Oceanside Park wrapped in hundreds of twinkling lights. Liam dropped my hand and turned to face me, his finger caressing my chin. "Happy Christmas, Annie Murray."

"Happy Christmas, Liam Donovan," I repeated, standing on my tiptoes as his lips reached down to mine.

What a happy Christmas, indeed.

# A LETTER FROM THE AUTHOR

Huge thanks for reading *A Holiday Homicide*! I hope it hit all of the right holiday notes and has you in the holiday spirit. If you want to join other readers in hearing all about my new releases and bonus content, you can sign up for my newsletter!

www.stormpublishing.co/ellie-alexander

If you enjoyed this book and could spare a few moments to leave a review, it would mean so much to me. Even a short review can make all the difference in encouraging a reader to discover my books for the first time. Thank you, thank you!

I can't believe this is the fourth book in the series, and I can't thank you enough for joining Annie and me on this journey. When I first started to sketch out Redwood Grove and her story, I wasn't entirely sure where it would take me, but the one thing I've quickly learned is how it's connected me with you.

I'm humbled by your notes, DMs, letters, and emails. Thank you so much for sharing reviews and sharing the series with your friends and family. It's so wonderful to hear that Annie is resonating with you, and there's more to come.

Thanks again for being part of this amazing journey with me and I hope you'll stay in touch—I have so many more stories and ideas to entertain you with!

Ellie Alexander

# KEEP IN TOUCH WITH THE AUTHOR

elliealexander.co

 facebook.com/elliealexanderauthor
 x.com/ellielovesbooks
 instagram.com/ellie_alexander
 tiktok.com/@elliealexanderauthor

# ACKNOWLEDGEMENTS

My deepest thanks to Tish Bouvier, Lizzie Bailey, Kat Webb, Flo Cho, Jennifer Lewis, Lily Gill, Courtny Bradley, Mary Ann McCoy, and Ericka Turnbull for being the most amazing brainstorming and hype crew! I'm so grateful for your input, suggestions, and support. You mean the world to me.

I can't say enough about the team at Storm Publishing and my incredible editor, Vicky Blunden, who has truly developed this series with me. It takes a village to write a book, and I'm so lucky to be part of the Storm village. From cover design to marketing, editing insight, and everything in between, you really are taking the world by storm!

To my friends and family who have been with me book by book, I couldn't do it without you. A special thanks to Gordy, Luke, and Liv for the book chats, the constructive feedback, the dinners, the late-night ice cream runs, and for letting books take over our entire world. You are my world.